Sign up to my newsletter, and you will be notified when I release my next book!
Join my Patreon (patreon.com/jackbryce) to get early access to my work!

ISBN-13: 9798870072555

D1528202

FRONTIER SUMMONER 3

A SLICE OF LIFE FANTASY ADVENTURE

JACK BRYCE

To thongs… again.

Frontier Summoner 3

David's Character Sheet

Below is David's character sheet at the end of book 2.

Name: David Wilson

Class: Frontier Summoner

Level: 4

Health: 50/50

Mana: 25/25

 Skills:

Summon Minor Spirit — **Level 10 (4 mana)**

Summon Domesticant — **Level 6 (6 mana)**

Summon Guardian — **Level 1 (8 mana)**

Bind Familiar — **Level 1 (15 mana)**

Identify Plants — **Level 6 (1 mana)**

Foraging — **Level 7 (1 mana)**

Trapping — **Level 7 (1 mana)**

Alchemy — **Level 5 (1 mana)**

Chapter 1

I awoke to the smells of sizzling bacon and brewing coffee drifting up from downstairs. Taking a deep whiff, I cradled a happily purring Diane a little closer to me.

"Breakfast smells good," I said, voice still heavy with sleep.

"Hmm," Diane agreed. "Leigh's looking out for you." She stretched lazily, arching her delicious backside against me. "Why don't you go on ahead? I'll be there in a minute."

Grinning, I gave her butt a pinch before rising. After washing up briskly, I found Leigh already bustling about her kitchen, cheerfully humming to herself as she cooked up a hearty breakfast.

"Mornin' sunshine!" she chirped by way of greeting as I entered. "Figured we'd want a good meal before hittin' the road today. Explorin' the Wilds to find a Dungeon is hungry work, after all!"

"This smells amazing, Leigh," I said appreciatively, snaking my arms around her waist and giving her a kiss on the neck that made her giggle.

"Go on," she hummed. "Grab some coffee, baby, and take a seat. Diane still nappin'?"

"She'll be down in a sec," I said as I poured myself some coffee from the pot. "Thanks for taking care of breakfast for us."

Leigh waved away my gratitude as she scooped up eggs, bacon, and toasted bread onto three plates. "My pleasure! Gotta start big adventures on full stomachs after all," she replied, setting the heaping plates on the table along with little bowls of fresh berries she had taken from the store downstairs.

The simple but hearty fare had me grinning in anticipation even before I took a bite. A moment later, Diane joined in a cute, oversized shirt, stretching lazily before she placed a kiss on my cheek and sat down, licking her lips at the sight of the tasty breakfast Leigh had prepared.

Over breakfast, we discussed our intended route one last time as we ate. I traced the path Waelin had shown us on the map, tapping certain waypoints. "So," I began. "It looks like about two days' travel through this forested region here. I suggest that, at the end of the second day, we camp in the forest. We wouldn't want to hit the Blighted Land at night, I don't think."

Diane and Leigh exchanged looks and nodded, turning a little more serious at the mention of a more dangerous part of our journey.

"Past the Blighted Land, we should find the

hidden pass into the secluded valley where the Dungeon of Nimos Sedia is located." I gave both girls a pointed look. "That's where we'll find the Star Jewel to help save Celeste."

"So, a three days' journey?" Leigh asked.

"At least," I said. "We should prepare for ten in total, I think. Caldwell said it would take us no more than ten days, and I trust his judgment. It looks like the forest and the mountain will have plenty of fresh water. I wouldn't drink from a stream in the Blighted Land, so we'll have to stock up on water before we cross into that area."

Diane nodded, looking anxious but determined as she chewed her bacon. "I just hope we don't run into too much trouble. Do you really think we're ready for this?" Her big blue eyes were uncertain. I gave her hand a reassuring squeeze.

"We've got this," I said supportively. "Between your crossbow, Leigh's animal skills, and my summoning magic, we can handle whatever gets thrown at us out there."

Leigh gave Diane an energetic pat on the back. "David is too right! We got all our bases covered."

With her friends' encouragement, Diane's expression firmed with resolve. We continued eating heartily, fortifying ourselves for the long miles ahead. Outside, the sounds of Gladdenfield Outpost awakening drifted in through the open windows — merchants setting up stalls, a smithy's distant hammering.

After we had polished off second helpings, I rose and started gathering up our packs and equipment. "Alright, let's do one final check we've got everything." Together, the three of us began methodically taking stock.

Sorting through my own pack, I verified we had matches and a lighter, our tent, bedrolls and sleeping bags, rope, a flashlight, spare batteries, my Farming and Ranching skillbook in case I had downtime, and other camping gear.

I also carefully checked my potion satchel, satisfied to see an array of mana draughts — I had brewed those myself — and the antidotes and healing potions Waelin had furnished for the expedition to save his niece, Celeste.

Meanwhile, Diane ensured we had enough food

supplies. There were trail rations, dried meats, pickled vegetables, but also fresh supplies that we could eat on the first few days. Her keen eyes missed nothing as she inspected each item before stowing it neatly.

Leigh whistled cheerily as she took stock of cookware, spare sets of clothing for each of us, first aid supplies, a compass to help us navigate, and some of the imbued lures that she, as a Beastmaster, could craft and use to befriend animals.

Before long, we had three sturdy packs stacked by the door containing all the essentials for wilderness survival thanks to our combined efforts. I did one final weapons check — rifle and handgun cleaned and loaded, knife sharpened. The girls also gave their chosen arms a quick inspection — Diane her crossbow, and Leigh a simple six-shooter. Both girls also carried a long knife.

"I'd say we're all set!" Leigh proclaimed proudly, hands on her hips as she eyed our assembled equipment.

Diane gave a determined nod to agree with her

harem sister. I knew my competent companions were the best guarantee for success of any venture we would undertake beyond Gladdenfield's secure walls.

After tidying up the remains of breakfast, we shouldered our packs and stepped outside into the bustling frontier settlement. The sun had just crested the distant hills, washing Gladdenfield's dusty streets in golden dawn light. Gentle woodsmoke hung in the crisp morning air.

Townsfolk were already up and about on various errands. Many called out greetings to Leigh or nodded respectfully to me as the victor of Lord Vartlebeck's tournament. Their well wishes for an uneventful journey followed us as we made our way toward the main gates.

"This is it, girls," I said, feeling the excitement for the journey in my bones. "A new adventure."

Diane and Leigh made excited sounds as they clung to one of my arms each, and we nodded at the guard as we passed beneath the tall timber palisades, leaving behind Gladdenfield's secure borders.

Ahead, the open wilderness beckoned, both thrilling and daunting in its vast scale and unknown dangers that lurked within. This was it — together we were stepping into the Wilds on another great adventure!

Chapter 2

Stepping past Gladdenfield's gates, we set off down the winding path leading into the dense forest. Ancient trees with gnarled trunks and leafy canopies towered on all sides, filtering the morning light into golden beams that painted the forest floor.

The crisp scent of pine and earth surrounded us as we hiked beneath those silent sentinels. Here and there, massive boulders and fallen logs offered reminders of the primordial forces that had shaped this land over eons, with strange rocks or cracked pits showing the signs of the Upheaval that had united our world with the magical realm of Tannoris.

Ferns and bushes clustered along the sides of the trail, rustling gently in the breeze. Tiny wildflowers peeked out from the undergrowth, their fragile beauty contrasting with the ancient strength of the mighty oaks and pines.

We made good time, but we still admired our lush surroundings. Leigh paused frequently to point out interesting plants she recognized from her wilderness training, regaling us with her knowledge of which beasts fed on such plants and which were avoided because they were poisonous.

Now and then, the excited chatter of squirrels or birdsong filtered down through the leafy canopy overhead. Shafts of golden light slanted between the trees, illuminating swirling motes of pollen.

There was a timeless serenity to this ancient wood that eased the mind and spirit.

As we continued deeper into the forest, the terrain gradually grew more rugged. Exposed roots crossed the path, and we had to pick our way carefully over them. Moss-cloaked boulders offered respite, so we paused atop one to share some dried fruit and nuts.

Diane's nerves about the journey ahead seemed to have settled. She pointed upwards, a smile lighting her face as she traced the path of a hawk soaring lazily on the thermals high overhead. Its keen eyes were likely scanning the spaces between the trees, searching for prey stirring in the undergrowth.

After our brief rest, we continued onward. The pleasant chill of the recent night still lingered beneath the sheltering boughs. Our packs felt lighter, our steps coming easier as our muscles adjusted to the gentle rhythm of the hike.

Around late morning, we came upon a small brook glinting merrily over smooth stones as it wound its way through the woods. I refilled our canteens in the cold crystal water while Leigh pointed out tiny silver minnows darting amongst the pebbles.

"Oh, I would have loved to catch a few of those," Diane said, licking her lips at the sight of the fish.

I chuckled, amused by her love of the catch. "Well, we have plenty of food and a long journey ahead. Maybe on the way back, we'll take a little more time to relax. Unless you can catch one in the, say, fifteen minutes we'll take a break here."

Of course, that was a challenge to Diane.

Leigh and I enjoyed the soothing babble and glimpses of darting fish, smiling as we watched Diane at play, trying to catch one of the nimble minnows with her hands. Her delighted laughter when one evaded her grasp warmed my heart. Unfortunately, she didn't manage to catch any of the sprightly fish.

After our pleasant stop beside the brook, I pulled out my compass and map, confirming we remained on course through the trackless wood. With Leigh's wilderness skills, I had few qualms about getting lost even this far from civilization.

As the sun climbed towards its zenith, dappled shadows danced around us in the gentle breeze. All was tranquil aside from woodland birds conversing back and forth in the leafy canopy high overhead. The pungent scent of pine enveloped us as we followed the brook for a while, and the air out here was wholesome and purifying.

As we hiked, I reflected on how different this was from the tame parks and recreation areas of New Springfield. Out here, one was reminded viscerally that we were simply guests passing through a domain shaped over eons by implacable natural — and magical! – forces. It instilled humility.

The winding trail took us up a steady incline as the terrain grew increasingly rocky. Soon we were navigating between house-sized boulders draped in vibrant ferns and moss. Their craggy surfaces were pleasantly cool to the touch as we passed.

When the path forked around a massive fallen oak, I calmly oriented us using my compass, so we remained on course through the trackless ancient wood. Diane and Leigh assisted, and I had few qualms about getting lost with this company.

As we hiked, the girls pointed out small wonders along the way — a family of raccoons peeking from a hollow tree, ripening wild berries, or the pellets of an owl at the base of a tree. Each new discovery was a delight that kindled a spirit of outdoorsmanship within us all.

Now and then, the excited chatter of squirrels or a snatch of birdsong would filter down through the leafy canopy overhead. Shafts of golden light slanted between the trees, illuminating swirling motes of pollen.

When weariness crept into our limbs as noon approached, we agreed to start looking for a suitable spot to pause and eat a midday meal. A clearing carpeted in emerald moss between towering elms seemed ideal.

There we rested for a time, talking lightly as we shared hunks of cheese, dried meat, and sips from our canteens. Overhead, the swaying boughs murmured in the gentle breeze. All around us, life went on as it had for millennia untold.

Our strength and spirits were renewed after lunch, so we soon resumed our trek with reinvigorated steps. Rounding a lichen-speckled boulder, we stumbled upon something unexpected — the crumbling facade of some ancient structure, nearly swallowed by the encroaching forest.

My girls and I exchanged amazed looks at this remnant emerging from the mists of ages past before we stepped closer.

Approaching cautiously, we noted fluted pillars and elegant statuary peeking from the vibrant blanket of ferns and ivy. Strange symbols adorned weathered arches carved with artful precision from now-cracked stone. It was old, much older than any building in the Americas.

"It's Tannorian architecture," Diane whispered in awe; her eyes wide.

Having come from that realm originally, she recognized subtle hallmarks in the alien design.

"This must be thousands of years old, left here by the Upheaval."

"That's amazing," I breathed, studying the magical mystery of another world with fascination. Even for those living on the frontier, discovering such wonders was rare.

"Let's take a closer look," Leigh suggested.

Mouth agape, I walked under the moss-covered archway and into the enchanting ruins.

"Has to be elven," Diane said. "The kin don't build like this."

Spellbound by the lingering grandeur amidst decay, we carefully picked our way through the ruins, marveling at the otherworldly craftsmanship. Vines snaked over once-ornate balustrades, and windows framed nothing but leafy boughs.

Slowly and in their gentle way, the trees were taking this place back. But that only added to the mystery of the ruins.

Pushing deeper into the abandoned edifice, we entered a small courtyard open to the sky. There, enthroned atop a crumbling plinth, rested an exquisitely carved figurine of swirling stone — an elven woman with flowing robes and a serene countenance.

"Wow," I breathed at the sight, stepping closer to the plinth.

Her delicate features were so finely wrought that it seemed impossible she was mere cold stone. Mesmerized, we circled the statuette, noting lifelike details from gracefully pointed ears to individually articulated folds in the robes.

"She must have been a goddess or mythical heroine," Diane mused, studying the elegant sculpture. "I wish I knew more of the old lore." Her eyes were sad, likely thinking of all the history lost in the Upheaval.

"Maybe Waelin will know," Leigh said.

I nodded. "We could show it to him."

Diane cocked her head. "Take it with us, you mean?"

"Yeah," I said. "It's beautiful. And this place is a ruin now. It belongs to no one. It would be nice to give it a second home."

Diane nodded. "Maybe on our hearth?"

I smiled. "Exactly."

Kneeling before the sculpture, I brushed away caking dirt to reveal an ornate plaque etched with looping symbols in the elven script. Though inscrutable to me, their flowing shapes had an innate beauty.

Leigh kneeled next to me and studied the symbols. I looked sideways at her, a puzzled smile on my lips.

"*Ilmanaria*," she said. The winged woman gazed back as if in silent affirmation.

I blinked. "Wait… You can read elvish?"

"A little," she said. "I don't know many words, is the problem. But I can read the letters and know the sounds they're supposed to make."

I laughed. "Well, aren't you full of surprises! You'll have to teach me!" I glanced at Diane. "Ilmanaria. Does the name ring any bells?"

Diane considered it for a moment. "I think I recall her name from childhood tales. She was a guardian spirit of mages or something. I don't know any more."

"Well, let's take it with us! Waelin will know

more."

Gently, I took the statuette from its place. For a moment, I hesitated; I did not want to desecrate this place or steal from it, but I sensed only tranquility. Those who had dwelled here in the past were long gone, and this beautiful artifact would receive a second life in our home.

Afterward, we jointly explored side chambers shrouded in cool shadow. There, painted frescoes still clung to otherwise bare walls. Strange creatures and unfamiliar landscapes had been meticulously rendered in pigments that defied time.

"These must be magical," I said, amazed by how intact the depictions remained. "They have survived for so long, even when exposed to the elements."

"It's certainly possible," Diane agreed. "The elves often use magic in their works, and it wouldn't surprise me at all if they had some kind of way to make their art last longer!"

We watched in amazement, and the images seemed to dance before our eyes... sweeping vistas of majestic towers and rich castles unlike anywhere on Earth. Elven warriors with plumed helmets rode dragons into war, and mages in immaculate robes bent the very elements to their will. This art offered visceral glimpses into Tannorian realms both wondrous and alien.

As we lingered, admiring those masterpieces, I couldn't escape the melancholic realization that we were likely the first in a long time to look upon them. All great civilizations crumble, often leaving only these haunting echoes behind, and much of the elven glory that once lived on Tannoris had passed.

When we finally tore ourselves away to continue our forest trek, the ruined sanctuary still occupied our thoughts. We all felt imbued with an almost spiritual vigor from experiencing the last lingering grandeur of that place.

But we needed to be on our way. Part of the joy of travel was certainly exploration, but we wanted to complete our quest as well.

We moved on, leaving the ancient structure behind us now. I glanced back frequently, appreciating this marvel that fate had put on our path.

"Can you imagine what it was like before the Upheaval?" Diane wondered aloud. "Great sprawling cities, magical academies filled with elven sages, dragonriders..." Her voice held melancholy longing for a past irretrievably faded.

As we resumed our trek, the sun had begun its gradual descent toward the distant hills. I felt vibrant and full of life, appreciative of what I had seen so far and looking forward to what was to come.

Chapter 3

As the sun sank lower in the sky, we sought out a suitable clearing to make camp for the night. Finding a nice flat area surrounded by sheltering pines near a brook flowing with fresh water, we set down our packs with a collective sigh of relief.

"I'd say this is a mighty fine spot to settle in for

the night," Leigh declared, hands on her hips as she surveyed our chosen campsite. I had to agree. The dense trees would provide good cover from wind or rain, and the nearby brook provided fresh water. Visibility would be limited, but that was an issue everywhere in the forest.

We quickly fell into a smooth routine, working efficiently together to get camp established before full dusk settled. Diane and I worked on assembling the tent while Leigh busied herself gathering dry tinder for a fire.

Before long, the canvas shelter was erected, and our bedrolls arranged neatly inside. Meanwhile, Leigh had a good stack of firewood ready, and I busied myself with getting a campfire underway.

Soon enough, we had a modest fire crackling, the cheery flames dispelling the encroaching gloom beneath the trees. The smoky scent of burning pine filled the little clearing.

With camp readied, we turned our attention to preparing a hearty trail supper. Leigh hummed as she filled a pot from the nearby stream to boil over the flames. Diane sliced strips of smoked venison while I measured out portions of beans and rice.

Soon the simple but nourishing meal was bubbling away over the fire as we watched the sunset paint the sky in brilliant hues of orange and pink through the trees. The tantalizing aroma of meat and beans mingled with woodsmoke made my stomach rumble.

When it was ready, Leigh carefully dished out portions of the hearty meal of rice, beans, and venison into our tin bowls and mugs. We settled on logs around the fire to enjoy the well-earned fare after a long day's hike through the forest.

"Mmm, this hits the spot!" Diane said appreciatively between bites. The tender venison and savory beans perfectly sated our appetites built up from a day's worth of fresh air and exercise.

Leigh smiled, clearly pleased her efforts were being enjoyed.

As we ate, fireflies began to blink into existence, their otherworldly lights flickering like tiny stars amidst the ferns and bushes just beyond the fire's cheery glow. The effect was beautiful, and we all smiled with delight at the beauty of it.

Our hunger gradually diminished as we cleaned our bowls, leaving only comfort and drowsiness. Diane stifled a yawn. The excitement of the day's discoveries was catching up rapidly, it seemed.

When Leigh began preparing a pot of tea to keep us warm as the night's chill crept in, curiosity got the better of me again regarding her unexpected knowledge of the elven language we'd encountered.

"So, Leigh, you never did explain earlier — how'd you pick up reading the elven letters?" I asked once we all had steaming mugs in hand.

Leigh's expression turned thoughtful. "Well, it's kind of a long tale…" she began slowly.

Diane and I nodded eagerly for her to continue.

She took a slow sip of tea, gathering her thoughts. "Ya see, when I was just a youngin' first setting out to be a wandering Beastmaster, I happened to meet this elf lady named Rahael. She was awful old and grizzled but one heck of an animal trainer who made her bones in Tannoris."

As she spoke, Leigh's eyes took on a faraway cast

as if peering back through the mists of memory. The firelight danced over her fine features. "Ol' Rahael kinda took me under her wing for a spell. I guess she took a likin' to me. She taught me a lot about befriending critters and living off nature's bounty."

I listened raptly, fascinated to learn more of Leigh's past mentors and tutelage. Even Diane seemed enraptured by the tale, absently turning a twig over in her hands as Leigh spun her story.

"I was with her nigh on a year, I reckon. We were roaming all over before she settled down in a frontier town called Fallhaven to retire. Anyhow, while we traveled together, she'd teach me all sorts of things." Leigh smiled wistfully. "Elven writing was among her lessons. I... don't really have a head for it, so I never really picked up much of that stuff, but the letters kinda stuck. Don't know why."

She shook her head as if in lingering awe. "But Rahael was a good mentor. She knew more than most folks ever will about the beasts of Tannoris. You'd expect the kin to know more, and they do in certain ways, but Rahael knew all the lore. I suppose I was just a humble pupil soaking up whatever she saw fit to teach."

As Leigh elaborated on her mentor's wisdom and unusual longevity, I found myself picturing those bygone days when a young Leigh had wandered the wilderness guided by the elf woman's profound knowledge. Rahael sounded like a remarkable figure.

"I'll never forget those days we had together before fate split our paths," Leigh concluded. "She gave me the foundation that's served me so well as a Beastmaster. I hope she's doing well in Fallhaven."

Leigh smiled wistfully down at her now-empty mug before meeting my eyes across the flickering flames. "Anyhow, that's the long and short of it! Guess Rahael's lessons stuck with me."

"That's really amazing you crossed paths with someone like that," I said sincerely. "A good mentor can make all the difference in a place like this."

Beside me, Diane hummed agreement, clearly as enthralled as I was by Leigh's poignant tale.

As the embers burned lower, a tranquil hush fell over the little camp. Somewhere in the distance, an owl hooted its lonely night song. Weariness began seeping into our bones from the long day's hike. After tidying up the remains of dinner, I told the girls I'd take first watch. We kissed each other goodnight, and they headed into the tent.

I was tired but also looking forward to sitting a while longer, soothed by the muted symphony of the forest at night.

Chapter 4

The next morning, I awoke from a deep, restful sleep with Leigh curled up against me. I blinked awake slowly, savoring the tranquility of the still, quiet forest. Leigh's breathing was deep and even, and I took a moment to savor the sight of her like this.

Moving carefully so as not to disturb Leigh, I slipped on my boots and emerged from the tent, inhaling deeply of the crisp morning air. Wisps of mist clung to the undergrowth and ferns, illuminated by the first golden rays piercing the canopy. The babbling brook provided a soothing backdrop.

"Morning, sunshine," Diane said with a smile. She sat on a boulder, crossbow on her lap, and shot me a warm smile.

I stretched and yawned. "How was the last watch?" I asked.

"Oh, nothing special," she said. "It's nice and quiet out here. I actually enjoyed it!"

I smiled before heading over and giving her a kiss on her forehead. "So did I!"

After washing up briskly in the chilled water, I got a small fire going and put a pot of coffee on to percolate. The rich, earthy aroma soon filled our little camp, complemented by strips of sizzling bacon I had set to fry in our iron skillet.

Before long, my efforts roused Leigh from her slumber. She emerged tousle-haired but bright-eyed, eager for some of the hot coffee and breakfast I was preparing. We ate heartily together as the forest came to life around us.

Over breakfast, we discussed hopes to cover more miles today. The map showed we were making steady progress, but the Blighted Land still lay some distance ahead through the trackless wood.

"Should be no more than a day's march," I said. "We'll camp near the edge of the forest. There's no point in wandering out into the Blighted Land at night."

The girls nodded, a little apprehension showing. Knowing its menacing moniker, they were not particularly eager to reach its borders.

After breaking camp and concealing signs of our presence, we continued our forest trek as shafts of morning light illuminated our path. The subtly shifting terrain kept us alert. Trees clustered densely, suffusing the woods in primordial mystery.

We frequently checked the map and compass throughout the day, ensuring we maintained the right heading. The remote location left no visible paths to follow. Our progress relied solely on navigation skills and attentiveness to our surroundings.

Around late morning, a snarl of exposed roots crossing the forest floor forced us to pick our way carefully. But teamwork saw all of us across the hazard safely. Beyond, we discovered a tranquil glade carpeted in lush moss and swaying ferns.

We gladly paused there to rest and take on sustenance. A fallen oak provided ample space to lounge. From my pack, I passed around strips of dried venison to gnaw. The sheltered glen was tranquil, perfect for regaining strength.

Our hunger diminished; we spent a few extra minutes simply absorbing the ambiance. Wind swaying the canopy above, beams of light dancing amidst the ferns, the musty scent of earth and leaves — all combined to soothe body and soul.

But the winding trail beckoned us onward all too soon. We hoisted our packs and pressed deeper into the ancient forest. The hoar trees here were gnarled with age, the very embodiments of patient wisdom. Their whispered secrets went unheard.

Through the afternoon, the terrain grew increasingly rugged. Twisting roots snaked across the shaded forest floor, making the going slow. The winding path threaded narrowly between sheer ridges and plunging ravines now.

Navigating a particularly difficult stretch, I lent Diane a steadying hand until she was over safely. Leigh whistled cheerily, undaunted by the rough terrain. But we all breathed easier when the route leveled out again beneath enormous, moss-blanketed pines.

Gradually, the character of the woods shifted around us. The ferns and undergrowth thinned away, leaving bare earth and stone. The air seemed heavier, and fewer birdsongs filled the oddly muted forest. An intangible gloom permeated these older stands.

As we hiked briskly onward, weariness settled into our bones beneath packs that now felt heavier. But neither sunset nor suitable campsite presented itself yet. Anxiety nagged me about taking rest in this faded section of wood that felt strangely vacant.

Without warning, the tree line ended abruptly up ahead. We hurried our steps, emerging from brooding shadow into late afternoon sunlight that dazzled the eyes. Pulling up short, we found ourselves overlooking a stark, eerie valley shrouded in unnatural haze. Dead trees clawed at the sky, and leafless shrubs with thorns covered much of the dry soil.

"The Blighted Land," Leigh breathed, voicing the recognition in all our minds. Spread below, the accursed valley exuded an air of malevolence that raised the hairs on the back of my neck.

Bordering the Blighted Land, the woods resumed, but the trees there appeared sickly and gnarled. Little healthy wild growth remained, as if the valley's very soil was poisoned. In the distance, the mountains reared up in forbidding majesty under the darkening sky.

"We should backtrack and make camp," I said, glancing at the position of the sun. "We made good time and hit the Blighted Land a little earlier than expected, but I still don't want to be out here exposed after night falls."

The girls readily agreed, looking askance at the unnerving valley.

Retreating into the cover of the trees, we hiked until the ominous vista was lost from view, putting a ridge between it and us. In a sheltered hollow near a freshet, we established camp as dusk deepened. An eerie silence hung beneath the boughs.

As we prepared a simple meal of rice, vegetables, and dried meat, no one felt much like talking. The cloying sense of dread inspired by the Blighted Land had diminished our spirits. We focused on bolstering our defenses, gathering extra firewood and concealing the camp as best we could amidst the trees.

Afterward, we sat by the fire in silence for a bit, until Diane began humming softly, and her lyrical voice lifted gently into song:

"O wanderer, never fear the dark,
The dawn will come, shadows depart,
Brave the night that hides the way,
Take heart, see light of new day.

The road ahead lies veiled from sight,
With perils strange on moonlit night,
But keep one step before the next,
Your soul's own flame will light your quest.

Let fears unspoken fade away,
Like mist before the sunrise ray,
Hold to hope through darkest hours,
Until the forest sunshine flowers."

The melancholic folk melody was beautiful and heartening, and I soon found myself invigorated by Diane's words. As Diane sang, the gloom permeating the muted forest seemed to retreat, if only for a fleeting span.

When the song ended, she shot Leigh and me a tremulous but hopeful smile. "Just a little something I learned on the trail once upon a time," Diane explained with a melancholy sigh. "Music has a way of soothing the soul and keeping the dark at bay."

I reached over and gave her hand an appreciative squeeze. "That was beautiful, Diane," I said sincerely. "And you're right, it's exactly what we needed tonight." Diane's singing had never failed to stir the spirit.

Once we had eaten, we hastily stuffed our trash into bags and stowed it safely away to minimize any scents that might attract creatures in the night. Anxiety still nipped at me as I checked and rechecked the simple fortifications encircling our camp. Whatever unnatural things lurked in the Blighted Land, I wanted no encounters with them under cover of darkness.

Diane's song echoed still in the back of my mind, keeping the all-pervading gloom at bay. None of us would get a full night's unbroken rest, but caution felt essential this close to the Blighted Land.

I took the first shift of the watch, determined to let the girls sleep as long as I could let them. I occupied myself tending the fire as they retired.

Seated beside the crackling flames with my rifle close, I frequently cast glances into the encroaching darkness between the trees. Any hint of movement or sound put my senses on high alert. The dismal valley's proximity infected even dreams, lending them a bleak quality.

In the night, strange sounds and animals' growls bounced between the trees, telling tales of strange creatures wandering about. Now and then, something flittered in the canopy, rustling the leaves. After several hours had passed, I woke up Leigh, who took the second watch. I handed her my rifle to be on the safe side.

Gray light eventually spilled through the forest, waking me and Leigh up and stirring birds to song again. We found Diane patrolling the perimeter of the camp with her crossbow, and we hastily prepared to continue our journey.

As we departed the hollow, I glimpsed the Blighted Land ahead through the trees. The time had come for a more dangerous part of our journey.

Chapter 5

The morning sun rose, casting pale light across the ominous valley of the Blighted Land. Its twisted trees and thorny undergrowth seemed even more unnatural and threatening now that we stood at its threshold. An uneasy silence hung in the air, broken only by our footsteps crunching on the dry earth as we reluctantly pressed onward.

The further we ventured, the more oppressive the stillness felt. Even the morning birdsong was muted here.

Diane walked closer beside me, her eyes wide and scanning our surroundings warily. Leigh's usual cheer had faded into tense focus. We all felt the foreboding that permeated this cursed valley and moved with heightened caution.

Strange shapes loomed out of the haze — monolithic shards of stone jutting at odd angles from the dusty earth as though thrust violently skyward long ago. They were pitted and scarred, devoid of any life.

Merely looking upon them gave me a sense of primordial dread. Diane and Leigh had no idea what they signified, and we gave the disturbing formations a wide berth as we navigated deeper into the Blighted Land.

The sparse vegetation appeared simultaneously dead and alive. Shriveled gray trees clawed at the sky with bare, twisted branches that seemed to creak and groan of their own volition. Dark, oily plants sprouted from cracks in the earth, their thorns glistening with sinister secretions. The further we ventured, the less anything resembled healthy flora.

"This whole place feels... *wrong*, somehow," Diane whispered uneasily. "Like it doesn't belong in this world."

I murmured agreement, unnerved by the unnatural geography surrounding us. Each step took us deeper into a domain that felt almost malevolently aware of our presence.

"Remember what Waelin said," I recalled. "Dark magics tainted this strip of land at one point."

Leigh frowned, her head swiveling watchfully. "All the more reason we'll stay sharp," she cautioned tersely. "Critters that dwell in a place this creepy won't be natural or friendly."

Her warning only heightened our guardedness. We scrutinized every whisper of movement.

As we navigated down barren slopes, the dusty earth gave way beneath each step, replacing secure footing with disconcerting loose shale that shifted treacherously. Diane and I supported one another to prevent a tumble. Cresting a rise, we got our first glimpse of the valley's heart.

A murky land lay below, its dark waters choked by coils of massive thorns snaking out upon the surface. Shadowy shapes moved ponderously in the shallows. Though at a distance, a palpable menace emanated from the noxious pool. We steered our course to arc widely around it through more arid high ground.

Strange skittering sounds sent a chill up my spine. I paused, peering toward a formation of jagged boulders — and froze.

A veritable herd of leathery reptilian creatures were clambering over the stones below, hissing to one another in some abrasive tongue. Their forelimbs were long tendrils that grasped like hands.

My breath caught, but Leigh placed a warning hand on my arm before I could react. "Don't move a muscle," she breathed. "Those are Grapplejaws. They hunt by vibration. They're small, but their bite is venomous. In high enough doses, it can be lethal."

Heart pounding, I remained utterly still, barely daring to breathe, as the pack of dreadful things scrambled unnervingly by. Luckily, they did not head toward us. Only once they had passed, we exhaled in relief.

We quickened our pace through that stretch, eager to put distance between us and the monsters. As we moved, Diane gasped and pointed skyward. Drifting lazily overhead were bizarre creatures that resembled massive, asymmetrical jellyfish, trailing a confusion of organic tendrils. Their forms pulsed and rippled hypnotically in the sky.

"What on Earth are those?" Diane murmured, staring agape as the things floated by.

Leigh squinted at them critically. "Not of this Earth, I reckon," she muttered darkly. "Likely some Tannorian aberrations. I ain't never seen them before either."

The outlandish creatures soared with the wind currents, oblivious to us. Their alien biology was like nothing I had ever glimpsed, seeming to defy reason itself. We watched uneasily until distance obscured them from view over the jagged horizon.

As we navigated through that unsettling domain, the air remained still and oddly muffled, as if the strange geology somehow smothered the wind. Dust eddied lethargically around our feet. It felt like the Blighted Land itself resented our presence. Diane slipped her hand into mine for reassurance as we walked.

As the morning came to an end, the heat intensified, reflecting up from the pale earth in shimmering waves. We were all too glad to take shelter briefly in the scant shade of a crumbling rocky overhang to rest and drink. No one spoke much, our minds and bodies burdened by the oppressive atmosphere.

Once we had regained a measure of energy, we again ventured forth into the unrelenting sunlight. I tried to hold the image of Celeste's beautiful but frail face in my mind's eye — we endured this hellish place for her sake and Waelin's hopes. That fragile life depended on our fortitude.

And if we succeeded, Waelin would put his magic at the disposal of the Frontier Division, which meant that many more humans would be able to venture out of the cities. That would mean more food, freedom, and prosperity for humans.

As we continued, we were beset by strange phenomena that defied reason — skittering movements with no source, dust eddies swirling in opposite directions, distant echoes as though from caverns invisible to our eyes. The Blighted Land itself seemed capable of madness-inducing trickery.

When Leigh paused abruptly, staring hard at a mound of loose shale, I frowned and stood guard. But she merely furrowed her brow, deep in thought, before beckoning us onward again without a word. Her tense silence unnerved me, but explanation would have to wait. Survival was our priority.

The terrain remained harsh and barren, with landmarks that all resembled one another. But my keen sense of direction kept us oriented correctly. I had studied the map well, and we kept close to a gorge that ran roughly in the direction we needed to go.

Afternoon saw us clear of the valley's heart, thankfully. The mountains' foothills rose ahead. Cleaner air stirred, and some semblance of ordinary vegetation emerged from the parched earth as we neared the far border. Relief swelled within me, tempered by weariness. We were almost out of the Blighted Land.

But our respite was short-lived. "We're being trailed," Leigh stated bluntly, her expression grim. "Something's been shadowing our steps most of the day." My stomach dropped even as Diane's eyes widened fearfully. Leigh's intuition was seldom wrong. If she said we were hunted, we were.

Leigh chewed her lip pensively. "From the signs, I reckon it's one of them Landcrawlers. Giant burrowing beast, tough as an old boot. Must've caught our scent." She shook her head. "Damn shame, 'cause it's an aberration. My Class abilities won't allow me to befriend unnatural beings like that. And it looks like the clever girl looped far wide around us but couldn't fully hide the signs from me. She won't attack until dark or until we leave her territory."

I frowned, pondering this new challenge. "So… this thing is attacking us either way?"

Leigh nodded. "We're not a large enough party to scare it off, and these Tannorian creatures have some kinda sense for levels. If we had about fifteen levels between us, the beastie would back off. But with Diane and I both level 2 and you level 4, it's gonna try its luck."

"That means we get to choose the battleground," I said. "At the edge of its territory if we just keep walking, or any place within its territory if we stay there until night."

"Yeah, but if we choose a battleground, that would also mean we'd have to be in the Blighted Land at night," Diane put in. "Because it won't come out until night, right?"

She was right about that. I turned to Leigh. "Any idea how big its territory is?"

She touched her plump bottom lip for a moment

as she considered my question. "I reckon it should be up to the foothills," she finally said. "Ain't no way to be a hundred percent sure, though."

"Is it a big beast?" I asked. "Could it reach prey up in the branches of those stunted trees?" I pointed at a copse of trees closer to the foothills."

Leigh gave a lopsided smile as she pondered that. "That's a good idea," she said. "No, it couldn't. But it's got a pretty big body with lots of strength. It could uproot one of them trees by rammin' it."

"So we need something to distract it," I said and grinned broadly. "Good thing I'm a summoner…"

The girls exchanged a look and smiled. "Sounds like you have an idea?" Diane said.

I nodded. "If we take to the trees, I can summon two or three minor spirits to distract it. I'm thinking a storm and a fire spirit. They can pelt the Landcrawler with their minor attacks, which will hopefully annoy it. Meanwhile, we'll be in the trees. Rifle, revolver, and crossbow should solve the problem, right?"

Leigh nodded. "It'll take a couple shots, but it

should work."

"Well, that settles it, then," I said. "We'll head to those trees over there and prep our ambush. Leigh, is there any chance you can give us an accurate window for the attack?"

She wagged her head. "After the sun's down but before midnight is about as narrow as I can make that window."

I nodded. "Right, well... We'll be a little uncomfortable then, tonight. Once we deal with the Landcrawler, we will continue marching. I want to clear the Blighted Land before we make camp."

The girls nodded agreement, and we quickly headed toward the trees. We moved as swiftly as our tired limbs allowed across the remainder of the valley.

At times I swore the Landcrawler's tremors reverberated faintly through the ground beneath our boots as it tracked us relentlessly. But I led us onward unerringly toward the copse of stunted trees.

We made a temporary camp among the dead trees to have a quick bite to eat before the sun would set. The mood was tense, but I had every confidence that we would succeed. The plan was solid, and our resolve was firm.

Chapter 6

The sun sank below the mountains, casting the Blighted Land into ominous shadow. We had taken up positions in the tangled branches of stunted trees overlooking the dusty valley floor. My rifle was loaded and ready as we awaited any signs of the Landcrawler's approach.

The strange land remained eerily quiet, our ears straining for the slightest hint of movement. Leigh squinted into the deepening dusk, tense as a drawn bowstring. She gestured subtly that the creature was nearby.

My heart quickened; senses primed for confrontation. I allowed myself a look at my strong and resolute women. Diane had taken up position among the branches with the natural agility of her kind. She looked completely comfortable as she moved from branch to branch, keeping overwatch.

Leigh was a little less at ease, but I could tell she had found a stable position that would allow her to fire and deal with the recoil of her revolver. Both girls had their share of experience and knew how to handle themselves.

"Here it comes," Leigh said. "I feel its presence."

It took me a moment to feel it too, but then it was there. A faint tremor shook the dead branches beneath us.

I tightened my grip on the rifle stock, breathing controlled and steady. The Landcrawler was drawing closer, each quiver through the earth marking its progress underground. Its emergence was imminent.

The trembling intensified, and I saw the ground being upturned as it burrowed its way toward us now. It was immensely fast, which meant it had sturdy and sharp claws. It came straight toward us.

With a spray of dirt, the beast suddenly burst from the barren soil with a bone-rattling roar. It was about twenty feet shy of our circle of trees — perhaps the roots barred its way, but it was facing us and lumbered on in our direction.

My eyes widened — it was enormous, easily the size of an SUV, its thick scaly hide the dull brown of the valley floor. Curved claws tipped its burrowing forelimbs, and a lashing, armored tail whipped behind it. Leigh had been right: that thing could bring down a tree with no trouble.

The Landcrawler's huge head swung from side to side, nostril slits flaring wide as it scented for us, but the creature had no eyes to see with. Still, its sense of smell was impeccable.

I swallowed hard, signaling Leigh and Diane to aim their weapons. The creature took another thudding step toward my tree, dust billowing around its gnarled feet.

Now was the time for my magic!

As it drew nearer, I began summoning my nature spirits. Wisps of mana coalesced before me, taking the forms of first a crackling being of lightning and a small flaming creature. They awaited my command, floating in the air beside me, and I mentally directed them to attack our foe.

Casting the spells consumed 8 of my 25 mana, so there was room for reinforcements if necessary. I could try the guardian, but I expected the quick and agile spirits stood a better chance.

"Look at them go!" Diane said, excited as she watched my little spirits engage.

Twin bolts of lightning and fire rained down, pelting the Landcrawler's armored flanks. It reared back with an infuriated roar as the spirits' barrage continued. The assault served its purpose — the beast's attention fixated fully on my ephemeral allies, oblivious to us hidden above.

With the creature distracted, we steadied our aim upon its vulnerable spots — nose, throat, and underbelly between the plates of natural armor, exposed whenever it lashed out with its tail. On my signal, three shots simultaneously cracked out, echoing off the valley walls. My rifle's recoil was serious, but I had braced myself for it.

Our volley struck home. My shot pierced the unprotected throat, while Diane's bolt struck the underbelly. Dark ichor sprayed out of the wounds. Leigh's shot, however, ricocheted off the thick armor plating.

But we had hurt it! The Landcrawler howled in agony, limbs flailing wildly. My spirits continued their harassment, evading the creature's mad thrashing with supernatural quickness.

I rapidly took aim and fired again, seeking to further incapacitate the rampaging beast. Leigh and Diane added their own barrage, bullet and bolt tearing mercilessly into our foe. The Landcrawler's roars became choked gurgles as vital fluids poured forth.

But then, its tail struck my little Storm Spirit, and the summon flailed and despawned, dissolving into air. And as it turned out, the Landcrawler was not stupid. It realized *we* were bigger threats than the summons, and it lumbered toward my tree.

"David!" Leigh called out. "Watch it!"

I had seen the danger. With a quick word of magic, I summoned my guardian for 8 mana.

Out of my swirling mana, a hulking, spectral form coalesced. The guardian was almost seven feet tall with a radiant body that appeared to be made of glass but was in fact much stronger. Its form was etched with glowing runes.

As the guardian manifested at the base of my tree, two boulder-like fists rested at its sides, one of which held a massive kite shield. I commanded the guardian to protect my tree, and it braced itself, gripping its shield with two fists as the Landcrawler came on.

It was a clash of titans. With a furious roar, the Landcrawler slammed its tail against the guardian's shield. The guardian staggered but held. I knew it would not endure an endless barrage of such strikes, but it held for now.

"Keep shooting!" I called out at the girls, who had been frozen for a moment in awe. At my command, they resumed their attacks, and we barraged the creature with bullet and bolt.

Yet still the monstrous thing remained standing despite the grievous damage we inflicted. On the third strike of its massive tail, my guardian dissolved, accepting its return to the spirit realm stoically. I narrowed my eyes and called for another with a quick casting of my spell. It protected my tree with the same steadfast power. I was down to 1 mana now, and I would have to down one of my potions if I would need to cast more spells.

I resumed firing, joining my attacks with those of my women and the fire spirit. Pinned by our combined assault, the creature could only shudder and spasm violently beneath the onslaught. One of the beast's legs crumpled, sending it crashing down heaving on its side and raising a cloud of dust. The fire spirit circled the beast warily as it thrashed weakly.

But our quarry was tenacious, and defiant fury still burned in the creature as it slammed its tail into my guardian — a little weaker this time. This thing would fight on still. I steeled myself, taking careful aim once more.

My next shot pierced that snorting nose in an explosion of fluids and tissue, blinding the Landcrawler as its sense of smell was destroyed. It loosed an ear-splitting shriek of anguish, thrashing madly and gouging the earth with its claws as it tried to escape. But we continued bombarding the incapacitated thing without mercy.

Leigh calmly sighted her revolver and fired it at the creature's exposed throat until naught was left but a ragged, gaping hole, pumping out its blood. I joined in, driving two more rounds home into its gore-spattered underbelly, while Diane reloaded her crossbow.

Only now did the frenzied death throes begin to weaken beneath the combined firepower. The fight was nearing its end.

On the next volley, the beast jerked violently, a final guttural groan issuing from its tattered maw. Then all at once, the strength fled its limbs, and it slumped heavily into the dirt. For a moment, I watched, wary of any last quiver of life, as my fire spirit and guardian hovered or stood over the corpse.

But the Landcrawler did not rise again. Gradually, its heaving flanks stilled. The acrid tang of blood hung heavy on the air.

Satisfied it was truly finished, I signaled Leigh and Diane. We descended cautiously from our perches to inspect the carcass.

"We did it," Leigh breathed, wiping the sweat from her brow. That was quite the confrontation!"

I gave a satisfied grin as I kissed both of my women. "You girls did well," I said. Then, I looked around. "But this valley holds plenty of other dangers. We'll celebrate once we're out of the Blighted Land and have made a safe camp."

Leigh nodded. "You're right," she said. "We should get moving. No tellin' what else prowls here under darkness. At least the shrieks might keep some of them at bay. I reckon the Landcrawler is one of the most formidable foes around here."

Diane murmured agreement, already having reloaded her crossbow as she watched our surroundings.

"Let's go," I said, giving the carcass another look. It didn't look like there was anything of value there.

We gladly quit that place of death. I took the lead with sure steps, shouldering my pack. Together, we navigated toward the foothills looming ahead.

Chapter 7

Exhausted but vigilant, we hurried on through the darkness. The mountains loomed ahead, but the way remained perilous. Strange sounds echoed across the desolate valley in the Landcrawler's wake. It seemed as if the death of the creature had roused many other things, now that the tyranny of the apex predator was over.

Sticking close together, we scrambled over the uneven terrain. My eyes constantly raked the gloom, rifle ready. After that confrontation, we couldn't afford to be caught off guard.

A dry gully provided temporary cover to pause and check our heading. I quickly oriented us toward a pass through the foothills. We had to keep moving.

We were halfway up a crumbling slope when a chorus of unnatural shrieks shattered the night. I froze and peered into the darkness behind us.

"What is that?" Diane muttered, fear edging her voice.

Leigh stood limned against the moonlight, her dark blonde eyebrows furrowed as she peered into the gloom. I moved to stand beside her, rifle at the ready.

I saw at the same time as she did: dark, sinuous shapes poured from cracks in the earth.

"Grapplejaws!" Leigh and I said at the same time.

At least a hundred of the reptilian horrors

swarmed toward us, tendrils grasping! They moved with horrid speed, apparently having sensed our hurried steps as we made our way toward the edge of the Blighted Land.

"We can't handle this many," Leigh said. "We need to move. Find a body of water to cross. They won't follow."

I nodded as I stepped forward. "Run!" I shouted. "I'll be right behind you." As I spoke, I aimed at the incoming mass of writhing lizards and fired at the nearest one. The rifle's retort boomed, and the little creature practically exploded as the round struck it. But more slithered relentlessly on.

We scrambled higher as fast as the treacherous footing allowed, shots ringing out desperately to slow our pursuers. But the Grapplejaws kept coming, hissing and shrieking, eager for their meal.

"David, behind you!" Diane cried. I whirled, slamming one of the Grapplejaws with the stock of my rifle as it slithered up from a rock. It was just about to pounce, and its venomous jaws snapped a hairsbreadth from my throat as the stock of my rifle pulverized the skull.

Step by step we battled up the slope, seeking higher ground. My rifle blazed until empty; the bolt locked back; magazine spent. Similarly, Leigh's revolver was empty, and she hadn't had the time to reload it. Still, they came!

"Keep moving!" I called out to the girls as I reached for my bandolier and hastily uncorked a mana potion to down it.

The liquid burned my throat, but I immediately felt my mystical energies replenish. I restored 10 mana, bringing my total back up to 11.

But even as I finished my potion, Diane's foot slipped on the loose shale in the dark. "No!" she called out as she started sliding back toward the Grapplejaw pack.

But I was there in a breath, and I grabbed her arm just in time, bracing myself to pull her up. Leigh — a few steps ahead — pivoted around, but I nodded for her to keep moving.

But now Diane and I were trapped against the slope with the creatures surrounding us. Their tendrils lashed out, seeking to enclose us. I smashed one away with my rifle stock, shattering its skull, and the others gave pause at that.

Leigh cried out as another Grapplejaw seized her leg. I desperately kicked the thing off of her before its inner jaws could strike. But we were soon to be overwhelmed. Our only chance was the slight hesitation at the end of the Grapplejaws as they made ready to accept that some of them would die if they tried to overwhelm us.

Gritting my teeth, I summoned a guardian right before Diane and me. It materialized in a whirl of magical energy, and the Grapplejaws croaked with worry at the sight of the tall, powerful being. They reeled back, blistered and howling, as I commanded my guardian to protect us.

As the guardian braced itself, Diane and I turned and prepared ourselves to fight our way through the line of hesitant Grapplejaws to make our way back to Leigh. Just then, Leigh focused her energy — she had been touching her forehead with two fingers — and magically glowing hearts appeared over the heads of some Grapplejaws standing between her and us.

At once, those Grapplejaws turned on their allies

with a snarl, and the distraction was enough for us to break through their enclosure while the guardian shielded our backs, and we reached Leigh again.

"Go, go!" I urged the girls.

Shielding Diane and Leigh, we fought our way up the slope, while the guardian stayed behind to hold off the advancing swarm, aided by the Grapplejaws that Leigh had charmed with her Beastmaster ability.

A narrow gorge opened ahead — the way through the foothills! — and I heard water streaming. "This way!" I called out, and we pushed for it relentlessly. But the pack pursued, having overrun the guardian and their turncoat fellows. They were now flanking us to cut off escape.

But ahead, the stream shone in the moonlight. Almost there! My heart soared when I realized we would make it.

Breaking forward, we staggered into the stream. The water was chilling but wonderfully real after the nightmare valley.

Behind us, at the bank of the stream, the

Grapplejaws milled in confusion, their pursuit stymied by the flowing water. Apparently, they did not like it. And even if they had, the current would be strong enough to wash them away. They paced the bank, hissing balefully but were unwilling to follow into the shallows.

"We made it!" Leigh panted. "I almost thought we were goners back there."

I splashed some of the cool water over my grime-streaked face, scarcely believing our escape. Diane doubled over gasping beside me, then flung herself around my neck, thanking me for saving her.

Soon enough, Leigh joined in our hug, whooping triumphantly at the creatures now retreating back toward the Blighted Land. We had made it across.

As the stream carried away the dust and sweat of our harrowing flight, relief nearly overwhelmed me. But there could be no rest yet. We had to put distance between us and that cursed valley before I would feel safe enough to make camp.

"Come on, let's keep moving," I urged gently. Diane and Leigh nodded, weariness in their eyes. But determination still propelled them onward.

Step by weary step, we ascended into the rugged foothills. The Grapplejaws' cries eventually faded behind us. Sheltering rock walls closed around the narrow path as if swallowing us from that malignant place. I did not look back.

Chapter 8

Exhaustion weighed heavily on our limbs as we climbed higher into the craggy foothills. The further we trekked from the Blighted Land, the lighter the atmosphere felt, as if a physical miasma had been lifted. Still, we remained wary, ears straining into the darkness for any signs of pursuit.

Eventually, the path leveled off, and we came upon a sheltered hollow tucked between two cliffs. A tiny spring bubbled up from between mossy stones — fresh, clean water unpolluted by the valley's evil.

Gratefully, we slipped off our packs and dropped almost in unison onto the cool earth, muscles aching, and skin grimed with dirt and sweat. For a time, we simply focused on regaining our breath and gathering the energy to erect camp.

Once I had caught my second wind, I set about getting a small fire going in the lee of the stone while Leigh unpacked our bedrolls. Diane helped prepare a modest meal to revive our flagging strength after the desperate escape.

Soon, we were gathered around the flickering campfire, nursing mugs of hot tea and chewy trail rations. The events of the last day felt almost surreal in retrospect. We sat in weary silence for some time, processing it all.

"That was too close," Diane finally murmured, staring pensively into the fire. "If not for your quick thinking and magic, David, we'd have been overwhelmed."

I gave her thigh a gentle squeeze. "We made it thanks to all of us working together. Your warning saved me from that Grapplejaw." Diane managed a tremulous smile in response. "And Leigh's ability helped us break out. I don't know if we could've fought our way through that line of Grapplejaws without getting bitten once or twice."

Leigh winked at me and smiled. "I must admit, when I saw all those critters pouring outta the dark, I thought we were done for," she remarked before taking a long swig of tea. "I ain't sure if I agree with Waelin's assessment of the place."

I nodded grimly. "I think he may have underestimated it. Or perhaps the place has grown more dangerous since he last got his information. And the land itself felt heavy and watchful..." I shuddered at the memory. "We'll have to go through that land once more on our trip back, but we'll be more careful the second time around."

"With the Landcrawler gone," Leigh said, "we shouldn't have to be there at night. And during the day, we should be able to spot those swarms of

Grapplejaws long before their little tendrils feel us out."

"Agreed," Diane said fervently. "Still, let's be careful."

For a time, we sat in pensive silence as the moon rose higher, casting silver light and black shadows over the secluded hollow. The simple joys of firelight and hot tea took on new meaning after the day's travails.

Eventually, I asked Leigh if those Grapplejaws and Landcrawlers were common creatures. The Beastmaster furrowed her brow contemplatively before responding.

"In the Wilds, you'll see more of 'em," Leigh admitted. "But there were a lot of 'em here in the Blighted Land. They usually ain't *that* aggressive or in such big swarms. The taint on this land must've touched them. As for Landcrawlers." She shook her head. "Don't see many of those in the deeper Wilds. But you ain't gonna like the reason why?"

"Oh?" I said.

She grinned. "Deeper in the Wilds, there's more dangerous creatures. And they *hunt* the

Landcrawlers."

I smiled and nodded. "Eat or be eaten, huh?"

"Something like that," she said with a wink.

"Still," I continued. "It must be pretty dark magic that turned the Blighted Land into what it is today."

Leigh nodded sagely. "Ain't nothing in nature that conjures things so… unnatural, not even from Tannoris. We want no part of whatever went down back there."

Diane peered up at the emerging stars in thoughtful silence before adding, "My people have tales of four great mages in the First Age whose hubris sought to twist creation to their will." Her blue eyes were dark with memory. "They battled each other with terrible magics, and their folly unleashed catastrophe in many places before they were finally defeated, if the legends hold true."

I stared at her in amazement. "You think powers like that could have had a hand in the Blighted Land's fate?"

Diane gave an elegant shrug, unwilling to speculate further. But the notion left me intrigued.

Perhaps these places were sites where those ancient mages had fought.

The reminder of such ancient, cosmic forces served as a sobering capstone to our journey through that accursed valley. We had survived, but who knew what lingering traces of darkness remained etched upon the land. Perhaps one day, it would be dealt with.

Shaking off the feelings, I glanced at the beauty of the moon and felt the simple joy of having my companions at my side. "Well, whatever evil befell that place, let's simply be thankful we passed through without worse incident," I said at last.

Leigh gave a wry chuckle. "I'll say! Why don't we talk of cheerier things, like how nice it'll feel to finally get a proper rest tonight now that we're out of that nightmare valley."

Diane perked up a bit at the thought. "Yes, I could certainly use some uninterrupted sleep after the past twenty-four hours!" She playfully nudged Leigh. "Don't go snoring now like you did last night?"

"Me?" Leigh exclaimed in mock affront. "I think

you've got us confused! I have it on good authority that you're the snorer. Whenever you're out on watch, it's blissfully silent!"

Diane stuck out her tongue, and just like that, the somber mood was dispelled in a bout of much-needed laughter.

The simple act of bantering lifted our spirits immensely. With full bellies and the glowing embers warming our toes, drowsiness stole upon us rapidly. We were happy to leave any further discussions for the morrow's light.

I let the fire gradually settle into coals while Diane and Leigh readied the simple bedrolls and blankets we carried. It was warm and dry, and we would not put up the tent tonight as the rocky soil didn't really allow for it. The girls' eyes shone with gratitude when I announced I would take first watch so they could get some rest first.

Snug in their sleeping bags, Leigh was out almost before her head touched the pillow, while Diane drifted off, gazing dreamily up at the glittering tapestry of stars overhead. As their breathing deepened into sleep, I gazed around the shadowed hollow with a smile, willing away my own fatigue to stand sentinel a while longer.

Tomorrow would bring a fresh set of challenges navigating the rugged peaks to locate the hidden Dungeon. But for now, in this serene interlude, warmed by the dying firelight and my companions' steady slumber, contentment washed over me.

Chapter 9

It had been a long night, so we took our time the next morning. Still, not having raised the tent, the early light woke us. After a quick breakfast, we swiftly broke camp, eager to make an early start.

"Hopefully," I said. "We'll find the entrance to the Dungeon today. I think we shouldn't enter it yet, unless we still have plenty of energy left." I shot a look at Diane and Leigh. "That is, assuming that a Dungeon is a place that will take several hours to explore?"

Both girls nodded at that. "Yes," Leigh said. "I haven't done many Dungeon runs, but they tend to take a while."

"I have only done two," Diane said. "Both took about… three hours, I think? They were level 1 Dungeons, and I cleared them with a party of foxkin."

I nodded. "What can we expect?"

"Traps," she said. "And the monsters that Waelin announced."

I nodded. "Mainly summons and bound creatures."

"Yep," Leigh said. "It'd be smart to let someone scout ahead when we venture in." She flashed a grin at her harem sister. "And who better than Diane, a Scout?"

Diane grinned and nodded.

"Alright," I said. "Sounds like a plan. But let's find this place first."

Consulting Waelin's map once more, I traced our intended path deeper into the secluded basin. Nimos Sedia's location remained a cipher, but the day's first light kindled fresh hope within me of unraveling its secrets.

We set out at a steady march, breathing deep the crisp air scented of pine needles and weathered stone. White-capped peaks framed the horizon, standing sentinel over the valley's hidden enigmas. Far above, an eagle's piercing cry rang out — some of the creatures of Earth still flourished after the Upheaval. In fact, many were doing a lot better.

Trudging downslope through stands of hardy brush, we began methodically scouring the area for any signs of subterranean construction — shards of worked stone among scree fields, depressions concealed amidst the undergrowth. But as the morning aged, no revelations manifested.

Pausing in the shade of a towering pine, I once again closely perused Waelin's map, searching for any subtle clue I might have missed. Each smudged contour and faded notation had been seared into memory. But even now, the parchment kept its secrets.

As we continued searching the gradual western incline, I lamented not having any kind of magic that could unveil what our mortal senses had failed to discern. Luckily, Diane's skill as a Scout helped us search the mountain pass with great detail.

The search of the western incline proved fruitless, but there was much more space to cover. However, the chances of entering the Dungeon this same day were growing smaller.

With determination, we fanned out to thoroughly scour the area, overturning stones and probing depressions for any signs of subterranean architecture or concealed entrances. I remained hopeful some subtle clue would manifest to unravel this enigma.

But as the sun rose toward its pinnacle, no hidden passages or structures emerged. The Dungeon's location continued baffling our searches. Still, Diane's calming presence and Leigh's irrepressible humor kept my frustration from surfacing or taking control.

Taking a break, we sat upon a weathered boulder

to eat a bite, gazing out over the rugged basin.

"Is it always this hard to find the entrance to a Dungeon?" I asked.

Leigh shrugged, seeming a little dejected. "I don't know," she said. "Someone else scouted them for my previous party, back when I still roamed and hadn't settled in Gladdenfield yet."

But Diane shook her head. "Normally, they are easier to find."

Rising, I decided we should shift focus to the pass's northern extent. Consulting my compass and map, I oriented our course toward a stark ridge line. Perhaps from that lofty vantage some new prospect would reveal itself to keen eyes. Diane and Leigh readily agreed, trusting my instinct to search farther north.

As we headed toward the northern stretch of the pass, the path turned arduous, switch-backing relentlessly up the slope. Jagged outcroppings and loose scree fields made traversing treacherous, forcing us to move with care. But the toil would be rewarded if the ridge's height exposed some hint of our elusive quarry.

Breathless but unbowed, we crested the ridge as the day reached its zenith. I hurried to the edge, squinting out over the windswept pass now sprawling below us. But aside from meandering pines and the occasional bald peak, details remained maddeningly obscured by distance and haze. If Nimos Sedia was still there, it continued camouflaging itself cunningly.

Soul weary but not disheartened, we descended the ridge to resume the search. There were still hours of daylight left and numerous secluded hollows and thickets yet to be scoured. And we had one another's company to keep spirits kindled when the fruitless seeking grew most monotonous.

Afternoon found us combing the mossy banks of a winding creek, seeking any tunnel openings suggesting an underground complex. But the stony soil yielded only damp and dancing lightflies that flitted playfully about us. Their luminous beauty raised my spirits some before weariness set in once more.

As the sun dipped behind the western crags, we climbed a gentle slope to establish camp within a sheltered hollow between towering pines wreathed in shadow. A tiny rill burbled over smooth stones nearby, allowing us to refill our waterskins with the freshest and sweetest runoff.

While I got a modest campfire going, Diane and Leigh prepared a humble stew from our dwindling supplies. We had been underway for four days now, and I was happy I had insisted on bringing supplies for at least ten days. Over our dinner, talk turned to hopes tomorrow would finally unveil the hidden Dungeon's whereabouts. If not, we would run out of time.

With bellies filled, I again unfolded Waelin's map to meticulously recheck each smudged contour and notation, hoping renewed eyes might glean some previously missed clue. But the parchment's secrets remained locked away, to my continued vexation. Sighing, I carefully folded it before turning eyes skyward.

Arrayed above in breathless glory spread the night's first emerging stars, their gentle luminosity kindling perspective within me. Our quest's fulfillment remained paramount, but brief respites like this beneath the majestic firmament were to be cherished as well. I said as much to my companions, eliciting smiles.

When the embers had dimmed to a ruddy glow, I took first watch, soon to be relieved by Leigh. My own dreams were untroubled by frustrations of the day, focused instead on the silver web of stars glimpsed through sheltering pine boughs.

Chapter 10

The next morning, we awoke determined to uncover the hidden entrance to Nimos Sedia. As we finished our modest breakfast, I turned to the girls, still pondering the conundrum.

"There must be a reason it's been so difficult to locate," I mused aloud.

"It's probably really well hidden," Diane mused.

Leigh nodded. "The elves are crafty architects — in many ways even better than the dwarves. If they want something to remain hidden, that's how it's going to be."

"So," I said. "We'll just have to be sharper then." I hopped to my feet and brushed off my hands. "Let's hop to it."

The girls nodded their agreement, and together we resumed our systematic search of the mountain pass. As we combed the rocky slopes, I tried to put myself in the mindset of the ancient elves who had constructed this place. Why would they conceal the Dungeon's entrance so cunningly? Perhaps for defensive purposes in times of conflict.

"Maybe the entrance blends in with the natural topography as camouflage," I mused aloud. The notion struck me as we squeezed between two massive boulders. Their craggy faces were scarred by centuries of wind and rain. What if the facade hid worked stone behind?

Signaling Diane and Leigh, I began scrutinizing the rocks and stone debris surrounding us.

Weathered cracks and crags could easily mask cut blocks placed artfully. We broadened our search, looking for anything suggesting artificial shaping.

The early morning hours passed swiftly as we tapped and pressed on the landscape, seeking hollow echoes hinting at empty space behind any surface. But our efforts continued to come up empty. Yet we persisted, down on hands and knees in places, digging away loose gravel and dirt.

It was Diane who first noticed it using her Class abilities — scuff marks in the dusty earth near a sheer cliff face that suggested recent disturbance. She had activated her Tracking skill, and the gentle bubbling of water below suggested some hidden stream where critters went to drink.

"If there's a hidden stream," I mused, "there might be more hidden. Let's follow this trail."

Tracing the subtle signs brought us to a cleverly concealed crevice in the rock. It was practically invisible from every angle, and only the murmur of water gave it away. The crevice was wide enough to admit a single person at a time, and it could only be seen when standing above it thanks to the boulders piled around it.

"This might be it," I said. "I'll have a look."

"Be careful," Diane urged.

Diane and Leigh helped clear away enough loose stone for me to gingerly enter the crevice. I raised my flashlight beam as I descended, wary of loose footing on the damp, uneven surface. Rough-hewn steps led tantalizingly down into darkness before me — no natural formation could have created their deliberate, sequential contours. These had clearly been fashioned by skilled hands, and I knew in my bones this passageway would lead to Nimos Sedia at last.

A little farther down the crevice, water burbled, collecting among the rocks before slipping away again. Next to the little pool, time-worn steps descended into darkness. These had been fashioned by hand, and I knew this was it.

"We found it!" I exclaimed, excitement ripping through my voice. "It's here."

Diane and Leigh squeezed into the hidden cleft after me, our eyes shining in the lantern light. After a day of searching, Nimos Sedia's lost entrance lay before us at last!

Like cunning chameleons, the elven architects had merged Nimos Sedia's facade seamlessly with the surrounding topography. Without knowing precisely what to look for, the concealed entrance remained invisible to the naked eye. But our persistence had finally unearthed its secret.

As we gathered around the top of the carved steps, I turned and grinned at both women. "I knew we'd find it if we just kept looking!"

Leigh whooped joyously, and Diane laughed, both girls swept up in my elation. The promise of exploration and discovery crackled between us like electricity.

But we had to stay focused, I reminded myself. This was just the first step, albeit a crucial one. The greater challenges likely still awaited somewhere in the lightless depths below.

"What are we waitin' for then?" Leigh said enthusiastically. "Let's see where these here stairs lead!" She made as if to start down them immediately, but I gently pulled her back.

"Hold on," I cautioned, wanting to be smart

about this. "We should take some time first to prepare before venturing inside. Check weapons and supplies, get our flashlights ready. It's going to be dark down there."

Leigh rubbed the back of her neck, looking abashed. "Right, got ahead of myself for a second there," she admitted. "Good idea to be cautious."

Locating this lost entrance had required every ounce of wit and tenacity Diane, Leigh, and I possessed. It had been well hidden by elven skill, but we had managed to unearth it.

But the greater trial still awaited somewhere in the lightless depths under our feet. Yet now, standing together at the threshold and brimming with cautious excitement, I knew we were ready to brave whatever ancient enigmas lay hidden within this dungeon.

After we ate, rested up, and packed what we would likely need in the darkness of Nimos Sedia, we were finally ready to venture in.

Taking a deep breath, I led the way down the carved stone steps into the yawning darkness, one hand trailing along the rough wall to steady myself. The air grew steadily colder and heavier as we descended.

Soon the last of the daylight faded away behind us. Up ahead, my flashlight's narrow beam illuminated patches of the worn steps and dripping stone walls.

"Stay close together," I cautioned over my shoulder.

Diane and Leigh's own flashlight beams bobbed along just behind me. Their tense silence told me they shared my heightened sense of foreboding in the smothering blackness all around us.

After what felt like an eternity of careful descent, the stairs finally ended in a small circular chamber with two arched doorways leading off into further gloom. Strange symbols were carved around each entrance whose meanings were lost to the mists of time.

Halting to get our bearings, I swept my flashlight

systematically around the room. Thick cobwebs drooped from the ceiling, stirred faintly by some unfelt draft. The cracked stone floor was dusty, with no tracks or signs of recent passage.

"Which archway should we take?" Leigh asked.

"I think we should scout ahead," I said. "Get a feeling of what's down these corridors."

"I can check the tunnels, then come back to report," Diane suggested, her hushed voice loud in the heavy silence.

I nodded, still studying the archways. "Do you think you can remain hidden in case you come across any guardians?"

"Yes," she replied. "Anything out there will have difficulty seeing me. That is, if it's not much higher than level 3."

"This should be a level 3 Dungeon at most, so that should work. But Waelin's information was off on the Blighted Land. It might be off regarding Nimos Sedia as well."

She nodded, her jaw set. "That may be so, but I still stand a fair chance to remain hidden from monsters up to level 5. After that, it'll become riskier…"

"Do you want to try?" I asked, deciding to let her make the decision.

She gave another firm nod. "I do."

I smiled and gave her a kiss on the cheek. "Go on, but don't get too close to anything and report back if there's trouble."

She grinned and slipped through the left archway, her padding footsteps swiftly receding into the dark.

Leigh and I awaited her return anxiously. The very air itself seemed oppressive this deep underground, as if the weight of eons pressed down upon us. Each minute crawled by. There were no sounds down here aside from occasional drips of distant water. Even our breathing and the scuff of our boots on stone sounded muffled and flat.

After several tense minutes had dragged past, I frowned and opened my mouth to suggest one of us go look for Diane. Before I could speak, her faint footsteps echoed out of the leftmost tunnel again. I exhaled in relief as her slender form materialized out of the gloom.

"The left passage leads to a few empty chambers," Diane reported. "No signs of life or movement that I could detect. There may be some old elven artifacts still inside worth a look."

I nodded. "Good work. Let's check it out but stay sharp."

Falling into single file again, we proceeded cautiously through the left archway. The tunnel beyond twisted and branched confusingly before emptying into a circular room.

As Diane had indicated, the chamber appeared untouched for ages. Thick layers of dust clung to ornate stone benches carved along the walls. Strange symbols decorated the high domed ceiling, their meanings opaque to me.

While Leigh stood guard, Diane and I quickly investigated the adjoining rooms — various chambers and alcoves all equally still and neglected. In one side room stood an ancient stone altar stained with dark splotches I desperately hoped were not blood. The deeper we delved, the more unease swelled within me. What had this place been used for in ages past?

"Right, doesn't seem to be much else here," I finally announced, a slight edge in my voice belying my desire to hurry up. "Let's try the other tunnel. The Star Jewel must be deeper inside."

Retracing our steps, we reconvened in the central chamber then passed through the right archway into another rough-hewn tunnel. Here the stagnant air smelled slightly metallic. The winding passage ended at an elaborately carved set of double stone doors. Strange runes and figures adorned their surfaces.

Exchanging a look with Leigh and Diane, I grasped one of the large iron rings set into the doors and pulled cautiously. The ancient door scraped open reluctantly, stone grinding against stone. Beyond lay impenetrable darkness. Raising my flashlight, I began carefully sweeping the narrow beam around.

The light revealed a high-ceilinged chamber containing row upon row of large metal braziers, all cold and empty. At the chamber's far end rose a towering statue of some robed elven figure wielding a staff. The iron sconces lining the walls were empty, with no fuel source now to light them.

"A shrine of some sort, perhaps," Diane whispered. Her sharp eyes darted nervously about at the shadows clinging to the room's edges beyond the flashlight beams' puny reach. The place felt heavy with elapsed time and arcane purpose inscrutable to us now.

"It looks like a wizard," Diane mused, studying the statue.

I nodded agreement. "Let's search the room," I said. "See if there are any exits. And be mindful of traps."

The girls inclined their heads in agreement, and we began our methodical search of the chamber.

Chapter 11

Moving cautiously, we began searching the shadowy chamber for any hidden exits, wary of traps. My flashlight's beam darted across the dusty floor, alert for any subtle signs of danger. Meanwhile, Diane investigated the perimeter, her sharp eyes allowing her to navigate the gloom with ease.

Leigh stood watchfully near the entrance, one hand resting on the revolver at her hip. The echo of our careful footsteps seemed unnaturally loud in the oppressive silence. As we moved, the arcane statuary seemed to leer watchfully down at us.

Halfway across the chamber, a faint click from beneath my boot froze all of us in our tracks. I looked over at Diane as she lifted her foot slowly. She had stepped on a stone tile, and it had cracked. From both edges, dark liquid oozed out in thin rivulets, meeting in the seam in the center. When the two streams touched, there was a hiss, and a cloud of noxious vapor rose to envelop Diane.

"Poison trap!" I called out in warning. Swift as lightning, I pulled one of the antidote vials Waelin had provided from my bandolier and tossed it to Diane. She caught it as she stepped away and downed the antidote, giving her a better chance to fight any toxins she might have inhaled.

"You alright?" I asked worriedly, hurrying over once she had downed the potion. The vapor had already dissipated.

She nodded, wiping her mouth with the back of her hand as she winced at the antidote's taste. Any effects seemed neutralized.

"Yeah," she said, smiling at me. "Thanks... This is an alchemical poison... The antidote countered it, or else I would've already gotten very ill."

I nodded slowly, watching the cracked tile. All the liquid had gone, and the vapor had dissipated. It was as if nothing had happened. "You sure you're okay?" I pressed.

"Yeah... I should be more careful."

"David's sharp eyes saving our hides again," Leigh remarked from the back of the room, shaking her head as she peered at the stone tiles. "Coulda been nasty business."

Diane bit her lip. "If traps like this one are still active, there could be others lying in wait as well..." she murmured uneasily.

I squeezed her shoulder supportively, though I harbored the same concerns now. "We'll just have to keep eagle eyes out and stick to searching the perimeter of any chamber," I said. Though eager to press forward, caution was clearly critical in here.

Danger lurked beneath seemingly innocuous surfaces.

Diane nodded firmly. "I'll take point and search the whole place for more traps," she volunteered without hesitation. "I'll be more careful. It'll take longer, but we'll be sure."

With Diane tentatively scouting a path around the outside edge of the chamber, I conducted a wary examination of the walls. Stretching up on my toes, I checked above the empty sconces, lest anything was concealed atop them.

Meanwhile, Diane's sharp gaze traced over every crack and crevice, seeking subtle hints of switches or catches camouflaged in the stonework. But the ornate walls appeared solid, with no cracks or openings suggestive of hidden doors.

Finally, Diane completed her cautious circuit of the tiled floor, but she found no more traps — similar to the poisonous one or otherwise. Unfortunately, she or I hadn't found any doors either.

Diane blew out a frustrated breath, hands on hips as she critically surveyed the ostensibly solid chamber again. She then gave me a helpless shrug. I frowned, rubbing a hand over my stubbled chin. This couldn't be the end of the Dungeon.

"No way forward from here?" Leigh asked from the back of the chamber. "We must've missed an opening somewhere back…"

Her words abruptly died as a deep rumble shook the foundations beneath our feet. Dust drifted down from above and the empty braziers rattled ominously.

We exchanged wide-eyed looks in the quavering flashlight beams, dread clutching my insides. Was the whole ceiling about to come crashing down on us? But the tremors swiftly subsided again, leaving only ominous silence once more.

"Okay, on second thought, maybe there *is* something back here," Leigh amended shakily.

Gripping my flashlight like a torch, I played the beam slowly over the chamber's perimeter again, seeking any cracks or openings that the tremors might have revealed. Then I glimpsed it — barely discernible seams marking out the outline of a door-sized section of the wall.

The tremors — whatever they were — must've laid them bare!

Rushing over, I confirmed the subtle groove and pressed my palm flat against the section of wall. Slowly, almost reluctantly, it began to grind backward and then slid fully out of sight into a recess, exposing a stygian portal beyond. The rumbling had been the hidden doorway opening somehow.

"You did it!" Diane cheered, though her expression was still taut with anxiety.

Peering inside, I swept my flashlight over stairs descending deeper underground. There was no other option but to follow them and see where they led.

""Stairs," I said to the girls as they came over. "No way to go but down." I steeled myself and stepped over the threshold.

As I stepped forward, there was a sudden metallic clang that made me jump back. From the ceiling, a portcullis came down, slamming so hard into the tiles on which I had just stood a moment ago that chips of stone sprang up.

Another trap... I was learning some hard lessons about Dungeons and Dungeon safety.

As I took a deep breath, a deep rumbling issued behind us. I whirled, flashlight beam darting upward.

The girls gasped as they saw the same as I did. The statue of the elven wizard began to writhe and shift subtly, pieces of stone falling to the floor as it rolled its shoulder. Then, its baleful gaze fell on us...

Chapter 12

The towering statue shifted and stirred, stone scraping loudly against stone as it ponderously turned to face us. Intricate glyphs etched across its surface began smoldering with eldritch purple light, casting our faces in an eerie glow. Eyes widening, I quickly stepped back and readied my rifle as the enormous granite golem lifted its carved staff.

"Get ready, it's about to attack!" I warned urgently.

Leigh swiftly drew her revolver from its holster while Diane fitted a steel-tipped bolt to her crossbow with deft fingers. My mind raced — normal bullets would likely just chip the statue's stone, but there had to be a weak point where we could damage it.

"Aim for the joints, they're weaker!" I shouted over the grating noise of the golem lumbering toward us. Normal attacks might be less effective, but I could see the elbows and knees crumbling with each step — they were the only vulnerability I could spot.

As the girls took position, my free hand traced quick sigils in the air, channeling my will to summon a guardian. We had mere moments to act before the colossus was upon us.

With an arcane word, my swirling blue mana coalesced into a powerfully-built spectral warrior gripping a massive tower shield. The translucent entity planted itself staunchly between us and the stone behemoth, shield raised as I ordered it to protect us. The girls swiftly took flanking positions on either side, slightly behind the creature.

In unison, Leigh and Diane opened fire, shot and bolt sparking brightly off the statue's lumbering granite limbs. The ancient golem staggered slightly under the barrage but kept coming.

The thing's mossy stone robes crumbled with each thudding step. Glowing emerald eyes fixed upon my guardian with preternatural hatred as it made ready to attack.

With a resounding boom, the towering construct's carved staff hammered down. My guardian caught the crushing blow on its spectral shield, the deafening reverberations rattling my bones even from yards back. Fragments of stone cracked and fell from the point of impact.

Seizing the chance while the golem was overextended, I focused my will and traced another quick summoning sigil, shouting the words of power. A second guardian manifested in a swirl of azure mist just as the first guardian staggered under the crushing staff blow.

I was already 16 mana down, leaving 9. I wouldn't be able to keep this up; we needed to coordinate our attacks if we were to emerge victorious.

"Keep aiming for the joints!" I reminded the girls as I unslung my rifle.

The girls continued peppering the lumbering statue relentlessly with their weapons. More cracks were spider-webbing across the stone, but the thing seemed largely impervious still. Only sustained structural damage or overwhelming arcane force would drop it.

My twinned guardians moved in, raising their shields side-by-side to divert and absorb the golem's wild swings while allowing Diane and Leigh clear shots. As they approached, I nestled the buttstock of my rifle in the pocket of my shoulder and fired at the knees, the report booming in the chamber.

The creature staggered, then resumed its attacks. Stone chips flew with each thunderous impact of the statue's massive staff against the spectral shields. The construct reeled from our coordinated barrage but did not relent. Then, with a particularly vicious swoop, it smashed both of my guardians to bits, making them dissolve and return to their spirit realm.

"David!" Diane called out as she placed another bolt in the groove of her crossbow.

"I know," I said, and I swiftly cast another Summon Guardian spell. The ethereal warden manifested and moved up, distracting the animated statue before it could move on to attack one of us. As it braced itself for impact, I downed another mana potion and immediately cast another Summon Guardian spell, directing the second guardian to join the first. We needed tanks out there as one swing of that staff could kill any of us.

"Keep up the fire!" I called out to the girls. "Keep targeting the joints."

The thing staggered under our renewed barrage. Sighting along my rifle barrel during a lull, I aimed for a cracked joint at the statue's granite knee and fired.

Stone exploded from the wound in a burst of

dust, and the leg crumpled awkwardly beneath the listing golem. It toppled forward heavily, staff clattering away across the tiled floor.

But still the animated statue tried dragging itself forward using its thick arms, weight scraping loudly over the debris-strewn tiles, then slammed with its fists at the guardians. But the attacks were weaker now.

Together, my guardians braced their shields in a shield wall and shoved mightily to keep the downed but still dangerous golem at bay. The statue slammed and smashed, but the guardians handled the attacks well.

The girls and I continued firing relentlessly, blowing chunks out of the thing's stone torso and arms. It writhed and thrashed beneath the onslaught, limbs grinding as it attempted in vain to rise and face us once more. Glowing glyphs flickered erratically across its cracked surface.

Slowly but surely, our coordinated assault was overpowering the arcane sentinel. With a final massive heave, it smashed one of my guardians out of existence before another barrage made the thing stop moving, the glyphs on its body gradually going dim and darkening.

Cautiously, I moved closer and prodded the crumbling pile of rubble with my rifle barrel. When no response came, I nodded in satisfaction — the arcane energies animating the ancient golem had apparently been depleted fully. It was inert once more.

"That was a close shave," Leigh muttered with an exhaled breath, though her hand still trembled slightly as she pushed new rounds into her revolver's chamber.

Diane lowered her crossbow, visibly awed. "That was incredible teamwork and bravery, David," she said sincerely, placing a soft hand on my shoulder. "Without your guardians shielding us from those crushing blows, I fear that we…"

I pulled her into a relieved hug. "We made it," I said, smothering her projections. "We did very well."

Leigh let out a low appreciative whistle as she toed the nearby pile of carved rubble. "Gotta say, Ol' Rocky put up one heck of a fight, but it didn't stand a chance against us in the end."

Despite the quip, her eyes remained wary as she scanned the shadowy chamber again. "Let's hope that's the last surprise guardian down here, or we may not get so lucky again."

I wholeheartedly agreed with the sentiment. As I was about to speak, a flashing in the corner of my eyes drew my attention. "I leveled up from that," I said. "Level 5!"

Both girls gave an excited chirp. "Hey! I think I leveled too!" Diane said; her eyes unfocused for a moment as she checked the notification. "I did!"

"Yep," Leigh said. "Me, too! Level 3!"

"Perfect!" I said. "Let's break here for a moment. We can take turns applying our levels. We might need any advancement we can get!"

Chapter 13

With the stone golem vanquished, I could feel the new power thrumming through my veins. It seemed that, as a side effect of leveling up, my mana had restored as well, which was welcome, as it had been at 3 at the end of the harrowing battle with the animated statue.

"You level up first, David," Diane said. "Leigh and I will stand watch."

"Yeah," Leigh said. "Looks like the defeat of that thing made the portcullis rise." She peered at the stairs behind the secret door. "I'll stand guard, and Diane can double-check it for another nasty surprise."

I gave the girls a thankful nod before I sat down on a stone bench, closed my eyes, and focused to assess my new abilities after advancing to level 5. As expected, my maximum health had increased by 10 points to 60. My mana reserves were now 30, up from 25.

I was also interested to see that Summon Minor Spirit had reached level 15, and that had decreased its mana cost by 1! Additionally, I could bind a second familiar to me — reinforcements for Ghostie! But most excitingly, I had also unlocked access to a new spell.

Concentrating, I reviewed the options now available to me. The first was a defensive summon — Summon Mistwraith. For only 4 mana, I could summon a misty wraith to obscure my presence or that of an ally, making them more difficult to hit from a distance.

The second spell was Flame Lance — a 10 mana fiery attack conjuration that dealt a lot of damage. Finally, there was an offensive summon: Summon Goblin, which would call forth a goblin warrior for 6 mana.

As I pondered the options, a special alert won my notice.

Unique spell option unlocked due to condition "Blessing of Aquana": Summon Aquana's Avatar.

Excitement rushed through me as I quickly perused the spell. It was a costly one at 10 mana, but it allowed me to summon a physical manifestation of Aquana. Of course, the avatar would not be as powerful as Aquana actually was, and I could only have one active at the same time, which was not bindable with my Bind Familiar spell. But it would be a formidable combatant. Closer study revealed that it would be a water elemental.

To me, it wasn't really a choice. Sure, each of the spells had their benefits, but the unique ability to summon an avatar of Aquana dwarfed everything else. How many mages even had this spell?

Without further consideration, I chose Summon Aquana's Avatar. Its capabilities seemed invaluable. I felt the knowledge of the spell's incantation imprint itself on my mind. When next I applied my magic, I would be able to manifest this new ability.

Excited, I gave my character sheet a review.

Name: David Wilson

Class: Frontier Summoner

Level: 5

Health: 60/60

Mana: 30/30

Skills:

Summon Minor Spirit — Level 15 (3 mana)

Summon Domesticant — Level 11 (6 mana)

Summon Guardian — Level 8 (8 mana)

Summon Aquana's Avatar — Level 1 (10 mana)

Bind Familiar — Level 2 (15 mana)

Identify Plants — Level 8 (1 mana)

Foraging — Level 9 (1 mana)

Trapping — Level 9 (1 mana)

Alchemy — Level 12 (1 mana)

Satisfied, I dismissed the sheet and excitedly related my advances to the girls.

"Wow!" Diane purred. "You can actually summon Aquana?"

"Well, it's not actually him," I said, "but it's his avatar — the next best thing. It's pretty powerful, I bet. I'd try it out, but it would cost me mana that I'll likely need farther into the Dungeon."

"Nice!" Leigh enthused. "It sounds really useful."

"I wonder if Leigh and me might also get access to a special ability due to the blessing of Aquana?" Diane mused.

I smiled at them. "Only one way to find out. You girls advance now, and I'll stand guard."

Humming excitedly, the girls went to work while I stood guard. It didn't take them very long, and Diane was first to finish.

"The Blessing of Aquana gave me an ability to deal extra water damage with my weapons," she said. "It also becomes magical damage, which would make a battle with creatures with damage resistance — like the statue just now — a lot easier!"

"That's very useful," I said. "We need to up the damage output, and with my new spell and your imbued weapons, we'll do a lot better."

Leigh piped up next. "The Blessing of Aquana gave me a new option, too! I got a new ability called Calm Waters. I can suppress any water beasties, including non-animals, and make them non-hostile toward us and hostile toward others. Might come in useful whenever we gotta cross a stream or lay an ambush!"

"Excellent," I said, smiling at both of them proudly. "That's very useful, indeed! I'm thrilled we all gained new abilities. They should really help us moving forward. I'm feeling pretty confident we can clear the rest of this Dungeon."

The girls nodded their agreement, and I did a quick rundown of our supply situation, taking stock of potions and other equipment. The fight had depleted some resources, but we still had antidotes and healing draughts left thanks to Waelin's provisions, as well as a few mana draughts of my own making.

"Looks like we're ready to move," I said. "No more traps?"

Diane shook her head. "None."

"Alright, let's press on," I said firmly.

Diane nodded. "I'll take point and scout ahead again." Moving cautiously, she approached the hidden door. Beyond lay the stairwell and whatever deeper secrets awaited discovery.

With Diane scouting the way, Leigh and I followed single file down the worn steps into the benighted depths. Our flashlight beams sent monstrous shadows leaping up the dripping stone walls on either side as we descended.

With weapons at the ready, we proceeded down the ancient stone staircase, senses primed for any signs of movement in the darkness below. The air grew heavier and colder with each step, our breath misting faintly in the flashlight beams.

At the base of the long descent, the claustrophobic stairs opened into a high-ceilinged hall lined with towering statues of armored elven warriors. Their stern stone faces glowered down silently, clutching spears and swords. The place had a solemn, tomb-like feel that raised the hairs on my neck.

"Hope these don't wake up, too," Leigh muttered.

"Let's check for traps and be sure," I replied.

Moving cautiously, we fanned out to check the shadowy perimeter of the hall, alert for traps or triggers that could animate the imposing statues. But all remained still aside from occasional drips of water and scurrying of some unseen creature in the cracks and crevices.

Reaching the far end of the hall, we halted before a set of intricate bronze doors etched with arcane symbols. Studying them closely, Diane pointed out subtle grooves suggesting the doors could slide apart. Soon enough, we found a handle to open them. A wide hallway yawned beyond.

"Maybe you can scout ahead?" I said, looking at

Diane. "Try to find any traps or enemies."

She gave a firm nod and moved toward the side of the corridor, studying her surroundings with intricate care as she moved. We watched her disappear into the shadows, relying on her keen foxkin eyes in the gloom. Leigh and I stood watch, waiting for her return.

After several minutes, she hurried back to report. "There are fire elementals up ahead guarding the next doorway," she whispered. "I counted at least six of them."

I frowned. Fire elementals could be dangerous foes. "Alright, let's get into position and plan our attack," I said, leading us back up the steps out of sight.

Once we were ready, Diane crept back down to keep lookout on the elementals. When she gave the signal, Leigh and I swiftly followed, guns raised and ready. Up ahead, the hall glowed with the flickering light of the six fiery guardians mutely patrolling before a set of sealed bronze doors.

Wasting no time, I focused my will and spoke the magical words to summon Aquana's avatar for the

ql_2edx

first time.

I watched in awe as my mana coalesced into a lean and powerful water elemental wreathed in shimmering vapor. The elemental resembled a man rising from a tide of water pooling up to his ankles. The waters roiled with primeval power, and I had no doubt that Aquana's avatar could dish out a serious amount of damage.

Bidding my minion to halt for a moment, I also cast Summon Guardian to have a protector for the avatar.

"Amazing," Diane whispered as she saw the crystalline, shield-bearing creature take up position next to the shimmering water elemental.

I grinned broadly. "Let's see what the two of them can achieve together."

At my mental command, the duo floated forward. The guardian remained a few steps ahead of the avatar, and it raised its shield as it came to a halt, while the avatar unleashed a roaring jet of water that blasted two of the fire elementals, steaming them away into wisps of vapor.

"They seem to work together," Leigh said.

I nodded agreement, a little perplexed. I had only given them the combined mental command to advance, and they had applied a joint tactic that had the guardian shielding the advance of the avatar, and it employed its ranged attack from the safety behind the guardian's shield.

Of course, they had now been spotted. The remaining four elementals converged chaotically on my guardian, seeking to overwhelm it with scorching flames and fiery blows. But it raised its shield and weathered their assault, while the avatar retaliated with more torrential jets that drove them back, making fire elemental after fire elemental dissolve with a hiss.

Under the cover of my summons, Leigh and Diane opened fire, their shots puncturing the mutable forms of two elementals and disrupting their fiery cores. With furious hisses, the injured beings dissipated into smoke, while the avatar got rid of the last one standing.

As the last elemental fell, the intricate bronze doors at the far end of the room abruptly split down the middle and slid apart with a grinding rumble. Diane, Leigh, and I tensed, swiveling with weapons ready in case more guardians emerged. But there was only stillness and silence beyond the now open portal.

Cautiously, I moved up to peer through the widening crack between the bronze doors. "Looks like another hallway beyond," I reported.

Sure enough, they had opened into a rectangular passageway with an arched ceiling. I waved for Leigh and Diane to follow as my summons dissipated.

Moving slowly, we swept our flashlight beams over strange friezes carved into the walls depicting fiendish creatures I did not recognize. The air here felt even colder, tinged with an acrid, organic scent. Some greater evil likely lay ahead, and we proceeded on high alert.

The snaking tunnel ended at an ornate marble door marked with a complex circular glyph that appeared magically sealed. I traced my fingers over the intricate grooves, frowning. "Any ideas on how to open it?"

Diane scrutinized the glowing sigil closely. "If I

had to guess, I'd say we need a key of some sort attuned to the door's magic," she said at last. Her sharp eyes began scanning the ground around the doorway.

Meanwhile, I scrutinized the neighboring walls, seeking any cracks or hidden switches that might reveal a concealed compartment containing the key we required. But the stonework appeared flush and seamless. This portal was clearly meant to be impervious to intruders.

"Over here!" Leigh suddenly called out excitedly. Diane and I hurried over to find her shining her flashlight beam on something half-buried in dust in the far corner — a gleaming crystal disc etched with runes to match the sealing mark on the door.

Brushing it off reverently, I felt a thrum of power within the artifact. This had to be our key. Moving back to the door, I carefully fitted the disc into the central groove atop the glyph. Immediately, the sigil flared brighter, and the marble portal rumbled open. By the time we moved through, my avatar and guardian had dissipated.

Beyond lay a shadowy chamber far larger than any previous one. Our flashlight beams were swallowed entirely by the cavernous gloom. But in the light, I discerned tombstones, crumbling pillars, and wooden doors framed and adorned with bones at the far side.

"Keep alert," I whispered. "No telling what could be lurking in a place like this..."

My words abruptly died in my throat as I glimpsed shapes shifting in the darkness ahead. A second later, a chorus of unearthly shrieks split the still air.

"Get ready!" I shouted in warning, swiftly backing up and summoning a guardian just as the things attacked. Blurs of raking claws and gnashing teeth swarmed my guardian from the shadows. I heard Diane and Leigh open fire beside me, muzzle flashes strobing the chamber.

As my guardian valiantly shielded us from the frenzied assault, I was able to glimpse our attackers — emaciated gray-skinned humanoids with sunken black eyes and mouths full of jagged fangs. They moved with uncanny speed, frustrating our attempts to draw a bead on them.

"Ghouls!" Leigh called out over the cacophony.

Chapter 14

My guardian held fast against the snarling tide of undead as Leigh, Diane and I struggled to get a clear shot on the darting forms swarming it. Ghouls were dangerous foes — their bite could paralyze, and their claws reap life energy.

"Try to bottleneck them!" I called out. Just before

my guardian fell, I quickly downed a mana potion to bring my mana up to 14 and summoned another to take its place, the magic draining my reserves back to 6. We had to turn the tide soon.

At my direction, the guardian retreated into the hallway creating a narrow gap where the doorway opened into the chamber, with Leigh and Diane taking position behind it. With the ghouls forced to come at us from one direction, we were finally able to target them effectively as they tried to push through.

Rifle shots and crossbow bolts took down ghoul after ghoul as they scrambled and pushed to reach us past my guardian's massive shield. Dark blood sprayed the dusty floor, and their eerie shrieks turned to gurgles as we systematically eliminated them.

Just when it seemed the tide was turning, an ear-splitting screech rent the air — the ghouls' leader had arrived! The hulking undead brute barreled toward us, smashing into my guardian with a sweeping blow.

"Focus fire!" I yelled, taking quick aim with my

rifle. If we didn't drop it fast, the monster's paralyzing venom could spell doom. Diane and Leigh reacted immediately, their shots tearing chunks from the ghoul leader's mottled blue-gray flesh.

My guardian swiftly moved to lock the burly ghoul in melee, but the thing lashed out with surprising speed, raking its claws across the guardian's torso. With a flash, my summon dissolved under the draining attack.

Having seen it coming, I had slammed back another potion and summoned two guardians, depleting my mana to 0. They manifested just in time to form a shield wall, keeping the ghoul leader away from my women and forcing it to attack the guardians in the narrow bottleneck.

I kept the guardians between us and the ghoul leader while lining up with my rifle, taking shots at the creature's center of mass — it was moving way too fast for headshots. Whooping, Leigh and Diane joined their shots to mine, with Diane's bolts imbued with her new ability to deal extra damage.

The hulking undead brute reeled under the

sudden barrage, black blood streaming from its gnarled face. At my command, the guardians seized the opportunity and pushed the ghoul hard with their shields.

The ghoul thrashed violently as it was pushed back, then was stunned for a moment. In that moment, I landed the perfect headshot, and the ghoul crumpled to the dusty floor with a rattling groan.

In the ringing silence that followed, no more ghouls emerged from the shadows. My remaining guardians stood sentinel as we caught our breath, eyes scanning warily for any renewed assault. But it seemed the threat was quelled.

"Nice work, ladies," I said with an exhausted grin.

Diane and Leigh smiled tiredly in return, hands trembling slightly as the adrenaline wore off. That had been another close call, but our teamwork had carried the day again.

"I think Waelin's information was off on this place, too," I muttered, looking around us. "We're levels 5 and 3, and this place is supposed to be a lot easier."

The girls nodded grim agreement, and I turned my gaze to them. "If you girls want to abort, then we can," I said, although I really didn't want to do so. Still, if either of them was unwilling to continue, they needed a chance to say so.

Leigh and Diane exchanged a glance, then both shook their heads. I smiled and gave them a nod, pride blossoming in my chest at their courage and steadfastness. "Alright," I said. "Good on you both! Let's take a short break before we continue!"

Pausing only long enough to sip some water and eat a few bites of dried meat from our packs, we pressed deeper into the vast chamber. More enemies could lurk within the gloom, and so I took a mana potion just to be on the safe side and have some mana reserves.

Once I was satisfied no ghouls remained lurking, we proceeded. We still had to locate the Star Jewel somewhere in these benighted depths. As we moved, my summons dissolved.

Sweeping light over crumbling pillars, our flashlight beams fell upon the wooden doors adorned with bones. With the ghoul threat vanquished, they had opened, revealing a black hallway beyond.

"Diane, can you check that for traps?" I asked, and she gave a resolute nod before moving up. I used the time to quickly push fresh rounds into my magazine, making sure it was full and ready.

Moving cautiously, Diane entered the shadowy corridor, eyes sharp for any signs of traps or triggers. Leigh and I waited tensely, listening to her receding footsteps echo faintly off the stone walls. After several fraught minutes, she reappeared unharmed and gave the all-clear signal.

With Diane scouting a few paces ahead, Leigh and I followed her into the unlit passage beyond the bone-adorned doorway. The air felt even colder and heavier as we delved ever deeper into sunless realms.

The claustrophobic hallway terminated at an

arched stone doorway opening into a circular chamber. Stepping inside behind Diane as she checked for traps, I swept my flashlight over intricate mosaics covering the curved walls and domed ceiling overhead.

The artwork depicted unfamiliar constellations and celestial bodies, perhaps chronicling the night skies of ancient Tannoris. Stacked along the walls were rows of stone sarcophagi sealed with heavy lids. The entire chamber seemed a shrine of the dead from millennia past.

While Leigh stood guard at the entrance, Diane and I conducted a methodical sweep around the perimeter. But the chamber's occupants remained undisturbed, with no hidden threats revealing themselves. Satisfied it was safe for now, I paused to study the faded mosaics more closely, reminded how fleeting even great civilizations proved over the inexorable passage of time.

Leaving the tombs sealed, we passed through the opposite arched doorway into another long passageway. The walls here were slick with moisture dripping down from somewhere overhead. The echoes of falling water grew louder as we navigated several twists and turns along the clammy corridor.

The passage terminated at a steep staircase delving down into the dark. Gripping the slick handrails, we descended cautiously into the gathering chill below. Through the clinging mists, I glimpsed an underground lake spread out before us, its glassy surface reflecting our flashlight beams. A simple wooden bridge extended out over the still onyx waters.

At the sound of our footsteps, luminous fish scattered from the dock where they had been nibbling some glowing moss. Ripples warped and danced across the lake's mirror sheen, casting wavering funhouse reflections of us standing at its brink.

Though anxious about what might lurk beneath that glassy facade, we had no choice but to proceed. To be on the safe side, Leigh used her Calm Waters ability on the lake.

Testing her weight gingerly first, Diane crept out onto the creaking planks. When they held firm,

Leigh and I followed cautiously. The ancient bridge groaned underfoot but did not give way. As we proceeded, we seemed wholly surrounded by this lightless lake sealed far beneath the earth.

Finally, the beams of our flashlights fell on a stone doorway that loomed ahead, beautifully inlaid with mosaics of colored glass that reflected the light. We exchanged hopeful looks as we proceeded.

Chapter 15

As we approached the intricately decorated doorway, I could feel the thrum of powerful magic emanating from within. This had to be it — the final chamber containing the Star Jewel. Gripping my rifle tightly, I stepped forward.

The glass mosaics flickered with light as the

heavy stone door slid open at our approach. A wide chamber lay beyond, dominated by a raised stone dais. There, resting atop a carved pedestal, a brilliant multi-faceted gemstone shone with blinding radiance — the Star Jewel!

But surrounding the pedestal lurked hulking, sinuous forms that turned to fix us with baleful reptilian eyes as we entered.

"Oh no," Diane muttered. "Those are drakelings!"

At least six of the massive creatures guarded the Star Jewel, uncoiling and spreading leathery wings as they prepared to attack. In appearance, the Tannorian monsters were much like a hybrid between a dragon and a man — they had wings, claws, and dragon maws, but they were otherwise bipedal.

"Take positions!" I shouted urgently, already summoning a guardian as the drakelings charged with bone-rattling roars. Diane and Leigh swiftly rolled behind stone pillars flanking the entrance while my guardian planted itself staunchly before me.

The leading drakeling smashed into the spectral warrior with devastating force, but my guardian held fast behind its tower shield. Meanwhile, the girls opened fire from their flanking positions. I hastily downed a mana potion, raising my mana back up to 12, and channeled my will, manifesting a shimmering water elemental — Aquana's avatar!

The avatar swept forward, unleashing twin torrents of swirling water that battered the drakeling horde. They reeled beneath the magical onslaught while my guardian continued blocking their frenzied melee attacks.

I added my rifle shots to the barrage once I had found cover. A well-placed headshot took out one of the drakelings as it tried to flank my guardian, while another following in its wake fell with Diane's water-imbued bolt in its throat.

But the hulking reptilians were incredibly resilient. Fighting in a coordinated pack, a trio of the beasts swooped upon my guardian from three sides, their claws and tails lashing out in a flurry of devastating blows. With a flash, my summon dissolved beneath the savage assault.

Cursing, I quickly downed my final mana potion and resummoned my guardian just as two of the drakeling broke through toward us. Diane cried out in pain as a lashing tail clipped her, sending her sprawling.

"Push them back!" I yelled, lining up a headshot and quickly dispatching the one who had attacked Diane, while Leigh helped Diane take cover. Then, Aquana's avatar joined in with the guarding, smashing its fists with the power of the tempestuous seas, crushing drakeling skulls.

The girls' shots joined mine, tearing into scaly hide and splintering horn. My avatar continued pummeling the staggered drakeling with ceaseless torrents, while the guardian held the line and advanced by pushing with its shield.

Step by step, our coordinated assault forced the vicious pack back toward the pedestal. But they fought like demons, their fury unabated despite injuries. Any lapse in our barrage would see them surge forward again. But when we made our way closer to the pedestal, I discerned the driving force behind their power.

A drakeling, at least two feet taller than the others, stood there, its draconic scales shimmering as it directed the others. It was their leader, and it looked like it had a Class or an ability that lashed its followers into a frenzy!

"Focus fire on the leader!" I redirected our efforts. The drakeling alpha towered over its brethren, ancient cunning glinting in its swirling red eyes. Diane's crossbow bolt pierced one directly as I gave the mental command to the avatar and combined our attacks.

The water elemental changed tactics and drove a concentrated jet directly at the drakeling leader's head. At the same moment, Leigh, Diane and I volleyed it relentlessly. Staggering beneath our focused assault, it bellowed an ear-splitting shriek of fury and agony.

Pressing our advantage, I directed my guardian to hold the other drakelings at bay for as long as it could so we could take out the leader. I aimed my rifle and fired a shot at the still gleaming red eye, even as the avatar punched it with the wild power of the oceans.

That did it! With a final gurgling roar, the massive drakeling toppled like an avalanche, crashing to the polished stone floor and laying still.

The remaining reptilians fell back with hisses of dismay at their leader's defeat. But bereft of its coordination, their defense swiftly collapsed before our sustained barrage. One by one we systematically shot them down until none were left standing.

As the last drakeling collapsed in a bloody heap, my avatar and guardian faded away. A stunned silence filled the chamber. Dazed, I lowered my smoking rifle and hurried to check up on Diane.

She winced, badly bruised, but gave me a tired thumbs up. The girls had made it through.

"That was a hairy fight if I ever saw one," I muttered, shaking my head as I surveyed the carnage around us.

"We made it, though," Diane said, rubbing her bruise as she smiled at me.

"We sure did," Leigh agreed. "Never doubted us for a second!"

Grinning, I pulled them both in for a hug. Then,

so entwined, we crossed the carnage-strewn floor to stand before the pedestal.

We crossed the chamber strewn with the corpses of drakelings arm in arm until we came to the dais where rested the treasure of Nimos Sedia.

The Star Jewel.

It glinted serenely as though oblivious to the havoc wrought around it. Reverently, I lifted the glittering gem from its stand, feeling a thrumming pulse of power within.

"We did it," I said softly, hardly believing our success. This mystical relic could restore poor Celeste. All our trials and tribulations had ultimately led to this moment.

Diane and Leigh exchanged exhausted but elated smiles. "I'd say we make a pretty darn good team in spite of the odds," Leigh quipped, slinging a weary arm around Diane's shoulders.

Carefully stowing the Star Jewel in my pack, I

did a hasty check of our remaining provisions while the girls bandaged wounds. We were battered and bone-tired, but triumphant. However, dangers likely still lurked between here and sunlight.

And even better: a notification told me I had achieved another level.

"Level 6," I muttered.

The girls frowned at that, then checked their own notifications. "Yeah," Diane said after exchanging a nod with Leigh. "We advanced too. These enemies must've been a lot stronger than level 3."

"Yeah," Diane mused. "But... even if they were. It took me years to get from level 1 to level 2..." She looked at me, eyes narrowed. "And you're level 6 already? That's... Such quick advancement should be impossible."

I shrugged. "Well, I can't help it," I said, smiling. "It's just happening."

"Well, I ain't complainin', though," Leigh hummed. "Whatever special mojo David's got, it's rubbin' off on us! Level 4, baby!" She pumped her fist.

Diane nodded slowly, still studying me. "It certainly is great, but we should look into it!"

I nodded. "Sure. I mean, I wasn't aware it was irregular, but we can certainly study this later. Now's not the time, though. We should get moving."

"Yep," Leigh agreed. "Monsters can respawn in Dungeons, and I'd hate to do this battle over again."

Diane gave a resolute nod. "You're right! We'll rest topside and look into this mystery later."

With Diane scouting a few paces ahead, we swiftly navigated the shadowy corridors and stairwells leading back up toward the surface. No further attacks or guardians materialized to bar our escape, much to our relief.

Step by weary step we climbed until the tomblike gloom gave way to shafts of sunlight illuminating a narrow fissure — the hidden entrance through which we had first entered Nimos Sedia earlier this day. One final scramble brought us blinking out into open air.

Basking in the golden light of late afternoon, we

staggered a few paces from the sheer cliff face concealing the Dungeon before sinking down on a sunny patch of fragrant grass. For several minutes, all we could do was sit, chests heaving, scarcely believing our success.

But from my pack came the unmistakable thrum of the Star Jewel, affirming this was no fantasy. In spite of the impossible odds, our tenacity, skill and teamwork had carried the day. Exchanging weary smiles of triumph, we set up camp to tend wounds and celebrate victory under the open sky.

Chapter 16

After successfully retrieving the Star Jewel from the depths of Nimos Sedia, we quickly set up camp a safe distance from the hidden Dungeon entrance. The warm afternoon sunlight felt glorious on our skin after the chill of the underground tomb.

Sinking down gratefully onto the soft grass, I let

out a long exhale, scarcely believing our success. Beside me, Diane gingerly stretched her bruised limbs while Leigh busied herself getting a small campfire going. For now, we simply sat gathering our strength after the harrowing escape.

Before long, the cheerful crackle of burning tinder and aroma of woodsmoke lent familiar comfort. Diane prepared a simple but hearty stew from our provisions while Leigh and I cleaned and checked our weapons. Soon we were all nestled comfortably around the dancing flames, bellies full and bodies finally relaxing.

As the adrenaline of battle receded, we gradually began recounting the day's events, reminiscing over each obstacle overcome and foe vanquished. Though exhausted, elation still shone in our eyes — we had achieved what few others could, braving the ancient Dungeon's sinister depths against impossible odds.

"I still can't believe we made it outta there in one piece," Leigh marveled over her mug of steaming coffee.

Diane smiled and gave my shoulder an

affectionate nudge. "We narrowly escaped doom a fair few times in there, but David's quick thinking and magic helped see us through." Her melodic voice swelled with pride.

"We all played a role," I demurred, though secretly very moved by their faith in me as leader. Our unique skills had complemented one another perfectly when it truly counted. United, we had done it.

As the afternoon sun waned, the flickering firelight lent our reminiscing a dreamlike quality. The quiet mountain pass around us almost made the day's nightmarish battles seem unreal in retrospect. But we had the Star Jewel with us, and we had succeeded.

The embers gradually dimmed, and I threw some fresh firewood on. I was about to suggest making dinner when Diane suddenly sat forward, an eager spark lighting her brilliant blue eyes.

"You know what," she declared. "This adventure deserves a proper song!"

In moments, she had retrieved pen and paper from her pack and begun scribbling verses by firelight. Leigh and I exchanged amused grins at her enthusiasm before leaving her to her creative efforts, both secretly intrigued to hear the final piece.

While Diane composed, I tidied up our modest camp then we climbed into the tent to arrange bedrolls. Before long, Diane slipped in to join us, an apprehensive but excited smile on her lips as she held up the parchment.

"It's finished," she announced. "I can't promise it's any good, but I tried capturing the spirit of our journey together. I hope you'll enjoy it."

Settling onto her blanket, Diane cleared her throat melodically and then began to sing in her rich, lyrical voice:

"Oh gather close and hear this tale,
Of seeking fortune, come what may,
Three brave souls on adventure set,
Each touched by the goddess' rays.

Through forest deep they took to road,
Past crumbling ruins, ancient, grand,
O'er rocky slope and burbling stream,
Together toward the Blighted Land.

There, dark beasts did bar their path,
And evil wills their courage test,
Still they pressed through darkest night,
Their bonds of friendship blessed.

Within the mountain, secrets lurked,
Forgotten perils slumbered deep,
Traps and guardians hindered their hunt,
Yet forward they dared to creep.

Giant golem of living stone,
And wraiths that feasted on life,
Drakelings with fury unmatched,
Met with spell and gun and knife.

Each foe they faced as one in heart,
Their skills shone as a guiding light,
From blackest depths they seized their prize -
The mystic Star Jewel bright.

Oh gather close and hear this tale,
Of seeking fortune, come what may,
Three brave souls on adventure set,
Each touched by the goddess' rays."

Enraptured by the haunting ballad and Diane's rich voice, Leigh and I listened eagerly until Diane finished weaving the tale of our quest. Her mellifluous voice rose and fell with each new verse, transporting me back to the events described.

As the closing notes faded, I found that her interpretation of events — focusing on the friendship and our bonds — touched me.

"That was beautiful," I said.

Beside me, Leigh blew her nose on her kerchief and clapped enthusiastically in agreement. "So sweet," she murmured, her voice a little hoarse. Apparently, she was deeply moved by the rhyme.

Diane's cheeks darkened, equal parts pleased and embarrassed by our reactions. "I'm so glad you enjoyed it," she said softly. "I know it's not exactly polished, but this adventure deserved commemorating through song."

"You perfectly captured the spirit of our time together," I said earnestly, leaning over to kiss her cheek. "I know I'll think back on this melody fondly for years to come."

Diane's eyes shone at the praise. She bashfully tucked the parchment containing the ballad into her pack. "Then I promise to keep composing songs for each new adventure," she declared. "To help us remember."

Leigh grinned and slung tired arms around Diane's and my shoulders. "Works for me! Though y'all will have to remind me of any lyrics I forget," she added with a playful wink. "I ain't really got a mind for this sorta thing."

I chuckled at that. "Well, it looks like the tent is nice and snug. How about we go outside and make some dinner? We can level up while we're at it!"

After enjoying Diane's commemorative ballad, we decided to step outside the tent and level up around the campfire before making dinner. The sun was sinking behind the western peaks, casting a rosy alpenglow on the craggy mountainsides.

I focused inward first, assessing the new abilities granted upon reaching level 6. As expected, my maximum health increased by 10 points to 70. My mana reserves grew by 5 points to 35. In addition, my maximum number of bound familiars increased by 1 to 3. This way, I could start deploying a guard around the homestead while having another domesticant to help out Ghostie.

I also gained access to three new spell options: Nature's Respite, Mass Heal, and Summon Storm Elemental. Nature's Respite was a restorative spell costing 8 mana that removed harmful effects and healed an ally. Mass Heal restored health to my entire party for 10 mana. Finally, Summon Storm Elemental cost 10 mana to call forth a being of roiling lightning.

After contemplating the choices, I decided to learn Summon Storm Elemental. Its offensive capabilities would pair well with my water elemental summon when facing multiple foes. After all, chucking lightning on wet foes would be quite the damaging combination. I felt the knowledge of the spell's incantation imprint itself upon my consciousness and looked forward to manifesting the ability soon.

With my advancement complete, it was the girls' turn next. Diane and Leigh sat together near the fire, closing their eyes in concentration as they allocated their newly unlocked attributes and abilities upon reaching level 4. In one Dungeon run, they had doubled their levels.

Diane finished first, opening her eyes with an excited smile. "I learned a great new ability called Mark Foe that allows me to mark an enemy, so it takes bonus damage from us all!"

"Ooh, that'll be mighty useful in a tussle," Leigh said approvingly. She then closed her eyes again briefly before reporting her own upgrades.

"Let's see... I finally got the ability to bind a pet! Now, I can get an animal to stay with me and respawn when defeated in combat." Leigh grinned. "I like the sound of that!"

"Excellent, we've expanded our capabilities nicely," I said, pleased with our collective progress. Though the battles had been harrowing, the experience had advanced us all.

With the leveling up complete, we gathered around the flickering campfire and began preparing a simple but hearty road dinner. Leigh mixed up cornbread batter while Diane opened a jar of preserved meat and peas. I sliced some wild onions and garlic bulbs to add flavor.

Soon the iron skillet was sizzling merrily over the flames, infusing the little camp with mouthwatering aromas that stirred our appetites after the day's adventures. Diane used a fork to turn over the meat and veggies while they browned.

Once cooked through, we crumbled the savory contents of the skillet into our bowls along with spoonfuls of the golden cornbread batter. The humble but nourishing fare perfectly sated our hard-won hunger.

As we ate, dusk deepened around us. The dancing firelight and close companionship kindled a restful mood. Tomorrow we would begin the long return trek, but for now, this secluded camp was haven enough.

Over second helpings, Leigh amused us with humorous anecdotes from past misadventures out in the frontier wilds. Her colorful accounts elicited frequent laughter that warded off the mountain night's encroaching chill.

With dishes cleaned, Diane prepared a pot of

steaming chamomile tea to further warm our bellies before sleep. I stoked up the fire, building a glowing bed of coals that would keep the darkness at bay till dawn.

Mugs in hand, we lingered awhile longer simply enjoying the fire's light and warmth. Our quips and idle talk gradually diminished as drowsiness set in. One by one, we began drifting off, weary to the bone but profoundly content.

Mustering a little more energy to stand guard, I bid Leigh and Diane goodnight with tender kisses as they headed into the tent. They were soon nestled cozily beneath blankets, their deep and even breathing signaling they had slipped into well-deserved rest.

After securing our perimeter, I sat down by the fire and continued my exploration into my Ranching and Farming skillbook. Sleep pulled at me, but I only had a few more pages to go before the book would be finished. I read the final few pages, which focused mainly on the various ways to harvest by hand in ways that didn't damage plants or harvests.

Finally, when I folded over the last page, the book disappeared with a poof, and two notifications vied for my attention in the corner of my vision: 'Farming Skill Unlocked!' and 'Ranching Skill unlocked!'.

Excited to see all the changes, I gave my character sheet a once-over.

Name: David Wilson

Class: Frontier Summoner

Level: 6

Health: 70/70

Mana: 35/35

Skills:

Summon Minor Spirit — Level 15 (3 mana)

Summon Domesticant — Level 11 (6 mana)

Summon Guardian — Level 11 (8 mana)

Summon Aquana's Avatar — Level 3 (10 mana)

Summon Storm Elemental — Level 1 (10 mana)

Bind Familiar — Level 2 (15 mana)

Identify Plants — Level 8 (1 mana)

Foraging — Level 9 (1 mana)

Trapping — Level 9 (1 mana)

Alchemy — Level 12 (1 mana)

Farming — Level 1 (1 mana)

Ranching — Level 1 (1 mana)

With a satisfied nod, I relaxed by the fire, taking in the sights and sounds of the mountain pass at night. I was level 6 already. The spells and abilities that came with that level made me a formidable combatant, as well as a great homesteader. The frontier was opening up to me, and things were looking good.

Chapter 17

After breaking camp, we ventured once more into the ominous Blighted Land, senses primed for the dangers lurking within. Our victory at Nimos Sedia had bolstered us, however, and we were now two levels higher than we were when we first came here.

Still, we advanced with utmost caution across the dusty earth. Diane's sharp eyes pierced the gloom for subtle signs of movement. The slightest skittering or tremor would see weapons raised in readiness.

Before long, faint vibrations rippled up through the desiccated soil. We exchanged looks, and each of us knew what was coming. We had felt these tremors before.

Grapplejaws.

With a quick casting, I summoned my Storm Elemental for the first time. Mana swirled at my beck and call, swiftly forming into a man-shaped thundercloud with lightning crackling within. Blue, powerful eyes gazed out from the stormcloud-shaped man.

"Impressive," Diane hummed, studying my newest summon.

"Look alive, folks," Leigh warned. "Here they come."

And indeed, a whole swarm of the lizard-like beasts, their little tendrils searching, came in our direction. Leigh and Diane took position, their weapons at the ready, and I unleashed my storm elemental.

Forked lightning blasted from the wavering form, smiting through the swarming Grapplejaws. They spasmed and shrieked beneath the torrential electrical assault. From our flanking positions, Leigh, Diane, and I opened fire until none remained.

It was over in moments, and we exchanged looks of slightly astonished confusion.

"That… that was very easy," I said. The storm elemental crackled as if agreeing.

"I'll say," Leigh muttered. "And I'm pretty darn sure that was the same swarm as the ones who drove us out of the Blighted Land."

Diane nodded. "So am I. We are so much more powerful now. David's magic is a force of destructive power!"

With the Grapplejaws swiftly dispatched, we continued on through the Blighted Land, still wary but without the overwhelming dread of days past. Though the alien surroundings remained unnerving, we were newly empowered and marched with heads held high.

Strange rock formations towered all around, their pitted surfaces scarred by some unfathomable ancient cataclysm. We gave the disturbing monoliths a wide berth, though they remained inert. For all their looming menace, they could not touch us now.

The lifeless trees continued to unnerve with their creaking, twisting branches that seemed to writhe of their own volition. But daylight robbed them of any true threat. We passed swiftly, and our moods remained high, with Diane humming the song she had written, and Leigh enjoying the outdoors despite the ominous setting.

But the Blighted Land still watched. In cracks splitting the barren earth, oily plants unfurled fleshy and colorful leaves that undulated as they beckoned insects to their deaths. Thorns glistened with viscous fluids, betraying that everything in this place was toxic.

And the lifeless soil remained difficult to traverse in places, shale shifting treacherously beneath our feet. Where needed, we lent each other balanced hands, crossing such hazards together until firmer ground lay underfoot once more.

As we progressed, the noxious oasis of the Blighted Land glinted darkly beneath the midday sun as we left it behind us, its surface choked in coiling thorns. The broken hills gradually smoothed into more traversable land as we neared the valley's far border.

Soon enough, cleaner air stirred, bringing scents of pine and mineral-rich earth once more. The atmosphere felt less oppressive, and the Blighted Land was fading away behind us.

Hardier mountain shrubs emerged from the parched soil, still twisted and stunted but recognizably akin to ordinary flora. Their tenacious roots weathered whatever malignant forces radiated outward from the Blighted Land, and we all breathed and walked easier. It was a delight to traverse this terrain that mere days ago had been one of the most dangerous places I had ever been.

The shadows in our wake seemed to creep less eagerly as the unnatural gloom retreated. Step by step, we reclaimed the path through stone and thin soil, no longer haunted or hindered by the nameless dread of the Blighted Land.

With a surge of relief, we emerged from the Blighted Land's borders at last, and we touched the verdant and living forest with tired feet. Vital beauty surrounded us, and we were far from the reach of crawling shadows now.

As we paused to look back from a safe vantage, I glimpsed neither malice nor menace lurking in that faraway rift. For all its past evils, it lay diminished, emptied of power to stall our steps. Together we had faced its perils undaunted.

"The rest of our journey will be easier," I said to the girls. "For now, let's find fresh water and make camp. We have two more days through the forest ahead of us, and I think it'll be a pleasant march!"

Finding a pleasant clearing after escaping the Blighted Land, we swiftly set up camp before dusk could settle. A cheerful and clean brook conveniently allowed us to refill our waterskins with deliciously fresh water.

I got a modest campfire crackling merrily, while Leigh and Diane prepared dinner. Leigh cooked up pasta, making a sauce with jerky and tomato paste, while Diane chopped wild onions and herbs. The mouthwatering aroma of food sizzling in our iron skillet over the fire stirred appetites sharpened by long hours of hiking.

Before long, Leigh carefully prepared the pasta sauce in the skillet, infusing it with the onions, herbs, and seasonings Diane had prepared. The combination of flavors made my belly rumble hungrily.

Working smoothly, the girls soon had a hearty campfire dinner ready to fuel our tired bodies — a beautiful pan full of pasta with a delicious sauce. They proudly served me a heaping portion, eager to see the fruits of their cooking efforts enjoyed.

"This is incredible!" I told them sincerely after my first delicious bite. The rich pasta was perfectly complemented by the flavorful sauce, and it was cooked to perfection despite the primitive implements. Diane and Leigh beamed indulgently as they helped themselves.

I ate with satisfied sighs, and the girls giggled as they watched me enjoy their food. They were exchanging mischievous glances, and something about the way they were acting made me smile.

As the sun sank behind the soaring pines ringing our snug camp, warm contentment suffused us all. Our bellies were happily full after the long day of hiking.

After the meal, Leigh unpacked a pouch of sweet, dried berries for dessert. Their tangy flavor was the perfect finisher. Stretching her long legs toward the fire, Leigh playfully nudged me.

"All that hiking sure works up an appetite," she remarked. "It's gotta be darn nice for ya to have your own personal chef keepin' you fed out here."

Diane laughed and gave her harem sister a playful poke. "I'm not his 'personal chef'! And if *I* am, then so are *you*! You made most of the food!" She stuck out her tongue.

I grinned at their banter. "Well, I'm happy to handle any cleanup needed," I volunteered sincerely. The girls had done a wonderful job preparing the meal while I simply enjoyed their efforts.

"Deal!" Diane said.

With a grin, I simply summoned a domesticant. Leigh broke out laughing as the little creature began dutifully cleaning up, and Diane pouted at me.

"No fair!" she hummed.

I laughed and pulled her close to tickle her, and she broke out laughing before snuggling up against me contentedly as we relaxed by the flickering firelight. Leigh moved up on my other side, her soft cheek resting against my arm as she lazily stretched her legs.

With no agenda pressing, we lingered around the campfire swapping lively stories and playful quips. When Leigh teased me about my cooking skills, claiming I was probably bad at it as she hadn't seen me cook often, I retaliated by tickling her feet, making her shriek with laughter.

Watching Leigh trying to squirm away from my tickling, Diane just shook her head as she laughed. "You two are incorrigible."

As the glowing moon rose overhead, a romantic atmosphere settled over our secluded camp. Leigh scooted closer, resting her head in my lap and gazing up alluringly. Unable to resist, I stroked her golden hair gently.

Diane cuddled against my other side, one arm draped proprietarily across my chest. Tilting her chin up, she stole a slow, lingering kiss conveying wordless affection. Nestled between two beautiful women beneath the moonlight, emotions swelled hotly within me.

Beside me, Leigh shifted restlessly before abruptly sitting up. "I gotta say — after days on the trail, I'm really feeling gross and grimy," she declared bluntly. "I could sure use a nice bath!"

Diane and I chuckled at her candid admission. "I know what you mean," Diane agreed, wrinkling her delicate nose. "It's been much too long since we've properly washed up. And all that fighting, too!"

"Well, there's a brook nearby," I said. "I was planning on washing up myself in the morning."

"Now that sounds mighty fine," Leigh purred, her big blue eyes settling on mine as she still lay on my lap. "I ain't gonna wait, though. It'd be a crime to climb into my sleeping bag like this."

Diane hummed agreement, idly twirling a strand of her raven hair. "It will feel so lovely to be clean again," she mused dreamily. "To wash away the grime and soak." She exchanged a naughty look with her harem sister. "I think I want to wash up now as well!"

Leigh sat up and fixed me with her eyes. "You should come too, David," she said in that delicious drawl of hers. "Ain't no way we're sleeping together tonight if you ain't clean."

I laughed and threw up my hands. "Fine, fine," I said. "You girls win. We'll bathe before we go to bed. The creek is right there!"

Giggling, Diane and Leigh hopped to their feet and pulled me up and along toward the creek, while we left the domesticant to keep watch.

Chapter 18

My mind swam as I watched my pretty women kick off their boots. Wearing their light dresses, they were like nymphs of the forest, and the sight of them roused my hunger and great need.

As I reveled in the sight of them, the murmur of the creek framed our secluded corner of the world, the water shimmering under the setting sun. The air was a mix of pine and the lingering warmth of the day, a perfect backdrop for the teasing spectacle unfolding before me.

I watched as Leigh shed her dress. It slipped over her curves like water, revealing a body that was every bit as enticing as her radiant personality and her ever-present optimism. Her light freckles, vivid against her creamy skin, ran like a constellation from her face, down her shoulders, and disappeared enticingly between her full breasts.

She gave me a naughty look as she twirled around, showing me that beautiful and round apple butt, and as she flashed me a look over her shoulder, she reached around to push her cheeks up a little, making me grin broadly as my cock bucked in my pants.

"Like what ya see, baby?" she hummed.

"Do I ever," I agreed, my voice already turning husky.

Diane giggled at the exchange. She was more coy than Leigh, and her shyness played out in the hesitant way she held her dress in front of her body before finally letting it fall.

The fox ears atop her head twitched, a telltale sign of her nervous excitement. Her sapphire eyes sparkled with mischief as she revealed her athletic body, every curve sculpted to perfection, a fitting compliment to Leigh's more voluptuous form.

Their laughter echoed through the trees as they moved towards me in sync, their bodies swaying with an intoxicating rhythm. It was a dance of seduction, one that had my heart pounding in anticipation.

"Let's get all of this off," Leigh purred, her blue eyes raking my clothes like they were physical adversaries.

"Hm-hm," Diane agreed, and I felt her delicate fingers at the waistband of my cargo pants, her fox tail brushing against my thigh as she knelt to help me undress.

Leigh stood close, her voluptuous body pressing against mine, her fingers tracing the hard lines of my muscles as she played with the buttons of my shirt.

I stood there, exposed to their hungry gazes, the

chill of the evening air doing nothing to dampen my arousal. I could feel their eyes on me, taking in the sight of my body. When Diane peeled away my boxer shorts, their gazes lingered on my cock, already hard with anticipation.

"My, my," Leigh said and licked her lips. "Wonder what the cold water will do to *that*."

I chuckled as I gave her a loud smack on her ass that made her yelp. "Wait and see," I said, and I took each of them by the hand and waded into the creek.

The creek water was cold against my heated skin as I led them into it, but I shrugged it off. Our bodies generated more than enough heat, and before long, their hands were exploring as they washed me. The sensation of their fingers on my skin, their giggles filling the air, was a feast for the senses.

Diane was the first to come closer, her lips finding mine in a kiss that was equal parts sweet and demanding. Her lavender scent wrapped around me, a heady mix of desire and anticipation.

Leigh followed suit, her lips capturing my other

side, her tongue teasing as she whispered, "You two look so pretty kissin' like that…"

I just hummed, totally lost in the softness of Diane's lips, of Leigh's teasing tongue. I grabbed a handful of soft flesh from both girls, squeezing and exploring as their sighs of delight turned needier by the moment.

The feel of their hands on me and their bodies pressed against mine was overwhelming. I was drowning in a sea of sensations, their whispers and touches stoking the fire within me.

I felt Diane's hand wrap around my cock; her touch firm yet gentle. Her eyes met mine, a silent question in their depths, a lingering shyness, and I nodded, encouraging her to please me.

Leigh's hand joined hers, their fingers entwining around my throbbing shaft. The sight was maddeningly delicious, their fingers wrapped around my hardness, their shared touch sending jolts of pleasure through me.

"It feels so nice, David," Diane purred, her tail wrapping around my leg in a bath of softness.

Leigh's fingertips teasingly ran over the surface

of my balls, making me grunt with need as I grabbed a handful of her firm and large breasts, playing with the nipple with my thumb.

"And these balls are so full, baby," she whispered. "They need to be emptied... all over us."

Her words had me biting back a groan, the image they painted too enticing to ignore. Diane's eyes widened at dirty talk. A blush spread across her cheeks, but her grip on me didn't falter. If anything, it tightened, her eyes locked onto mine, a wicked glint in them.

Their shared touch was exquisite, the combination of Leigh's boldness and Diane's gentle touch pushing me to the edge. Yet, they were in control, their pace slow and deliberate, driving me wild with anticipation.

The setting sun cast long shadows around us, the fading light playing on their bodies. Their wet skin glistened, their breasts wet and firm, nipples hard and begging for attention.

I reached out, cupping a breast with each hand, reveling in the feel of them. Leigh's were full and soft; her nipples pebbled under my touch. Diane's were firmer, the perfect handful, her nipples equally hard against my palms.

I squeezed gently, earning a gasp from Diane and a moan from Leigh. Their reactions spurred me on, my thumbs brushing over their nipples, the sensation making them squirm against me.

Leigh's hand moved faster; her strokes more insistent. "Ya like that, don't ya?" she teased, her eyes locked on mine. The sight of her, flushed and aroused, had me nodding, unable to form words.

Diane's touch mirrored Leigh's, her hand moving in tandem with the blonde's. Her eyes never left mine, the intensity in them matching the firm grip of her hand.

I could feel the tension building within me, my body primed for release. But they had other plans, their touches slowing, their bodies pulling away just when I needed them the most.

"I think we need to work on David just a little more," Leigh teased, shooting me a naughty look.

"Hm-hm," Diane purred. "I agree…"

With a giggle, they dropped to their knees before

me, their eyes on my throbbing cock. The sight was sinful, their plump lips parted in anticipation, their tongues darting out to wet them. As they sat on their knees, I had a perfect view of their toned backs, narrowing until they came to their beautiful asses — Leigh's was round and juicy, and Diane's was toned and firm, topped with her fox tail.

I watched, entranced, as Diane leaned in first, her fox ears twitching, her eyes wide with anticipation. Leigh followed suit, her hand resting on Diane's thigh, a wicked smile playing on her lips.

They were tantalizingly close, their breath warm against my sensitive tip. I could see the desire in their eyes, the way they licked their lips, their gazes focused on me.

It was a sight that had me gripping the edge of sanity, the anticipation a tangible entity between us. I wanted to bury my hands in their hair, guide them to where I needed them the most. I wanted to fuck their mouths and make them gag.

Yet, I held back, letting them set the pace, letting them control the moment. It was a test of will, one that had me clenching my fists, my body taut with expectation. I stood over them as they looked up at me, two pairs of blazing blue eyes, and the sensation of those plump lips so close to my hard cock nearly drove me mad with desire.

And now, it was time to indulge in our needs...

It was a scene straight out of some ancient Roman myth of nymphs and sylphs — those girls with beauty beyond compare, kneeling naked before me, ready to please and fulfill my every desire. Their bodies were glistening in the soft evening light, the droplets of water from the creek making their skin shine.

Leigh was the first to move, her blonde hair cascading down her shoulders, her freckles standing out on her sun-kissed skin. Her voluptuous breasts swayed with each movement — a sight that never failed to draw a growl from the pit of my stomach.

She reached for me, her hands soft and warm

against my cock. I felt my breath hitch as her fingers brushed against it, her touch sending sparks of pleasure through my entire body.

"Mmm, David," she purred, her accent making her words sound like a song of sin. "You're so hard for us." Her blue eyes twinkled with mischief as she gave my cock a firm squeeze, making me shudder with desire.

I watched as Diane, her fox ears perked and tail twitching with anticipation, moved to join Leigh. The scent of lavender filled my nostrils, adding a heady sweetness to the musky arousal hanging in the air. Her breasts, smaller and firmer than Leigh's, pressed against my thigh as she knelt next to her.

Diane's hand joined Leigh's on my cock, their fingers intertwining as they stroked me. I grunted, the sensation of two pairs of hands on me a delightful torture. "Fuck, girls…," I groaned, my voice husky with need.

Leigh leaned in first, her lips parting as she took my cock into her mouth. I could feel the warmth of her mouth envelop me, her tongue swirling around my length.

Diane watched, her eyes darkened with lust, her fingers rubbing her clit in rhythm with Leigh's movements. The sight of her touching herself while watching Leigh suck me was a sight that had me hissing with every delicious stroke and suck.

"Your turn, Diane," Leigh said after a while, releasing me with a wet pop. Her lips were swollen and gleaming, a wicked grin playing on her face. "Show us how good you can suck this delicious dick."

Diane looked up at me, her eyes wide. But she didn't hesitate. She leaned in, her lips closing around me. The feel of her hot mouth was different than Leigh's, but equally pleasurable.

"That's it, darling," Leigh cooed, her voice low and sultry. "Suck him like a good girl." Her words, dirty and provocative, sent a shiver down my spine.

I watched Diane take me deeper, her cheeks hollowing as she sucked. The sight of her, her ears twitching and tail flicking as she pleasured me, was intoxicating. I felt my control slipping, my body tightening with anticipation.

"Fuck, Diane," I gasped, my fingers digging into her hair. I moved with her, my hips thrusting gently into her mouth. The wet, warm tightness of her mouth was driving me to the brink.

Leigh watched, her fingers tracing Diane's back before moving to cup her breasts. She pinched her nipples, and Diane moaned around me, the vibrations sending a jolt of pleasure through me.

Leigh moved behind Diane, her hands sliding down to squeeze her ass. I could see her fingers digging into the soft flesh, and the sight of them, Leigh's hands on Diane's pretty ass, nearly brought me to my knees.

"I need you, David," Leigh moaned, her eyes meeting mine over Diane's shoulder. Her hand slid between her own legs, fingers disappearing into her wetness. "I want to feel your hot cum on my skin, baby."

Her words, coupled with the sight of Diane sucking me and the feel of her mouth around me, were too much. I felt my balls tighten, my body coiling with the impending release.

"I'm... I'm close," I warned, my voice shaky. Diane's mouth felt so good, her tongue working magic on me.

Diane pulled back, her lips releasing me with another wet pop. She looked up at me, her eyes glazed with lust. "Cum for us, David," she breathed, her hand still stroking me.

Leigh moved to kneel next to Diane, their bodies pressed together. Their breasts were heaving, nipples hard and glistening with the water from the creek.

"Yeah, cum for us," Leigh echoed, her hand joining Diane's on my cock. They stroked me together, their soft, warm hands bringing me closer to the edge.

I could feel it building, the pressure coiling in my lower belly. I was on the brink, teetering on the edge of a pleasure so intense, so overwhelming, I could barely breathe.

"On our tits, baby," Leigh whispered, her hand moving to cup her full breasts, offering it to me. Diane followed suit, her breast pressing against Leigh's as they both looked up at me with anticipation.

I grunted, my body shuddering as I came. My cock pulsed, streams of cum shooting out and landing on their breasts. The sight of my release coating their skin was as tantalizing and sexy as the act itself.

Leigh let out a soft purr, her fingers moving to spread the cum over her breasts. Diane followed her lead, her fingers drawing patterns in the sticky fluid on her skin.

They giggled, their laughter echoing in the quiet evening. Their eyes met, and they shared a look, a silent communication that spoke volumes. They were satisfied, pleased with their performance.

And so was I.

I gasped for air, watching with profound delight as the girls giggled and exchanged naughty glances, their heaving breasts slathered with my seed. Seeing them like that was enough to make me ready to go again, and that was good. I was far from done.

Already, my blood was pumping wildly, my need still rising as I saw my two beauties kneeling before me, naked, their delicious breasts covered in my cum. Teasingly, Leigh scooped some of it from Diane's firm tits with a slender finger and lapped it up like a kitten at the milk bowl.

"Now come fuck me, baby," she purred, licking up my cum.

There was no resisting that. Diane giggled as I surrendered to my need and flipped Leigh around, earning a yelp from the curvy blonde. She looked at me over her shoulder, and her blue eyes blazed with a hunger that matched my own as she turned to present herself to me. She was on all fours now, her voluptuous curves glistening in the evening light that filtered through the verdant pine trees surrounding the creek.

I watched as her firm, round ass lifted in the air, a tantalizing sight that had me hardening once again. Her blonde hair cascaded around her shoulders, slightly damp from our previous play in the creek.

"Come on, baby," she urged, the need in her voice spurring me into action. Eager to oblige, I stepped forward, my body casting a long shadow over her, the cool water of the creek lapping gently at our ankles.

With a firm grip on her hips, I guided my throbbing cock towards her inviting entrance, teasing her with my tip. The anticipation had me grunting with desire, and I felt Leigh shiver beneath my touch, her body yearning for more.

Without any further ado, I pushed into her, our bodies connecting in the most primal way. The feeling of her tight, wet warmth enveloping me was pure ecstasy. I began to move, my hips thrusting in a steady rhythm, each push sending waves of pleasure through both of us.

Her body bounced with each of my thrusts, her voluptuous curves jiggling enticingly. I could feel her tightening around me, her inner muscles clenching and unclenching as she rode wave after wave of pleasure, her moans and gasps filling the air.

Diane was watching us, her sapphire eyes wide with excitement. I noticed her fingers creeping down to her own lower lips, her touch gentle yet deliberate. Her other hand reached out towards me, her fingers wrapping around my balls and massaging them gently as I pounded her harem sister into submission.

The additional sensation heightened my pleasure, and I growled low in my throat, pounding into Leigh harder and faster. The sight of Diane touching herself as she watched us was tantalizing, and I found myself matching the rhythm of her fingers with my thrusts.

"Harder, David," Leigh moaned; her words a plea and a command all rolled into one. I obliged, my body moving with renewed vigor that had her crying out with pleasure.

Diane's touch on my balls was becoming more insistent, her fingers teasing and caressing in time with my thrusts. The sight of her, fox ears and bushy tail, her body writhing with her own pleasure, was adding another layer of excitement to the already charged atmosphere.

Leigh's body was shaking with the force of my thrusts, her cries growing louder and more desperate with each passing second. I felt her tighten around me, her inner muscles clenching hard as she neared her climax.

I could see it in her eyes, the unbridled pleasure that was threatening to consume her. "Fuck me, David," she gasped, her voice barely a whisper as she teetered on the edge of climax.

I could feel her pulsating around me as our skins slapped wetly together, her body convulsing with pleasure, her moans growing louder and more desperate. Her butt cheeks rolled with every thrust, and I could only reach out and grab them, squeeze them, massage them.

Diane watched us, her sapphire eyes filled with admiration. She was close to her own climax, her fingers moving faster and more frantically as she watched us, her body twitching with the building pleasure.

"Yes, David," she moaned, her voice a soft purr

that sent shivers down my spine. I could see her body trembling, her breath coming in quick gasps as she approached her orgasm.

I could feel Leigh's body tightening around me, her inner walls pulsating with a rhythm that matched my own. Her cries grew louder, her body shaking with the force of her climax.

"David," she gasped, her voice barely a whisper as her body convulsed with pleasure. The sight of her in the throes of orgasm was enough to send me over the edge, but I held back, wanting to prolong the moment.

Diane was watching us, her sapphire eyes wide with excitement. Her fingers were moving faster now, her touch more insistent as she neared her own climax. Her body was trembling, her breath coming in short gasps as she watched us.

"David!" Leigh called out. "Oh, fuck... I'm cumming, David!"

I slammed into Leigh again, grunting with lust as her body shook with the force of her climax, her cries echoing through the forest. I could feel her body tighten around me, her inner walls rippling with pleasure, her body convulsing with each wave of satisfaction.

The sight of Leigh, submissive on her hands and knees and completely lost in the throes of her climax, was driving me toward the edge. Her face was flushed, her eyes closed tight as her body writhed beneath me, her cries growing louder and more intense with each passing second.

"Oh... Oh... I'm... ahhnn!"

Half-lost in pleasure, I saw Diane's body shivering, her eyes wide with excitement. Her fingers were moving faster now, her touch more insistent. A moment later, her body shook with the force of her climax. She writhed with pleasure as she gasped for air, trembling in tune with her harem sister.

I almost came, but I stopped myself and pulled out of Leigh, my cock still hard and throbbing. I could feel her body trembling beneath me, her climax leaving her weak and trembling.

I was nearing feral now. A deep growl escaped me as my gaze fell on Diane. I was going to fuck her, too. I would fuck both of them senseless tonight.

The delicious little fox girl had risen from the creek and now leaned against one of the boulders that lined it. Her full body was on display in its sensual glory, waiting and begging me to take it.

She bit her lip, a bold challenge in her sapphire eyes. "Do it, David," she purred, her voice hoarse from her orgasm. "Come here and take me. Fuck me. I need it."

Biting her lip, Diane leaned back onto one of the boulders lining the creek. She let out a cute giggle as the cold stone touched her smooth skin, then looked at me with big eyes, begging for me to fuck her, spreading her legs. Before me, still on her hands and knees, Leigh was panting as she recovered from her orgasm.

"David," Diane pleaded, her voice carrying an unspoken yearning. "I need you."

I grinned, my gaze sweeping over her toned

Jack Bryce

frame — from her perky breasts to her glistening pussy — my cock throbbing in response. With a few steps, I was beside her, and I reached out, my fingers tracing over the curve of her calf before I lifted her legs up onto my chest, making her giggle as I placed her feet on my chest.

My cock twitched at her entrance, teasing her with the promise of what was to come. She squirmed beneath me, her body arching off the cold stone in response. Leigh, sitting off to the side, approached us with a gleam in her blue eyes.

"So eager to be fucked," Leigh hummed, her voice dripping with lust. "I can't wait to see him fill you up." She grinned at me. "Lemme help you, baby."

"Fuck, Leigh," I grunted as she grabbed my cock and pressed the head against Diane's slick folds. Diane's body shuddered beneath me, a mewl of pleasure slipping past her parted lips.

I pushed in, inch by tantalizing inch. Diane gasped with pleasure as my cock pulsed within her tight heat, and I began pushing, each thrust driving me deeper into her welcoming depths. Her body yielded to mine as if we were two halves of a whole, her pussy clutching me with a vice-like grip.

"Oh, David," she whimpered, her fox tail twitching in sync with her body's internal rhythm. Her breasts moved with each thrust, the sight of her hardened nipples begging for my touch. I acquiesced, reaching out to cup one in my hand, the feel of her soft mound sending sparks of arousal coursing through my veins.

Leigh's hand kneaded my balls, her fingers skillfully matching the rhythm of my thrusts. "That's it, David," she cooed, her voice laced with sinful delight. "Give that naughty little girl what she needs."

Her words spurred me on, each thrust becoming more forceful than the last. Diane's moans grew louder, her body writhing beneath me in the throes of pleasure. I reveled in the sounds of her satisfaction, my own arousal building with every second.

"You like that, don't ya?" Leigh taunted Diane, a wicked grin playing on her lips. "You like his big cock fillin' you up."

The dirty words spurred me on, my thrusts becoming more potent. I could feel Diane's walls gripping me tighter, her body indicating her impending release.

"I'm close, David," Diane whimpered, her fingers digging into my forearms. I could feel her body tensing beneath me, an indication of the pleasure storm that was about to hit her.

"Cum for me, Diane," I growled, my voice hoarse with desire. I could feel her pussy fluttering around my cock, coaxing my own orgasm closer.

"Yes, David!" Diane screamed as her second orgasm washed over her. Her body convulsed beneath me, her inner muscles contracting around my length in a rhythm that matched the pulsations of her pleasure.

The sight of her climaxing was exquisite, the way her body trembled, and her face contorted in pleasure. It was a sight that could drive any man wild.

I couldn't hold back any longer. With a final, powerful thrust, I released my load deep inside her. The sensation of my hot seed filling her was euphoric, my body convulsing with the intensity of my climax.

"Yeah, David!" Leigh exclaimed, her fingers tightening around my balls. "Fill her up! Cum in her!"

Diane's body writhed beneath me, her walls milking every last drop of cum from me. Her fox tail twitched erratically with the aftershocks of her orgasm, the sight only increasing my pleasure as I spurted my ropes of seed deep into her fertile, young body.

Leigh's dirty words filled the air, urging me on as I rode out my climax. "That's it, David. Give her that cum. Make her feel every inch of you."

Diane's body bounced with every thrust, the force of my orgasm making me lose control. Her moans and pleas filled the air, music to my ears as her body welcomed my seed. I gave one final push before I gasped for air. Diane hummed pleasure as I spurted my last inside her.

Then, with a sigh, I slowly pulled out of Diane, my cock still twitching with the aftershocks of my orgasm. Her pussy released me, my cum trickling out of her and onto the boulder beneath her.

Leigh watched with fascination, her fingers reaching out to trace the trail of my seed. "Such a pretty sight," she murmured; her gaze locked onto Diane's cum-filled pussy.

My shoulders shook from the exertion as I collapsed forward, placing my hands on either side of Diane.

"Gods," Diane murmured, barely able to speak. "That... That was so good."

All three of us were chuckling and grinning broadly as we loosened ourselves from the embrace, our naked bodies glistening in the last light of day. The smells of sex, sweat, and the fresh pine forest mingled in the warm evening air, creating a heady, intoxicating aroma.

I settled with my back against the boulder, in the cool water from the waist down. Diane snuggled up to my right, her fox tail curling lazily around my thigh, a soft, fluffy caress against my skin. My arm draped over her shoulder, fingers idly tracing the delicate curve of her waist.

"David," Leigh murmured as she lay down on my other side, "that was... amazin'." Her fingers traced lazy circles on my chest, her gaze shining with unspoken desire.

"Uhhhnn... I agree," Diane chimed in softly. She nuzzled her face into my neck, her lavender scent wrapping around me like a sensual shroud.

I chuckled, pressing a kiss to each woman's forehead in turn. "I'm glad you enjoyed it as much as I did." My voice was low, the words rolling off my tongue like velvet. "Perfect end to a long day."

The girls chuckled agreement. Soon enough, the evening descended around us, the chirping of crickets and the murmuring creek the only sounds breaking the silence. I enjoyed the afterglow, my skin still tingling from the intensity of our lovemaking.

We basked in the warmth of each other's bodies for a while, the sounds of the forest lulling us into a state of blissful contentment. Before long, we headed back to our little camp, completely fulfilled.

Chapter 19

After our intimate night by the creek, we awoke refreshed and ready to resume our homeward trek. While breaking camp, I smiled, thinking back on the pleasures shared under the stars and soothed by the murmuring water. Diane and Leigh seemed equally dreamy-eyed as we swiftly packed up.

They were very touchy-feely, and there was much kissing and hugging, even from Leigh, who was often quick to make light of things. In her eyes, I saw that love had blossomed. I knew we would have our talk soon.

Consulting my map and compass, I oriented our course through the forest. We estimated another two days' travel to emerge from the woods near Gladdenfield. I was excited to get back and apply my new skills and spells around the homestead.

We set out at an easy pace, our packs lighter now as most of the supplies were gone. We had enough for about three more days, so I wasn't worried — we'd even be able to handle a delay if we needed to.

As we walked, shafts of morning light shot down through the emerald canopy, and the refreshing scents of pine and loamy earth surrounded us. It was great to be in the forest again, away from the noxious Blighted Land.

Now and then, we paused to appreciate subtle woodland wonders — a flowering fern, chattering red squirrels, luminous mushrooms, a soaring hawk silhouetted against the blue sky. Each new discovery kindled appreciation for nature's wealth.

Around midday, we paused beside a mossy deadfall to share strips of smoked venison and dried fruit. A nearby bush was laden with juicy wild blackberries, allowing us to indulge our sweet cravings afterward.

Fortified, we continued our forest trek as the shadows shifted and shafts of golden light illuminated new tableaus. This tranquil realm felt untouched by strife or hardship, cocooned in its timeless natural rhythms.

As the sun sank toward the distant hills, we sought out a suitable campsite. Finding a sheltered hollow surrounded by whispering pines, we swiftly established camp and got a modest fire going. The dancing flames lent familiar comfort.

While I prepared the fire, Leigh and Diane busied themselves in making food and tea to revive our energies. We all smiled, reflecting on how seamlessly we worked together now even in this simple domestic routine. Our time together out here on the quest had brought us closer, and our actions were in sync.

Bellies filled, we passed the evening enjoying idle talk of hopes for improvements to make around the homestead, then turned in, lulled by the gentle hooting of a nearby owl. I kept first watch, then roused Diane for the second as stars wheeled overhead.

The next day brought more fair weather and smooth progress along the winding woodland trail. We paused frequently to soak in our surroundings' natural splendor — gurgling creeks and misty waterfalls around moss-cloaked boulders.

Ahead, flowering vines twined over crumbling remnants of Tannorian architecture half-reclaimed by the forest, and I soon recognized the ruins from which I had taken the statuette of Ilmanaria, tucked safely into my pack, next to the Star Jewel.

We had already explored that place in great detail, but we were in no hurry this time around. As such, we once more marveled over faded mosaics clinging to tilting walls, glimpses into a past faded yet not wholly forgotten.

Around midday, we stopped beside a clear

stream to eat a quick meal of jerky, crackers, and nuts, our supplies nearly gone now. Diane playfully immersed her feet in the bracing water, smiling dreamily as minnows nibbled her toes. Nearby frogs croaked a lazy chorus.

Our break concluded, we continued onward, keeping a brisk pace. The trees were starting to thin out, and we caught occasional glimpses of rolling grassland between their trunks ahead — the forest's edge drew nearer. Here and there were homesteads much like our own, and I knew we had once again reached the lands where hardy people carved out their living.

By late afternoon, the trail opened up ahead of us, and we passed beneath the final massive oaks onto sweeping plains dotted with stands of hardy trees. In the distance rose familiar log walls — we had reached Gladdenfield's outskirts.

As we traversed the plains, I reveled in the feel of the open breeze. A pair of merrily trilling bluebirds flitted by overhead. Though the forest's magic would be missed, civilization's comforts beckoned. I was looking forward to completing the quest for

Waelin, but also to returning to the homestead and using my new abilities. After all this excitement, it would be nice to return to the calm life for a bit.

Reaching the palisades as the sun sank low, we were warmly welcomed back by the familiar elven guards with assault rifles. They marveled hearing we had braved the Blighted Land and emerged successful. After that, they beckoned us to enter town, and we stepped through the gate.

Leigh took a deep whiff of air and smiled. "It's good to be back."

Eager to complete our quest, we hurried through the busy streets of Gladdenfield toward the ramshackle inn known as the Wild Outrider. The sun was on its way down, and we were happy to have made it into town before darkness fell.

Though bone-tired from the journey, elation thrummed through us — the Star Jewel rested securely in my pack, its mysterious power a constant presence in my mind. After so many trials, we had succeeded.

The lively sounds of the frontier settlement filled the dusty air around us as we walked. Sour notes from a saloon's piano drifted out into the thoroughfare along with raucous laughter. A peddler called out his wares from beneath sagging awnings. The lively energy invigorated our weary steps. It was good to be back, although Diane and I also longed to return to the homestead.

Before long, the timber facade of the tavern rose ahead. I quickened my pace, keen to reunite with the elf who had sent us on this perilous errand and see it through to the end. Diane and Leigh matched my urgency, equally eager for fruition.

Stepping into the crowded, smoky interior, I saw Darny busy as ever behind the bar. Rowdy regulars mingled with dusty travelers fresh off the trail. The warm glow of oil lamps and scent of cooking food greeted us like old friends.

We approached the bar, and Darny looked up with a smile for our arrival. His cheeks and nose were red.

"Full night!" I called out to him.

He gave an enthusiastic nod. "Indeed it is!" he said. "How'd your journey fare? Another quest for Waelin, I hear?"

I grinned. "We did well enough," I said. "Can you send someone upstairs to call for him?"

"I'll do that," Darny said while filling a tankard with golden ale. "You folks have a seat. There's stew, ale, and wine!"

My stomach rumbled at that, and the three of us made our way through the rowdy tavern past ale-swigging dwarves and laughing humans to secure a table near the back. I waved over a harried serving girl to bring ale and bowls of stew.

As we ate ravenously, our eyes strayed often to the stairwell in anticipation of Waelin's arrival, our quest nearing its end. The stew was good and rich, and it reinvigorated us. The ale was a good batch, and the taste was welcome after almost ten days on water in the Wild.

Halfway through the hearty meal, a stir of movement drew my eye. Emerging from upstairs came the expected sight of Waelin's purple robes.

He shuffled toward us, the crowd parting respectfully. I sat up straighter as the elf approached our table, sharp gaze weighing each of us in turn.

"You return successful," Waelin observed. Though his tone remained characteristically brusque, his eyes glinted with fragile hope.

I nodded, gesturing for him to sit. "Would you like to see it?"

"Not here," he said. "Come to my room when you finish your meals, and we shall talk further." With that, he gave a curt nod and headed back upstairs.

Exchanging a look with my girls, we dug in again to quickly finish our meals. After that, we made our way up to Waelin's room. The elf opened the door before I could even knock for the second time and beckoned us in. The light in his eyes betrayed how eager he was to see the result of our questing.

I placed my pack on the table and retrieved the Star Jewel. It shone with a light of its own, illuminating the dimly lit chamber stacked with

Waelin's books and alchemical instruments.

His eyes shimmered with the same light, and the brusque elf suddenly seemed very vulnerable in that moment as he looked at me. "May I..." he asked, his voice small.

I nodded and handed him the artifact. The elf's weathered hand trembled faintly as he reached to grasp the glittering relic, as though hardly daring to believe it was real. His Adam's apple bobbed sharply.

"By the gods... after all this time, you found it." Raw emotion strained his rasping voice as he finally clutched the treasure that would save his niece's life.

Chapter 20

We gave Waelin a moment to study the object he had so long desired to save Celeste's life. For a moment, he seemed to forget we were even there, but finally, he looked up at us. "Did it all go well?" he rasped.

"The Blighted Land and Nimos Sedia nearly

claimed us," I said. "But we persevered for your niece's sake."

As I spoke, I thought back on the harrowing clashes in the Dungeon with the statue, the fire elementals, the ghouls, the drakelings, and their leader, not to mention the Landcrawler and the Grapplejaws.

"It was an ordeal," I finally added. "But we have fulfilled our quest. The jewel can now help Celeste."

Leigh hummed agreement, smiling. "We're happy to be able to help," she said.

Regaining his composure, Waelin carefully studied the relic before placing it on the table. "My niece's salvation is assured now thanks to you three," he said fervently. "Your courage and dedication are humbling. Whatever you need, consider it done."

I clasped his bony shoulder. "The warding spell you promised Caldwell will help protect countless frontier settlements. That, and your help to expand the magical knowledge of the Frontier Division is payment enough."

Waelin inclined his head. "You shall have it. My transaction with the Frontier Division will proceed once I have administered the Star Jewel's power to Celeste. She is my priority, you must understand." His voice thickened with emotion once more.

"We understand completely," Diane assured him gently. "Can we wait until she wakes?"

"Unfortunately, no," Waelin replied. "The process will take several hours, and I require silence and concentration. The ritual's secrets are also things I am protective of. I am sure you understand…"

Diane nodded. "Of course," she said. "Please give Celeste our best once she wakes up."

I nodded, agreeing with that sentiment before turning to Waelin again. "So, we found that in the Blighted Land and Nimos Sedia, the enemies were a bit more challenging than expected."

Leigh nodded. "Some were certainly over level 3."

Waelin frowned at that. "Well… That is something I regret. Perhaps the taint of the Blighted Land has deepened since I last received information from there. It is possible that the malignant forces that rule there grow stronger. If you destroyed some of the monsters, you have culled the power for the time being, but a higher-level Geomancer or Priest — anyone with Light or Earth magic — should be required to permanently lift the veil. I will address this fact with Caldwell, and the Frontier Division will see if they can spare someone."

I nodded. "And we leveled — a lot. I advanced from level 4 to level 6, and the girls from 2 to 4..."

He blinked, now truly flabbergasted. "That... That is highly peculiar." He rubbed his jaw for a moment. "I have never heard of such swift advancement." He looked at the girls. "And you all experienced this?"

The girls nodded. "Yeah," Diane said. "But it took me years to hit level 2."

"As it should," Waelin said. "I am level 9, and I have spent a lifetime getting there. Reckoned in elven years, mind you..." He narrowed his eyes at me. "And you? How long has it taken you to advance to the level you were before you delved into Nimos Sedia?"

"I was level 4. That took me… well, a few weeks, I guess. I only recently acquired my Class: Frontier Summoner."

He nodded slowly, a new interest flaring in his eyes. "Then it is you," he said. "Something about you fosters this quick advancement. Perhaps it is a Bloodline advantage?"

I perked an eyebrow. "Bloodlines?"

"Yes," Waelin said. "There are several Bloodlines among adventurers. They do not always manifest, but they often do within the same family. If your Bloodline allows swifter advancement, it is invaluable… You should investigate this matter. There are Blood Mages who specialize in such things. Give me some time, and I will try to find one. They are few and far between."

I inclined my head, my mind already spinning. I knew my parents were both adventurers, and they had been lost in the early days, shortly after the Upheaval. "Thank you," I said. "I appreciate your help."

Waelin's jaw moved. "Well, it is not completely

given without expecting something in return..."

I raised an eyebrow. "Oh? You have something to ask of us?"

He nodded. "I... suspect I shall have to travel to the Frontier Division's headquarters in New Springfield. I do not wish to take Celeste with me, for she is young and full of life. The dull arcane affairs of gray-haired dotards like myself never interested her. She loves the outdoors, life in the wilderness. As such, she shall stay here. I will procure her a temporary residence in town." He fixed his eyes on me. "Perhaps, you will do me the service of calling on her occasionally — to make sure she is well?"

"Of course," I said. "It would be my pleasure to check up on your niece. I expect Diane and I will be in town again in a few days to offload some produce. If you leave her address at Darny's, I will visit her and check up on her."

"Excellent," Waelin said gruffly. His eyes drifted to the Star Jewel, and I could tell his thoughts already turned to his niece's treatment. "Give her some time to recover... If all goes well, I shall leave in about ten days. She should be fully recovered by then. If you would check up on her then, I would appreciate it."

"I will," I said. "But I have one final question for you, though."

He nodded. "Of course."

"We found a statuette among elven ruins in the wilderness." I reached into the pack and retrieved the statuette of Ilmanaria. "Do you know what this is?"

He narrowed his eyes at the statuette and beckoned for me to hand it over. I did, and he held it for a while and studied it before handing it back.

"This statuette represents Ilmanaria. She is one of the many spirits the elves worship, and she is said to protect mages. The once-shining city of Talas Ilmanarion was dedicated to her. Like many things, it fell in the Upheaval. I remember its golden spires fondly." His expression saddened for a moment before he looked at me again. "This statuette is a Hearth Treasure. Place it in your house to have its residents receive a passive boon. Likely, it will grant you some kind of magical advantage."

I exchanged an excited look with my girls. "That sounds promising," I said. "We can use every edge we get out there."

Diane grinned and nodded. "Indeed, we can!"

"Well," Waelin rasped. "I cannot properly express my gratitude, but if there are no further matters to discuss, I would like to prepare for the ritual. It is a harrowing process, and preparations will take some time."

I nodded. "Of course," I said. "And best of luck with the ritual."

Waelin gave a weary nod. "I shall do my best." With a final grateful bow, he moved to the door and held it open for us.

As the door shut behind us, the three of us shared a look heavy with meaning. It was done. We had achieved our goal against all odds, and now countless lives would benefit. Smiling, the three of us headed back down into the tavern.

Leigh loosed a long exhale. "I'd say this calls for a celebratory round on me!" Flagging down the harried serving girl again, she ordered a pitcher of ale for us all.

Soon we were toasting our success as the tavern's energy eddied around us. Though the details of the quest must remain secret, I knew tales of our exploits would spread across the frontier in time. For now, we simply enjoyed each other's company, our mission complete.

Over mugs of rich ale, we reminisced on the quest's highs and lows — the marvels witnessed, perils braved, and lessons learned about ourselves and each other. Laughter flowed frequently, our bonds enriched by shared adversity we had weathered together.

Chapter 21

With our quest finally complete, Diane, Leigh, and I left the noisy tavern and made our way through the darkened streets back to Leigh's cozy dwelling in town. The rowdy energy of Gladdenfield Outpost had faded as most folks turned in after a long day's work.

Letting ourselves in, Leigh quickly set about building a warm fire in the hearth in the living area above the store. Soon enough, its cheerful glow filled the living room. After so many nights camped out under the stars, it already felt wonderfully homey.

"Let me get the beds in order," she said after finishing work on the fire. And as she moved past, I saw that her usually jovial expression seemed to have faded a little.

And I had an inkling as to what was going on in her mind, because it was on my mind as well.

"Ahh, so nice to be back," Diane sighed contentedly as she sank onto the plush sofa near the fireplace and languidly stretched out her lithe limbs.

The flickering firelight played beautifully over her delicate fox-like features, making her brilliant sapphire eyes shine. I smiled as I gave her an appreciative look and nodded agreement, but my mind was still on Leigh.

"You two need to talk," Diane said, effortlessly guessing my thoughts.

I chuckled. "You know me well," I said.

She grinned and fluffed her tail. "I do," she said. "Talk to her and tell her how you feel. She knows I welcome her, but she needs to hear it from you, too."

I smiled and nodded. "I will."

After a minute, Leigh returned with a pot of tea and cups. She placed them on the table before adding another split log to the flames, stoking them higher. Finally, she came over to join us. The dancing fire immediately began devouring the fresh fuel, popping and snapping merrily, its warmth washing over us.

Stifling a yawn behind one dainty hand, Diane rose gracefully to her feet again. "I think I'll pass on tea and just turn in for the night," she announced, padding over to give me an affectionate peck on the cheek, followed by a wink only I could see. "That big comfortable bed is calling my name after so many long nights on hard, lumpy ground."

I chuckled. "We'll join you soon," I said. "Right after we finish our tea."

"Sleep tight!" Leigh said, forcing a little chirpiness to her voice as Diane gave a final wave before padding out of the cozy room.

Now alone, Leigh and I smiled at one another, the firelight playing softly over our features. Without needing to exchange a word, she came over to settle beside me on the plush sofa, casually tucking her long legs up beside her and leaning into my shoulder.

I instinctively wrapped an arm around her slender frame, and she nestled even closer with a content little sigh. Silences with Leigh were rare, but this was a comfortable one. After having spent so much time together, we simply reveled in each other's presence a while longer.

But as we relaxed together, I knew the time had come for our little talk.

For a long stretch of time, Leigh and I simply sat together in front of the crackling hearth, cherishing the intimate moment. Leigh idly traced her fingertips over my arm in slow circles as she lounged comfortably against me. The tender feel of her feminine body nestled so trustingly next to mine awoke a growing need that I could no longer ignore.

"You know," I said, beginning our conversation with some levity. "Despite nearly getting killed, I really enjoyed our time together out there."

Tilting her chin up, Leigh's sparkling blue eyes sought out my own, their depths smoldering with unspoken heat that must have mirrored the simmering emotions kindling within me.

"I did, too," she said, and her blazing blue eyes urged me to continue. For all her bluster and bubbliness, this was one topic the blonde struggled with broaching.

"Being out there together these last days," I continued, "getting closer each new day... Well, it's only served to strengthen the way I feel about you. About us."

She smiled softly, tears welling up in her eyes. "Oh, David," she hummed. "I feel the same way.

I... I've felt that way a long time. But I was scared to talk about it."

My pulse involuntarily quickened at her admission. Almost instinctively, I tightened my arm around Leigh's slender waist in a supportive embrace.

"Don't be sacred of those feelings, Leigh," I said. "You mean so much to me, Leigh. You belong with me, to my family. There's no need to bandy words around that... I love you. That's the pure and honest truth."

She gave a happy hum, teeth catching briefly on her full lower lip as if gathering her courage before meeting my gaze again unwaveringly.

"I love you too, baby," Leigh confessed in a sudden heated rush, her charming country twang especially pronounced. "I've gone and truly fallen for you, too. I'm... I'm startin' to see you as my man."

Hearing her finally give voice to the growing connection that had kindled between us throughout our time away washed over me with the warm intensity of a breaking dawn. Unable to resist, I drew Leigh up into a searing kiss, intending to convey wordlessly that her feelings were fervently returned rather than one-sided.

For long moments our lips clung together heatedly, exploring one another with steadily mounting passion. Leigh instantly melted against me, her fingers threading almost desperately through my hair to pull me even closer still. By the time we finally parted for air, her fair cheeks were endearingly flushed.

"You and me – we belong together," I told her, reaching up to gently cradle her delicate face between my palms. "Our time out there together, all that we went through side by side… it changed things between us, Leigh. Opened my eyes. Diane will forever own my heart, but so do you. It can have more than one owner, Leigh. I love you, and I want you to join my family."

Unrestrained joy instantly suffused Leigh's classically beautiful features upon hearing my earnest confession. Overcome by emotion, she threw both arms exuberantly around my neck in a fierce hug that toppled us sideways across the sofa cushions.

I couldn't help but chuckle affectionately at her enthusiasm. I simply held Leigh's curvy body snugly against mine for a long moment, savoring her feminine warmth and softness.

"Yes!" she breathed. "I want to be a part of it. I want to be with you, and I *like* sharing you with Diane. She is one of my dearest friends, and I love seeing her happy the way you make her."

I grinned and kissed her cheek. "It makes me very happy to hear that," I said. "I know she wants you to be a part of the family as well."

Eventually we sat back up, Leigh practically glowing with happiness and passion now that our true feelings were finally out in the open. Taking both of my hands meaningfully in her own, she searched my eyes with sudden solemnity.

"Where do we go from here then?" she asked, her tone vulnerably hopeful. "I don't wanna risk messing things up. But at the same time, I wanna be with you, David. I don't like that you live out there, and I live out here."

I considered her words carefully, wanting to ease

her concerns. "I think the best thing is for us to take it easy," I suggested gently. "You should keep running the store, as that is something you enjoy doing. But it's a twenty-minute drive — maybe a little longer if you ride Colonel. You should come over more often, and we can look to expanding the cabin."

Leigh nodded slowly, mulling this over. "Would Diane be okay with… sharing you a whole lot more like that?" The shy eagerness edging her voice made me smile.

"She told me that she is," I stated with total faith in Diane's kind and generous heart. "Our relationship has never exactly been conventional, after all. I am confident that, together, we can figure out how to make this work between the three of us in a way that feels right."

Leigh's answering smile seemed to outshine even the roaring fire as hope and passion suffused her gorgeous features. "Well, I think so too," she agreed fervently. "You two both mean the entire world to me. I'd never wanna do anything to jeopardize this special bond we all share."

Reaching down, her thumb idly stroked along the back of my hand in a tender motion. "I just know deep down that my feelings for you are as real and powerful as anything I've ever felt, David."

"I promise you, mine for you are every bit as strong in return," I affirmed without hesitation, lifting her hand to my lips to tenderly kiss the backs of her fingers. "Diane wants us to be open and happy, however we define that going forward. She has told me all about the way the elves do it."

Leigh chuckled. "The *elven marriage*, ya mean?"

I grinned and nodded. "Exactly."

"Well, that does sound kinda nice."

"You two should talk, too," I said. "You'll see that she wants to include you. You are her best friend, too, and she'll welcome you with open arms."

Leigh nodded, clearly reassured by my words and the conviction behind them. A comfortable silence fell over us both then as we leaned together gazing into the flickering flames, each privately pondering the new depth our relationship had reached. My arm remained wrapped warmly around her slender shoulders, holding her close.

Gradually the hour grew later and later, the lively fire settling into glowing embers in the sooty hearth. Leigh straightened reluctantly with a sigh, then tilted my chin down to gift me with a long, steamy kiss that transmitted thrilling hints of passion yet to come.

"Let's go to bed, darlin'," she drawled with a coy wink and playful smile as we finally rose together. "We'll see if Diane is still awake. Actions speak louder than words and whatnot, am I right?"

I chuckled as she pulled me along. Hand in hand, we made our way to the bedroom. There, we found Diane still half awake. And soon enough, the fox girl was fully awake and ready to play…

Chapter 22

The next morning, Diane and I awoke in Leigh's cozy bed, a tangle of tousled blankets and bare limbs. Leigh was already up and about, making us breakfast. Stretching luxuriously beneath the quilts, Diane gifted me a sleepy smile.

"That was a lovely night," I told her, giving her a

kiss on the top of her head, her fox ears tickling me.

"I'll say," she agreed before snuggling close to me. "I'm happy you and Leigh talked... I really look forward to seeing more of her."

I grinned, breathing in her scent. "So do I!"

"I suppose it's time we headed back to the homestead," Diane murmured, though her contented tone suggested she was in no hurry to leave the comforts of town. Outside, the lively sounds of Gladdenfield awakening drifted up through the open window.

I nodded, giving her a tender kiss. "You're right, we should get a move on. I'm sure Ghostie has kept the place orderly, but there's work waiting for us out there."

After a brisk wash-up, we dressed and tidied the room before finding Leigh bustling in the kitchen. The savory aromas of coffee and sizzling bacon greeted us. Leigh enveloped us both in warm hugs, apparently having gotten an early start on making breakfast.

Over hearty plates of eggs, bacon, and toasted bread with jam, we discussed our imminent departure. Diane would be joining me for the drive back to the secluded valley we called home while Leigh remained to run her store.

We took our time eating breakfast, recalling the tales of our adventures and laughing. But finally, the food was finished, and Diane and I had become more than eager to check up on our home.

"Y'all take care on those dusty roads now," Leigh admonished lightly as she walked us out onto the porch after breakfast. Her eyes shone with unconcealed affection for us both. "I'll drop by tomorrow evening if that's alright with you. Gotta get the store in order first."

"We're looking forward to it," I said, giving her waist a squeeze before lifting our packs into the Jeep. Diane moved to hug Leigh tightly. Their close friendship brought a smile to my face.

With our goodbyes said, Diane and I climbed into the Jeep and pulled away down the dusty street. Leigh stood waving brightly on the porch as we finally headed back home.

It gladdened me knowing she would visit the homestead soon, our new understanding kindling anticipation of deepening intimacy to come. For now, Diane and I relished the open road unfurling ahead through the wilderness toward our remote valley.

Bouncing along the winding trail, we admired the varied scenery flowing past from forested slopes to grassy meadows dotted with wildflowers. A pair of foxes peered curiously from their burrow, making Diane's eyes gleam with delight. The frontier held endless fascination and beauty if one knew where to look.

After a gentle drive of about twenty minutes, the dusty trail delivered us from the Springfield Forest to the banks of the radiant Silverthread River where we made our home. As our cozy cabin with its garden and farming plots and — as of yet still unused — pasture dawned between the trees, Diane smiled contentedly.

I shot her an admiring look as she sat in the passenger seat, her raven hair billowing in the warm breeze as civilization came into view ahead. I was looking forward to a few calmer days ahead with her.

As we drove the final stretch, trees heavy with birdsong closed around us, shielding the modest cabin and its fields nestled on the bank of that beautiful, winding ribbon of silver. We were home at last.

I parked the Jeep right outside the cabin and shot Diane a warm look that she returned. Climbing stiffly from the Jeep, I inhaled the wholesome loamy scents of the land we had shaped with our own hands. It was profoundly fulfilling to stand witness to the fruits of our shared dedication and labor manifesting so tangibly around us. And at first sight, the place was looking in good shape.

Beside me, Diane surveyed our modest homestead with a brilliant smile, her eyes crinkling happily. This sanctuary held meaning for us now that a sprawling city never could. Together we had built something lasting.

As we grabbed our packs, a familiar excited chirping heralded Ghostie's return. The domesticant drifted over to encircle us enthusiastically, clearly pleased by our homecoming after days away. Its diligent efforts keeping the homestead orderly in our absence were plainly visible.

"Hi there, Ghostie!" Diane laughed, reaching out to affectionately pat the domesticant's smooth spectral head. It bobbed cheerfully in response before zooming off to continue patrolling the property's perimeter.

Carrying our bags inside, I rekindled the hearth fire while Diane put on a kettle for tea. Soon we were nestled cozily on the braided rug in front of the fire, steaming mugs in hand simply soaking up the comfort of these familiar surroundings.

Outside, the end of the morning drew near, shortening the shadows across the fertile fields as the valley. There was work to do, but we would enjoy a simple lunch first.

Over baked potatoes from the pantry, smoked trout, and some preserved vegetables, we discussed plans and hopes for the days ahead. I was eager to inspect the homestead and see how everything had fared in our absence. I also wanted to apply my new summoning abilities around the homestead, while Diane looked forward to further fostering the valley's natural bounty through her scouting skills. There were fish to catch, but the dwindling supply of firewood also demanded attention.

Bellies filled, we let Ghostie clean up as we got ready to spend the afternoon working.

After lunch, Diane and I readied ourselves to inspect the homestead and resume the myriad tasks needed to maintain our self-sufficient home. I was eager to take stock of things after days away on our quest.

Stepping outside into the warm afternoon sunshine, I spent some time walking the perimeter, verifying the fences remained sturdy and watching for any breaches. Several split-rail sections needed reinforcing, which I marked for repair. Overall, though, Ghostie had kept interlopers at bay.

Circling around, I entered my small alchemy garden, kneeling to scrutinize the Magebread flowers, Wispsilk leaves, and Thauma Roots. All three were flourishing, with several plants mature enough for harvesting. That was good because I needed to make new potions. I would harvest them and make new brews tomorrow.

After inspecting the alchemical garden, I moved on to the smokehouse. We were running low on the supply of alderwood to keep the smokehouse running, and I decided to prioritize that over firewood.

My final stop was the garden plot where Diane and I had left fast-growing tomato and onion crops. I was amazed to find that the produce looked like it would soon be ready for harvest. The woodland and earth spirits had clearly had a beneficial effect, especially combined with the fast-growing magical properties of the seed.

As I inspected the plot, Ghostie hovered around happily, tending to the plants. The domesticant bobbed in greeting as it watered the fast-growing tomato vines heavy with ripening fruit.

It was looking to be a rich harvest, and we would enjoy it for weeks to come. The surplus could be sold or traded in Gladdenfield. Hopefully, it would all be ready for our next trip into town.

My inspection complete, I slung my rifle over my shoulder and hiked out to methodically reset each trap along my winding trapline through the woods and meadows. Kneeling in the grass, I carefully reset the empty snares using my Trapping skill.

I had not set them before we headed out on our journey, knowing that any trapped creature would be a waste, but now that we were back, we could do with trapping again. Along the way, I used my Foraging skill to gather fresh, edible mushrooms and wild vegetables.

Returning to the cabin, I found Diane by the banks of the Silverthread, fishing. She had already caught us a dinner of trout for tonight, and I was looking forward to a fresh meal from the river.

Together we cleaned and gutted the fish by the banks of the river while Ghostie cleaned the implements and tools we had used before moving to wash the clothes we had worn during our expedition.

When the fish was done, Diane and I retreated

inside. Soon, the kitchen was filled with mouthwatering aromas that had my belly rumbling. Diane fried the fish with potato chunks, wild carrots, and mushrooms while I stoked the fire for the night.

With the fire going and food being prepared, I stepped outside to use my spells to imbue the crops, once again manifesting woodland and earth spirits to enrich the soil and help grow the crops. While the spirits worked diligently, I moved on to the next part of my plan: a storm elemental to protect the homestead.

Speaking the words of power, I conjured my new storm elemental, marveling at its wreaths of roiling lightning as it manifested from my swirling mana. Then, I cast my Bind Familiar spell on the summon, and I felt the bond between us forge as it entered my service like Ghostie had.

The whole thing set me back 25 mana, leaving only 7 after all the skills and other summons I had used today, but I was not expecting combat, so it was fine to expend my resources.

I instructed the storm elemental to patrol and

guard the homestead and its grounds. For a few minutes, I watched with a sense of satisfaction as the storm elemental — my second bound familiar — began patrolling the grounds. In the waning light, the crackle of lightning from the man formed of roiling storm clouds was a magical view.

When I returned inside, Diane was dishing up piping hot plates of trout with potatoes and wild vegetables. I inhaled appreciatively as I took my seat at the worn table.

Diane joined me with a smile, and we enjoyed the simple but hearty dinner she had prepared using the day's bounty. The valley provided well thanks to our care and labor.

As we ate, soft dusk settled over the valley beyond the windows. I sat back with a satisfied sigh, looking over at Diane.

"It's been a productive afternoon around the homestead," I remarked. "I was able to summon some new nature spirits to enrich the soil and help the crops grow faster. Oh, and I bound a new storm elemental familiar to help patrol and guard the property."

Diane's eyes widened. "You bound another one? That's wonderful!" she exclaimed.

I nodded, smiling. "Yes, in addition to Ghostie, I now have a storm elemental bound to me. It can defend the homestead when needed. That should make it easier for us to sleep at night or to head out on an expedition."

"That's exciting!" Diane said. "I wonder if we'll actually do any work around here ourselves in a few months." She winked at me.

I laughed and shook my head. "Well, there will always be plenty to do. I don't doubt that. But the more time we get to relax..." I grinned broadly and sat back before wiggling my eyebrows. "You know..."

Diane giggled at that and playfully waved my comment away. "You're terrible!" she laughed before we returned to our meals.

When our bowls were empty and our hunger satisfied, Ghostie dutifully whisked away the dishes to be cleaned. I settled onto the rug by the hearth while Diane prepared mugs of mint tea to further soothe us after the meal. The humble domestic rituals of our life here never failed to fulfill me.

Savoring the fragrant tea, Diane nestled contentedly against me as we gazed into the flickering flames. The cozy crackle of burning logs filled a comfortable silence between us. Familiar comforts and closeness kindled a drowsy, tranquil mood.

When the emptied mugs had been set aside and the fire gradually dimmed to glowing embers, Diane took my hand, smiling softly. Without needing to speak, we rose together and climbed the ladder to the loft.

Beneath the snug quilts, we celebrated our reunion and the success of our quest in the most intimate way — with tender caresses and passionate lovemaking. Any lingering stress and fatigue from days on the trail swiftly melted away in each other's arms.

When at last we lay cradled in one another's arms, sweat-slicked and satisfied, I tenderly kissed Diane's cheek, conveying my gratitude for having her to share nights like these with. Joyful exhaustion soon claimed us both, sending us drifting into untroubled sleep still entwined.

Chapter 23

The next morning, I awoke eager to replenish my stock of alchemical reagents and concoct new mana potions. Slipping quietly from the bed so as not to disturb Diane's rest, I washed briskly and donned my work clothes before making my way outside into the cool dawn air.

My breath misted faintly as I crossed the dew-speckled grass to my enclosed garden where magical herbs flourished. Kneeling amidst the dark, moist soil, I scrutinized each plant, determining which ingredients had reached ideal maturity for harvesting.

Selecting several plump Thauma Roots that pulsed with violet radiance, I gently eased them from the dirt and trimmed away the fibrous rootlets. Next, I plucked Magebread flowers brimming with shimmering pollen, and clipped the ethereal leaves of the Wispsilk.

Carrying my harvest inside, I cleared my worktable and laid out the arcane ingredients. Taking up a small silver knife, I began the preparations — peeling, slicing, and grinding — needed to render the plants into alchemically viable forms. Soon I had added the harvest to what I already had, leaving me with several jars of prepared ingredients awaiting my alchemical manipulations.

I turned as the door to the lab opened, seeing Diane smile at me, limned with morning light. She was barefoot and wearing a light dress. "You're working already, silly?" she said. "Did you even have breakfast?"

I chuckled and rubbed the back of my neck. "I was eager to get started today, so no... not yet."

"Come," she said, reaching out, and I took her hand.

We walked over our land, laughing and enjoying the wealth of sunlight and cool and fresh air before Diane ushered me inside. There, she served me a quick fortifying breakfast that consisted of a delicious frontier mishmash of jerky and wild vegetables.

Ghostie tidied up, and I struggled to resist her as she padded barefoot and happy through the cabin. Needless to say, I took her to the loft for a quick, revitalizing rumble before heading out into the open air again, feeling like a man of steel.

Fully satisfied, I devoted my full focus to the alchemical process. First, the cauldron was filled with a minute measure of water and set to heating over a low flame. While it warmed, I triple-checked my notes and preparations.

Soon, wisps of steam arose from the cauldron. Adding pinches of dried ingredients in careful sequence, I slowly amalgamated the vital essences needed to produce mana potions. As the mixture heated, its color gradually shifted through opalescent tones, signaling the alchemical fusion unfolding before my eyes.

When the reactions had stabilized, I removed the cauldron from the heat and decanted the brew into an earthenware vessel to cool and settle. The final elixir had assumed the distinctive translucent silver-blue hue of concentrated arcane quintessence. My efforts had borne fruit.

Working swiftly before the potency could dissipate, I carefully decanted the finished mana potion into a row of waiting glass vials using a funnel. Each became filled with the glimmering turquoise liquid, ready for consumption.

By midmorning, my table was arrayed with two dozen vials freshly brimming with the precious mana draughts. Stowing them safely on shelves beside healing potions and antidotes furnished by Waelin, I tidied my workspace feeling deeply satisfied. Soon they could aid my mystical pursuits.

I was getting the hang of brewing these mana draughts, and I felt a rising eagerness to learn more of this arcane trade. I suspected that began with more recipes, which I would have to find in stores or in the wilderness, perhaps in the ruins of...

And just like that, I once again thought of the little statuette... Waelin had called it a Hearth Treasure.

I had left it in the Jeep, and I now practically bounded outside to retrieve it. The mystical statuette was where I left it, and I studied the exquisite work of flowing stone with its highly detailed robes and delicate features for a moment before taking it inside.

"Oh, the statuette! Ilmanaria!" Diane purred as she was busy in the kitchen making flatbread. "I forgot all about her!"

"Let's see what happens when we give her a spot!' With those words, I placed her on the mantle. At once, a notification popped up in the corner of my vision, and I focused on it.

Idol of Ilmanaria Hearth Treasure activated: +10

mana.

"Oh, wow!" Diane cried out.

"You got it too?" I asked, feeling the arcane energy pulse within me.

"Yeah!" she said. "Oh... This is *very* useful!"

"I'll say," I replied. "That brings me up to 45 mana!"

"We should find more of these," Diane said, laughing as she clenched her fists, letting the arcane power pulse in her channels.

Grinning, I gave her a kiss. "I hope we do," I said. "This will make work around here even easier."

Before I could turn away, she raised a finger. "Oh! Don't forget: Leigh's coming over tonight!"

I nodded enthusiastically. "Yeah," I said. "Looking forward to it!"

"I'll make us something special!" Diane said.

I kissed her on her cheek and headed back outside, eager to do some more work.

With my morning's mystical workings complete, I decided to spend the rest of the morning and afternoon focused on more mundane tasks vital for our self-reliance. After all, our wood stores were running low, so I took up my axe and set off for the surrounding woods.

I hummed an idle work tune as I traversed the whispering forest, inhaling refreshing scents of pine needles underfoot and listening to woodpeckers tap for insects. Selecting a stand of young alderwood whose rapid growth could be accelerated, I set diligently to felling thin trunks and delimbing them.

Soon I had amassed a sizable pile of logs to split into firewood. The vigorous swinging of my axe felt good, sweat beading as I exerted myself purposefully.

I was already keeping it up much longer than before, and blisters no longer formed so swiftly.

Our needs demanded such toil, but I undertook the labors gladly, taking satisfaction in providing for Diane and me.

Late morning had escaped me by the time my muscles pleaded for respite. I was happy with the wood accumulated, enough to restock our cellar and smokehouse. Pausing to quench my thirst from a secret forest spring, I watched a doe and fawns browsing nearby, content with my contributions so far this day.

I summoned a woodland spirit to speed up the recovery of the trees I had felled, then followed up with an earth spirit to imbue the soil, allowing the trees to grow back much, much faster than they normally would. Then, I summoned a second domesticant and bound him to me as my third familiar, instructing him to haul the felled logs back to the cabin with me.

It took us several trips — and Ghostie helped as well — before we had deposited my haul and cut it up to fit the woodbin. After that, I washed the sweat from my face, neck, and torso, preparing for lunch.

Diane greeted me on the porch with a smile and embrace that warmed me more than the midday sun. Together we enjoyed a simple meal of flatbread, cheese, and smoked trout by the banks of the Silverthread. We looked over the river, watching the sun play on the water as the playful bubbles of fish rose to the surface. It was a perfect life.

As we lingered over the restorative fare, I described my mystical and mundane morning activities. Diane listened bright-eyed, then told me all about what she had done so far today as we enjoyed the filling lunch.

Our hunger sated, we spent a lazy hour simply lounging in each other's arms beneath the rustling branches as life continued inexorably around us. Birdsong and the melodic river were our music as we traded tender caresses. But before long, the warm sun beckoned us back to fulfilling tasks.

While Ghostie and his fellow domesticant tidied the kitchen, I returned outside to further split the logs accumulated earlier. Soon I was lost in the repetitive swing of the axe, muscles easing back into the familiar motions. Our snug home would be kept warm thanks to this honest work of my hands.

By the time I finished up, the afternoon was nearing its end. I turned my eyes to the small road leading up to our smallholding, and a smile dawned on my lips when — like clockwork — I saw Colonel approaching, bearing my beloved Leigh, easily recognized by her voluptuous curves and her flowing blonde hair with a distinctive cowboy hat on top.

Chapter 24

I waved at Leigh as she cantered up the dusty path astride her loyal steed, Colonel. Golden hair streamed from beneath her wide-brimmed cowgirl hat, catching the rays of the lowering sun. Even from a distance, her brilliant smile when she spotted me made my pulse quicken.

I replaced the axe in the mudroom and called for Diane. Then, I waited outside the cabin as Leigh made her way onto our land.

"Hey there," I called out.

She grinned and swung down fluidly from the saddle. Leaving her horse, Leigh hurried over on long denim-clad legs to sweep me into an exuberant hug. I held her lithe, feminine body against mine, breathing in the scent of worn leather and prairie wildflowers that clung to her after her trek through Springfield Forest.

"It's good to see you," I said sincerely, hands lingering perhaps a beat too long on her waist before I stepped back. Having her here just felt right after our recent emotional talk and new understanding.

Leigh's blue eyes danced playfully. "Baby, you have no idea how much I've been looking forward to this visit," she confessed, absentmindedly fiddling with one of her golden locks. "I've been missing you something fierce!"

With Leigh's arm looped companionably through mine, we made our way onto the porch of the cozy cabin. There, Diane greeted our guest with equal warmth. The two friends embraced happily, laughing and chattering.

After they had caught up, I introduced Leigh to my new storm elemental familiar patrolling the grounds in looping arcs by pointing it out.

"Well, ain't he just a dangerous-lookin' fella," Leigh remarked, clearly impressed as she watched the wreathing lightning and heard the crackling energy. Turning, she gave me an approving wink that sent pleasant warmth spreading through me. "What ya gonna call that stormy thing?"

"Mr. Drizzles," Diane said before I could answer, and I couldn't do anything but break out laughing. Leigh joined in.

"Almost as bad as Mr. Toasty," I muttered once I had recovered, and Leigh gave me a playful slap at that.

"Mr. Toasty is a fine name, I'll have ya know!"

I laughed and shook my head before ushering the girls inside where Ghostie was already scuttling about to tidy up the house. Inside, mouthwatering aromas filled the air — Diane had prepared mashed potatoes and a meat pie brimming with chunks of meat and wild vegetables. My belly rumbled as she cheerfully ladled out steaming bowlfuls for each of us.

We settled in around the worn but lovingly crafted wooden table near the merrily crackling fireplace to enjoy our dinner together. Conversation flowed easily between the three of us as we ate. The savory meal perfectly sated our appetites sharpened by long hours working outside.

"This little place of yours just keeps getting more homey and lived-in each time I visit," Leigh remarked appreciatively once her plate was empty, leaning back contentedly in her creaking chair. "Y'all have already done so much to make this land your own."

Diane smiled happily, her dark braid sliding over one slender shoulder as she nodded. "It really is starting to feel like home now," she agreed softly, long foxtail swishing behind her in slow contented beats. "Oh! And David placed the statuette he found, which gives us more mana now."

"Is that a fact?" Leigh said, one dark golden eyebrow arching upward. "Well, that's just dandy. Sure seems like your magic abilities are only gettin' stronger and stronger there, honey." Unrestrained pride and admiration shone in her voice.

"It's a bonus for anyone who lives here," Diane purred at her friend, and the invitation in those words was clear.

Leigh grinned. "Hmm," she hummed. "It's starting to sound *even more* interestin' to come around here."

Before long, our empty bowls were scraped clean, appetites fully sated by the rich venison stew. We let the meal settle in joyful silence for a while as Ghostie poured us mead from the little supply that Leigh had brought as a gift.

The company was good, and the night was young, and I reveled in it.

As we lingered at the table afterward as we talked, eventually enjoying mugs of fragrant tea steaming gently, our idle talk turned toward hopes and plans for further developing the homestead.

"You know, with your mystical talents, I'll bet we could expand the cottage a fair bit," Diane said to me, sitting forward eagerly, her brilliant sapphire eyes gleaming. "Maybe even add a whole second floor for a real bedroom… or two. That would really open up the interior."

"Ooh, and perhaps finally get a few cute little goats!" Leigh suggested enthusiastically. "Just think of all that fresh milk and cheese. And you've got that Ranchin' skill now, don't ya David?"

I smiled indulgently, warmed by their visible excitement. "All very doable ideas," I assured them confidently. "Though establishing even a small herd means we'll have to fence in more pasture first."

Leigh waved away the concern dismissively. "Aw, fences are no trouble at all. Y'all will have that done in a day or two." She then threw Diane a playful look. "But what do ya need the extra room for?"

Diane bit her lip and blushed. "Well, you know…"

I blinked, now suddenly understanding the background of her desire to expand the house. Diane was upfront about her desire to have kits, and it made perfect sense that she would want to broach the subject soon. After all, we had a stable thing out here. And with Leigh coming by regularly, we'd have plenty of people to care for kits.

Although I wasn't sure if the offspring of a human and a foxkin would be kits…

"Well now," Leigh purred, giving me a meaningful look, but she decided not to tease her harem sister any more than that. Instead, she turned to me. "Wouldn't it be nice to have an actual tool shed and a workshop, since you do so much yourself?"

With that, our discussion turned lively as we debated various options and improvements. The familiar cadences of Leigh's drawl dancing in counterpoint with Diane's melodic voice kindled cozy contentment within me.

"You know, if you cleared more land, I bet you could even grow more surplus crops to sell in town before long," Leigh added after awhile, absently swirling the dregs of her tea.

I paused thoughtfully. "Yeah," I mused, leaning forward. "I've considered expanding the fields. With my nature spirits speeding up growth cycles, yields could end up pretty substantial. Especially with those imbued, fast-growing crops."

Leigh nodded, pointing at me approvingly. "Mark my words, before the year's out you'll have way more fruits and veggies than just you two can handle," she predicted confidently. "I'm always eager to buy up whatever fresh produce folks can grow, 'specially with winter coming on."

Diane's sapphire eyes lit up, and her fox ears perked forward with excitement. "Ooh, you're so right! If we grew more excess produce to sell, we could start buying some nicer furnishings and decorations for the cottage with the earnings," she realized eagerly.

Reaching over, I gave her delicate hand an

affectionate squeeze, smiling at her visible enthusiasm. "That's an excellent notion," I agreed. "Let's definitely plan to expand the farm a little."

Already, I felt a bubble of excitement at the thought of trading our surplus crops or goods. It would feel good to engage with the community.

"While you're thinking of expanding, no reason not to be ambitious," Leigh added with an expansive gesture at the cozy interior space around us. "Add a couple extra rooms for Diane's wild plans..." She gave her harem sister a wink that made her blush. "And, of course, a bigger kitchen and larder..."

I chuckled indulgently at her eagerness but had to admit the vision sounded idyllic. "You're getting a bit ahead of yourselves, but those all sound like wonderful ideas we can work towards," I said warmly. "Rome wasn't built in a day, but with patience and tenacity, we'll transform this place over time into our perfect refuge, I'm certain of it."

Leigh gave me a playful nudge with her boot under the table. "See, I knew you were the right pioneer for the job," she teased. But beneath the humor glinted sincere appreciation that touched me deeply.

"Maybe we could get Leigh a guest room," Diane teased.

"No way," Leigh said. "I sleep with you two!"

"Not in this loft, I'm afraid," I laughed. "Those beds are tiny."

"Well, that's what you'll need to fix first, then," Leigh said. "Now come on! It's a fine, warm night, and we had a fine dinner. Why don't we sit by the river, make a little fire, and enjoy the starlight? After that, you can have your lil' domesticants drag down the mattresses, and we'll sleep by the fire."

I nodded and rose. "That's a great idea," I said. Diane gave an enthusiastic chirp as she hopped to her feet as well. We left Ghostie and his new friend with the dishes and headed outside.

Chapter 25

The sun had dipped below the western hills, cloaking our homestead in soft dusk as we made our way down to the silvery banks of the river. I gathered an armful of dry branches and got a modest campfire crackling, the golden flames dispelling the gloaming shadows. Above, emerging stars glittered like scattered diamonds against an indigo canvas.

Diane hummed idly as she shook out a woven blanket and settled gracefully upon it, her luxuriant ebony hair spilling over her delicate shoulders. Beside her, Leigh sprawled comfortably on her side, propping her head up with one hand.

For a time, we simply lounged together quietly, watching wisps of pale smoke curl skyward and listening to the melodic burbling of the water over smooth stones. Overhead, the stars shone in nature's glorious display, and it was a wondrous sight as always. The stars had a way of making every earthly affair seem small and insignificant.

The occasional snap of burning wood punctuated the soothing susurrations all around us — rustling leaves, trilling crickets, frogs serenading any who would listen from the rushes. Here by the bank where the fishing was good and berry thickets grew nearby, it was a little paradise we had carved out together using grit, skill, and a touch of magic.

As the evening chill crept in, I added more

branches to the cheery blaze until it rose high, radiating welcome warmth. The dancing flames lit Diane's refined features in profile as she gazed pensively across the shimmering water.

"It's nights like this that make me glad fate brought me out here to the frontier," she said at length, a wistful smile curling her lips. "If not for you taking me in, Leigh, who knows where I might have ended up after my family disappeared."

Leigh reached over to pat her friend's slender hand comfortingly. "Aw, think nothing of it, hon," she replied in her amiable drawl. "You and I were just a couple of green gals trying to find our footing after the Upheaval shook everything up. I needed a roommate to afford my little place anyway."

I perked up with interest, always eager for more glimpses into my beloveds' shared past which predated my arrival in Gladdenfield by a couple of years.

Sensing my curiosity, Diane glanced over with a smile, her brilliant sapphire eyes warming in the firelight. "Did we ever tell you how Leigh and I met?" she asked. When I shook my head, she settled in more comfortably to relate the tale.

"As you know, I roamed into the wilderness alone after the Upheaval when my family disappeared. I was just a teenage foxkin girl, scared and overwhelmed. For weeks I lived hand to mouth, foraging and hunting small game, just trying to survive. But I was so very lost and lonely. Sure, I met parties of wanderers and adventurers and sometimes even banded with them, but I had no true friends."

Her expression saddened briefly at the memory before she continued. "Then one day I wandered into a frontier trading post looking like a half-drowned kit. But this compassionate human took pity on me, insisting I come home with her."

Diane shot Leigh a fond smile, which the blonde returned warmly. "That's right, this poor lil' critter was skin and bones when I found her," Leigh supplied, picking up the thread of the tale.

"My heart just broke, seeing her so vulnerable and afraid. Wasn't any way I could turn her back out on her own in good conscience. So, I brought her back to my apartment above the general store in Gladdenfield, and we became roommates. I'd only just taken over the store, so I could use a pair o' hands."

Leigh chuckled, absently brushing back a wind-tousled lock of golden hair peeking out beneath her hat. "Diane didn't have a mind for shopkeepin', though. Not very good with numbers and keepin' inventory." She winked at her friend. "She is, however, very good at cooking, daydreamin', and I did good business with the game she brought in. Anyways, we looked after each other, and the rest is history."

Diane giggled. "We've been inseparable ever since," Diane finished happily, playfully bumping her shoulder against Leigh's. "I'll never be able to fully express my gratitude for everything you did for me back then."

Leigh waved off her earnest words. "Think nothing of it, sugar. We helped each other out." Her sky-blue gaze turned introspective as she watched the firelight dance hypnotically.

"Still, as much as we cared for each other, I always missed a man," Leigh added in a softer tone. She then gave me a mischievous look. "After all, I need someone tall enough to stock the top shelves!"

We all shared a laugh at her gentle teasing. Then, Diane turned sincere eyes my way, reaching over to intertwine our fingers. "Leigh's right," she said softly. "Having you completes me in a way I never thought possible."

Deeply touched by her words, I lifted her slender hand to my lips, brushing a tender kiss across her knuckles. "Believe me, I'm the lucky one here," I replied earnestly.

For long moments, we simply basked together in stillness broken only by the murmuring river and crackling fire, our hands joined contentedly. Overhead, the spangled cosmos spun on above our haven in the wilderness.

Leigh lay back on the blanket, removing her hat, and stared up at the sky, giving me and Diane a moment, and I decided to use it. I tore my eyes from the dazzling view overhead to glance curiously over at Diane.

"Earlier you mentioned hoping for more rooms

added onto the cabin. Do you have any special purpose in mind for those hypothetical new rooms someday?" I asked innocently, already certain I knew the answer.

Diane bit her lip, cheeks coloring charmingly even in the firelight. The topic clearly awakened vivid dreams and hopes within her. "Well, I was thinking perhaps... a room for kits one day," she confessed, words spilling out in an excited gush. She averted her gaze shyly, fox-like ears low.

My pulse quickened at her admission. Reaching over, I gently turned her delicate chin back to meet my gaze. "Diane, nothing would make me happier than raising a family together out here," I said earnestly. "We'll start planning things out — make a little nest."

Her sapphire eyes immediately shone, and she purred her happiness. "A nest sounds great!"

"You two are gonna make the purdiest lil' kits," Leigh remarked happily, reaching over to squeeze Diane's knee. "Why, I can babysit the darling scamps, teach 'em little scraps of wilderness lore..."

Diane laughed; imaginations clearly spun up by our support. "I would love nothing more than to have you teach our kits," she said. "I'd even name one after you."

Leigh chuckled. "That would get confusin'…"

I laughed, wrapping an arm around Diane's slender shoulders and pulling her close. "We'll figure it out, but I'm not letting the two people who came up with *Mr. Toasty* and *Mr. Drizzles* name any of my kids."

At that, we all broke out laughing. Nestled cozily beneath the glittering heavens, we continued joking and talking about the beautiful things that the future might hold for us.

But eventually, I noticed Diane's eyelids growing heavy, her bushy tail curling around her hips as drowsiness visibly set in. Kissing her forehead tenderly, I suggested we all turn in for the night.

Diane tried and failed to stifle a yawn behind one dainty hand. "Mmm, yes, that sounds lovely," she acquiesced, silky braid slipping over her shoulder as she rose gracefully to her feet and smoothed out her dress.

On my other side, Leigh gave an exaggerated stretch before standing as well. "Woo! I'm about done to turn in too," she declared.

Together we made sure the campfire was safely extinguished and doused for the night. Arm in arm, we headed back up the grassy slope toward the cozy cabin, leaving the hushed riverside camp behind.

The melody of crickets and rustling leaves followed us up toward the light and warmth awaiting within our wilderness abode.

Chapter 26

The morning sun dawned bright and clear as we awoke refreshed in the cozy cabin. After a hearty breakfast together, we discussed plans for the day's tasks around the homestead.

"The traps need to be checked," I said. "And it would be nice if we could do a lap of the area —

see what has been moving in the wilderness these past few days." Knowing that Leigh and Diane would need to catch up, especially considering Leigh joining our harem, I thought it was a good idea for the two of them to do the job together.

Besides, I was overdue for an easy, quiet day fishing by the banks of the Silverthread River.

"That sounds like somethin' the two of us can do," Leigh said, and Diane nodded her agreement.

Smiling, I watched the duo prepare for a moment before getting ready myself. Donning my hat, I grabbed the fishing pole and creel and headed down to the banks of the river. Diane and Leigh were already chatting and laughing as they gathered up their gear for a day of tracking in the wilderness around our home.

I decided the trout would likely be biting down by the shady bend in the creek. I whistled cheerily as I made my way across my property through the morning light, breathing in the crisp air. The land made me proud — of our achievements and of our independence.

At the tranquil bend, I set up on one of the

smooth boulders, making sure I had everything I needed to be comfortable. Once I was settled in, I attached the bait — worms that Leigh had brought from the store — and I cast my line out into the rippling currents and waited patiently for a bite, taking in the beauty all around.

After some time, my bobber suddenly dipped below the surface! Keeping the line taut, I swept my rod up and felt the satisfying throb of a good-sized fish. With a splash, I reeled in a fat trout that would make for delicious eating tonight. I unhooked the catch and placed it in my creel.

Resettling into my spot, I recast the line, watching intently for the next nibble. This time, I used some of my magic, summoning a minor water spirit. The playful water elemental coalesced into shape, summoned by my mana, and it immediately heeded my mental command to start guiding the fish to my bobber.

Soon enough, another fat trout took the bait! We were set for dinner already, but with fresh alderwood for the smokehouse, I was going to keep at it for a while.

The sun rose high overhead as the morning wore on, but the fish were biting, so I was happy to keep at it a while longer yet. This skillful way of providing food filled me with quiet satisfaction.

Eventually, I decided to try my luck down by the deeper pool farther along the creek. Hefting my gear, I hiked down the fern-lined bank until arriving at the crystal-clear pool. Schools of minnows scattered at my approach. Getting settled, I flicked the lure out and waited for a predator to snatch the bait.

After several casts, the line suddenly grew taut! Using a steady retrieve, I reeled in my catch. A fat, shimmering brook trout soon broke the surface, writhing against the hook. Carefully unhooking the sizable fish, I added it to my growing collection in the creel. This would be a fine meal.

As the day grew warmer, the fish seemed to grow more lethargic. The bright afternoon sunshine sparkled on the rippling creek, but fewer strikes came. Still, I lingered contentedly in the shade, knowing the trout would likely get active again once it started cooling off.

Sure enough, as the sun dropped lower toward the horizon, the fish started hitting once more. Within an hour, I had collected a half dozen more good-sized trout. My creel was getting heavy, so I decided it was time to start heading back. I had caught enough for a feast!

Whistling merrily, I hiked back past the sun-dappled forest, creel full of trout. I took the long way around, skirting the edges of my property to forage some mushrooms and collect some wild onions to use for flavoring. The fresh bounty of the land never ceased to amaze me.

Arriving back at the homestead, I first gutted and cleaned my catch at the Silverthread River in the usual spot. Once that was done, I headed back up to the cabin.

I unloaded my haul and got to work preparing the fish. I cleanly and efficiently filleted each trout. I set some aside to smoke in the smokehouse for preservation. The rest I would fry up tonight. I wanted to make a nice meal for the girls when they got back from their day scouting the area.

Stacking the excess firewood I had chopped

previously, I soon had the stove ready for frying my catch. I set the cast-iron skillet with some fat atop the glowing embers, letting the fat gradually grow hot while I worked.

Once the skillet was ready, I sliced up wild onions and potatoes to sauté first. The humble vegetables sizzled merrily once I added them to the pan. Their mouthwatering aroma already had my stomach rumbling in anticipation of the coming feast.

When the onions and potatoes were just shy of done, I added the fresh trout fillets. I watched with satisfaction as the fish flesh turned opaque and flaky. The whole cottage soon filled with the incredible smell of freshly pan-fried trout.

Once they were done, I took the skillet off the fire at just the right moment. After garnishing the trout and vegetables with some foraged herbs, I set the table in anticipation of the girls' arrival. I had made plenty of food — much more than the three of us could eat, and it would be a feast!

Before long, I heard the door open to cheerful voices as Diane and Leigh returned from their day scouting the wilderness. They were chatting and laughing about something they had seen as they came inside, setting down their gear.

"Something sure smells delicious!" Diane exclaimed, her brilliant blue eyes widening when she saw the heaping platter of trout fillets and veggies I had prepared.

"Why David, you've been busy as a beaver while we were out!" Leigh remarked appreciatively, hanging up her hat and eying the meal hungrily. "And fresh-caught trout at that. You do spoil us."

I smiled, always happy to provide for my girls after a long day. "I wanted to do something special for you two! Have a seat and dig in while it's hot," I urged them.

Eagerly they took their places at the table, marveling over the perfect flaky texture of the fish and the medley of flavors from the herbs and vegetables. We talked and laughed as we ate our fill of the delicious fare, savoring the fruits of our shared labors around the homestead.

Over dinner, Diane and Leigh regaled me with tales of their scouting expedition through the surrounding wilderness, relating some of the fascinating discoveries they had made tracking various beasts and foraging for edible and useful plants.

"We stumbled upon a whole grove of wild blueberry bushes!" Diane said excitedly. "The bushes were just laden with huge juicy berries. We must have picked four buckets full!"

Leigh nodded enthusiastically as she bit into a trout fillet. "Ooh, and we found some wildflowers I ain't never seen before, with the prettiest violet and yellow colors." She smiled at Diane. "We wove them into flower crowns and wore them the whole way home!"

I grinned, picturing the two of them frolicking through meadows picking berries and flowers. Their evident joy warmed my heart. "It sounds like you two had a delightful and productive day out there together," I remarked sincerely.

As we enjoyed second helpings of the fresh fish and veggies, the girls continued regaling me with humorous accounts of their day — trying to befriend a grumpy porcupine, getting buzzed by a huge bumblebee that sent Leigh shrieking and running. Their lively banter elicited frequent laughter from us all.

Before long, our empty plates and bowls were cleaned of every morsel. Still chuckling over the girls' amusing anecdotes, I leaned back contentedly in my chair and sighed. "That was without a doubt the best trout I've cooked yet, if I do say so myself."

The girls beamed happily, agreeing with my assessment. Around us, the cozy cabin glowed invitingly in the firelight as evening shadows gathered outside. Our sanctuary in the wilderness felt more like home with every new day shared here together.

As Leigh sighed and stretched, an impish glint entered her eyes. "Why don't we head down to the river for a nice moonlight swim?" she suggested, exchanging a knowing look with Diane. "It's a perfect night for it."

Diane giggled, blushing slightly as she toyed with the end of her braid. "That does sound lovely after getting so dusty and sweaty out in the bush today," she remarked.

I nodded agreeably, a smile playing about my lips. Their intentions were clear, but a swim beneath the stars sounded delightful. I was happy to indulge such playfulness between us. "I think that's an excellent idea," I declared, rising from my chair.

Together we quickly tidied up the remains of dinner, letting Ghostie and his fellow domesticant whisk away the empty plates and dishes to be cleaned later. Their spectral forms bobbed merrily about the kitchen, dutifully getting things in order.

Arm in arm, the three of us then headed out of the cozy cabin toward the silvery shore, ready to enjoy both the pleasures of the cool water and each other beneath the moonlight.

As we strolled comfortably together through the

velvety night, the peaceful chirping of crickets and rustling leaves surrounded us. Overhead, the moon shone bright and full, illuminating our path in silver light.

"You know, we really should find a proper name for Ghostie's new helper around the cabin," Diane remarked thoughtfully as we walked. "It seems only right since he's become part of the family now."

I nodded agreeably. "That's a good idea. Did you have any thoughts on what we might call him?"

Diane chewed her lip contemplatively, foxtail swishing behind her. "Hmm, not yet, but we'll think of something perfect, I'm sure!"

Just then, Leigh suddenly snapped her fingers, eyes lighting up. "I know what we should call Ghostie's helper around here — Sir Boozles!" she proclaimed.

Diane burst into giggles at the absurd suggestion. Even I couldn't restrain an amused snort.

"Sir Boozles?" I repeated, shaking my head. "You can't be serious."

"I'm completely serious!" Leigh insisted, her eyes dancing playfully. "I think it suits him just fine. I had a cat once who bore that name with pride, I tell ya!"

Diane continued laughing, having to pause a moment to catch her breath. "It does seem rather fitting, I must admit," she said at last.

I just chuckled indulgently, pulling them both into an affectionate hug as we walked. If Sir Boozles made them happy, then so be it.

"You two are impossible sometimes," I teased. Their answering laughter was music to me.

As the riverbank came into view ahead, I took a moment to appreciate my good fortune. Life out here was not without its trials, but with Diane and Leigh by my side, I could weather anything.

Together beneath the spangled sky, we left shoeless footprints in the sandy shore before wading in to enjoy the pleasures of the cool water and each other's company late into the magical night.

Chapter 27

The cool water enveloped us pleasantly as we waded into the shimmering waters of the Silverthread beneath the moonlight. Diane gasped and giggled as she acclimated to the chill, while Leigh whooped loudly and splashed right in up to her waist. Grinning, I dove underwater, swimming with strong strokes out into the deeper currents.

When I surfaced, I turned to see Diane floating serenely on her back, dark hair fanning out around her like liquid night. Nearby, Leigh was amusing herself by trying to catch silvery minnows darting around her legs. Their carefree laughter carried sweetly over the gentle lapping of the water.

"Look, I'm a mermaid!" Diane declared playfully, flourishing her foxtail as she spun gracefully around, treading water. I swam over to wrap her in my arms, both of us laughing. The cool water felt amazing after a long day working outside.

Leigh paddled around trying to sneak up on us, but I noticed her approach and alerted Diane. Together we sent twin jets of water splashing toward the blonde, whose squeal of mock outrage echoed across the river.

"Oh, now you've asked for it!" Leigh laughed, immediately retaliating with sweeping armfuls of water. Soon we were embroiled in an all-out splash fight, our laughter ringing out under the starry sky.

I allowed the girls a couple of direct hits before I

suddenly dove and vanished entirely beneath the inky surface. Surfacing stealthily behind them both a dozen yards away, I waited until they were peering around trying to spot me.

When they had their backs turned, I swiftly and silently swam nearer, then erupted up right between them with a roar, pulling them both underwater. We bobbed up together, sputtering and giggling uncontrollably.

"No fair, you rascal!" Leigh exclaimed, giving my shoulder a playful shove once she caught her breath. But her eyes sparkled with delight at my antics. Nearby, Diane treaded water gracefully, smiling in wordless amusement.

As our energetic play dimmed, we transitioned into lazily circling around one another, simply relishing the soothing embrace of the river. I floated peacefully on my back staring up at the cosmos glittering across the vast heavens above. The water's gentle support felt hypnotic.

While I drifted, the two girls swam graceful circles around me, their occasional rippling movements setting eddies spinning outward. Now and then, one would glide near to steal a quick kiss or give me an affectionate splash. Their antics kept me smiling.

"Want me to show you how Scouts swim?" Diane asked playfully after a while. When I nodded, she took a deep breath and suddenly dove straight down, her foxtail following her underwater.

She remained submerged for at least a couple of minutes, no doubt exploring the river bottom. When Diane finally surfaced, she described playing with the fish and even finding some sparkling stones. She gifted Leigh and me each one.

"How do you stay underwater so long without air?" I asked curiously, turning the smooth stone over in my palm. It was etched with delicate natural latticework.

Diane grinned mysteriously. "It's one of my Scout abilities," she confessed. "I can stay underwater for a longer time at the cost of a little mana."

I laughed. "Well, isn't that a convenient trick when you're in a tight spot. I'm afraid my summoner abilities don't really help with swimming!"

She grinned and splashed some water at me, which I deftly dodged. "Maybe not," she admitted, "but you can summon Aquana's avatar or a water spirit. I doubt you need to do much else with water."

I laughed and gave a lazy shrug as I went back to floating in the water.

Meanwhile, Leigh had grown bored with just treading water. I noticed her eyeing a sturdy overhanging tree branch drooping low over the river. Before I could speak up, she suddenly hoisted herself up to stand balancing on the unsteady bough!

"Leigh, be careful up there!" I cautioned, but had to admire her boldness and agility, not to mention her perfect and voluptuous figure. Of course, wilderness swimming was in the nude. She just shot me a playful wink before leaping off with a fearless whoop, curling into a tight cannonball right between Diane and me.

We got drenched by the resulting splash, but I

just laughed. "You're incorrigible," I told her affectionately when she surfaced, pushing the sodden hair from her face. Diane nodded bemused agreement.

As the moon rose higher overhead, we playfully dared one another to swim out to a tiny island in the middle of the river. I let the girls beat me there easily despite my strongest strokes. Their competitive banter as we made our way there charmed me endlessly.

But all too soon, the deepening hour marked the inevitable end of our lively midnight swim. Wading ashore together beneath the moon's radiance, droplets glistened like diamonds on the girls' happy faces. Playfully, they shook their wet hair at me, eliciting laughter.

Retrieving the blankets and towels we had left above the flood line, I tenderly wrapped one around Diane and Leigh after admiring their beautiful bodies in the moonlight. Their appreciative smiles kindled a glow in my heart, as did the naughty lights that lived there.

"It's nice and warm out here," Leigh said.

"Especially with a towel around my shoulders. How about we stay a while longer and watch the stars?"

"Sure," I agreed. "That sounds perfect, to be honest." I thought for a moment. "Why don't you girls settle here on the boulder, and I'll run inside to get a bottle of wine and some firewood? We'll make a fire and make a little night out of it!"

"David, that's a perfect idea!" Leigh chirped, with Diane nodding in agreement.

With a smile on my face, I ambled over to the cabin to retrieve the promised supplies. I was looking forward to making the night last a little longer.

Towel wrapped around my waist, I swiftly gathered some split logs and put them into a basket, also taking kindling, some extra blankets, and a bottle of wine before hurrying back down to the silvery shore.

There I found Diane and Leigh nestled together on a flat boulder, wrapped snugly in their towels as they gazed up at the starry sky. The sight of the two of them lounging like that, shapely legs coming out from the towels bundled around their beautiful bodies, made my heart beat a little faster.

"Hey!" they both chirped, studying me with admiration in their pretty eyes as I set down the supplies.

I quickly got a modest campfire kindled, coaxing the flames higher until they radiated a pleasant warmth. The firelight dancing over the girls' faces as they chatted lent the moment an intimate glow.

With the fire burning, I squeezed in between my companions, draping an arm around each of their slender shoulders. Wordlessly, we passed the wine bottle between us, savoring the sweet warmth that spread through our veins as we watched the grand game of the stars above.

For a time, we simply sat gazing into the flickering flames or up at the sky in cozy silence, relaxing in one another's close company. Now and then, the popping of burning wood punctuated the gentle lapping of the Silverthread.

Eventually, our idle talk turned to reminiscing over the first days as we all met together back in Gladdenfield.

"Why, my eyes popped open when Diane first brought you into the shop, David!" Leigh teased, eliciting giggles from Diane. "Such a fine man I ain't never seen in the whole of Gladdenfield... Or even beyond that."

"I'll never forget that day," Diane said, laughing as she recalled our first meeting. "When I saw the way you were looking at him, I knew right away." She shot me a conspiratorial smile. "Leigh has this set of bedroom eyes that she keeps just for you!"

I laughed, rubbing my neck self-consciously. "I know," I said. "There's little I love more than Leigh's bedroom eyes."

Leigh put them on, just to tease me. There was such a naughty blaze in those big blue lookers that I felt my need rise at once.

"Like this, baby?" she purred in her most submissive, bubbly blonde voice. "I'm thinkin' these eyes snared you like yours snared me."

I grinned broadly, allowing myself a peek down Leigh's ample cleavage where the towel pressed bosom together. "It's true," I admitted. "The two of you are the best things that have happened to me, together with me coming out here and making a place for us."

Diane smiled and gave my hand an affectionate squeeze. "Well, likewise. You make me very happy." Her bright eyes shone.

As the girls continued reminiscing about those early days, I mostly just listened with a smile, letting their quips and stories wash over me. The lakeside setting made it all the more magical.

When a lull fell over the conversation, I gazed thoughtfully across the shimmering expanse of the river, my mind drifting.

"You know..." Diane began after a moment, a hint of dreaminess in her voice. "Now that we have this wonderful life established out here, we have a true family together. It is something I have wanted ever since I was a kit."

I turned to her and smiled, giving her an affectionate squeeze. I saw Leigh looking at me with meaning in her eyes, and I knew that Diane's mind was on the one thing she still wanted to add to this.

Diane bit her lip, looking introspective, but she didn't say anything. Still, I knew what she was thinking about, and I had been thinking about it a lot myself. Our life here was good, and we had settled into a steady rhythm that was promising.

A rhythm that could sustain more life.

I smiled at Diane again, watching the cute way she pursed her lips as she thought. "Why would we wait any longer?" I finally asked.

Diane's brilliant eyes instantly widened in surprise and joy. She sat up straighter at once, knowing exactly what I meant. "I... yes! But... only if you're ready too," she added hastily. "I mean... I'm ready. I've been ready. I'm... I'm *very* ready."

Leigh and I chuckled at her sudden enthusiasm. She seemed unable to sit still now, pressing herself up against me and giving me a big pair of glistening puppy eyes.

"She looks very ready, indeed," Leigh purred, her tone turning a little huskier.

I took Diane's delicate hands in mine, rubbing my thumbs over her knuckles. "I am ready, too," I said, realizing the notion filled me with anticipation. "I don't see a reason to wait."

"You are?" Diane breathed, scarcely daring to believe it. "Truly?"

I smiled and nodded, seeing joyful tears spring to her eyes. "Yes, my love. Let's start our family."

Tears of happiness sprang to Diane's eyes. "Oh David, I hoped so much you would say that!" she cried. "I've dreamed of this for so long. I... I can hardly believe it's really happening!"

Unable to contain her elation, she flung her arms around my neck in a fierce hug. I held her close, stroking her hair as she nuzzled against me. Her reaction washed away any lingering doubts. We were ready for this, and fate had reached a turning point.

As we sat back smiling at one another, Leigh gave Diane an exuberant grin. "Well, you two are gonna make some cute lil' kits!" she declared happily. "I call honorary auntie."

Diane giggled, fox tail swishing excitedly behind

her. "Of course! They'll need their Aunt Leigh to teach them all her wilderness tricks."

"Hm-hm," Leigh purred, leaning a little closer, her soft hand warm on my inner thigh. "But it takes a little more than talk to make kits." With that, she bit her lip. "And I'd be honored to help the two of you out a little…"

Chapter 28

I chuckled softly, my eyes raking over the two willing beauties wrapped in their towels, eager for my attention. "I don't think Diane and I would *need* any help making sure she got pregnant," I mused, "but we would certainly *like* the help!"

"Well, sugar, if you think you can handle the

kinda help *I* can offer..." Leigh drawled, her blue eyes twinkling with mischief.

"Sounds like a challenge," I said, grinning.

Diane giggled softly, her sapphire eyes shining with a mix of excitement and nervous anticipation as she bit her lip for a moment. "I certainly won't mind it," she whispered. Her voice trembled slightly, which told me that this was something she had been anticipating for a long time.

"Well," Leigh teased, giving Diane a little poke. "Take off the towel." Her gaze shot over to me. "Why don't you come closer, baby?"

I stepped forward, feeling my muscles ripple under the towel with anticipation. I allowed my gaze to trail from Diane's alluring fox ears down to her curvaceous body, watching as she let her towel slip away.

Her body was glistening, beads of water tracing paths down her athletic curves. Her breasts, firm and round, jiggled slightly as she moved. The sight was so tantalizing it made my heart pound in my chest.

My rod tented my towel as she stood there like a

goddess of the forest, slightly blushing, and I wanted little more than to take her right there and then. But instead, I decided to play along with Leigh's naughty game a little longer.

I turned my eyes to the curvy blonde. "So, what would your advice be?"

Leigh grinned and licked her lips. "David," she said in a voice as smooth as silk, "why don't you get Diane all wet and ready for you?" She smiled at Diane. "You can lie back, baby, and let David eat that hot little pussy of yours."

My cock twitched in anticipation as I watched Diane lie back on the towel, her fox tail twitching. She spread her legs invitingly, still blushing slightly, her pussy glistening wet.

I stepped forward, discarding my towel, and gently placed a hand on each of Diane's toned thighs as I sat down and surveyed my prize.

Leigh winked at me, then got on her knees next to me. "And while you're at it," she purred, "I'll make sure *you're* ready for her too."

I groaned as Leigh's hand wrapped around my cock, her firm grip making me gasp. "Leigh," I managed to grunt, "That feels amazing."

As Leigh worked her magic on me, I turned my attention back to Diane. Her enticing scent filled my nostrils as I lowered my head to her glistening pussy. I began by gently kissing her thighs and her toned stomach, and by the arching of her back, I could tell that she was ready for me to kiss her sweet little pussy.

With a sigh of delight, I ran my tongue up her slit, savoring the taste of her. She moaned, her hips arching off the towel as I teased her.

Her breasts jiggled as she trembled, her nipples hardening under my gaze. I could hear her panting, small whimpers escaping her lips as I continued to pleasure her.

"David," she moaned softly, "More..."

Leigh's hand moved faster on my cock, and she half-crept under me, her full breasts brushing my thigh as her mouth closed around the tip. I groaned at the dual pleasure, my eyes rolling back in my head.

I plunged my tongue deeper into Diane, tasting her sweet juices. She gasped, her body arching off the towel as she moaned. The movement allowed me to bring up a hand, and she sighed with pleasure as I teased her tight little rose with my finger.

My tongue flicked over her clit, making her shiver. Her muscles tightened, her body trembling as I brought her closer to the edge.

Leigh's mouth moved over my cock, her tongue swirling around the tip. I could feel the tension building within me, the pleasure intensifying with each of Leigh's skilled strokes.

Diane's moans grew louder, her body trembling as I continued to eat her out. Her muscles clenched, and her body tightened like a coil as she neared her climax.

The scent of her arousal filled my senses, driving me wild. I increased the pressure, my tongue swirling over her clit in a rhythm that had her gasping.

"David!" she cried out, her voice echoing through the woods. Her body convulsed, her pussy clenching around my tongue as she came.

I groaned against her, my cock throbbing in

Leigh's mouth as Diane rode out her orgasm. Her juices coated my tongue, the taste of her arousal making me even harder.

"Ahhnnn, David," she purred. "So... So good!"

I doubled down, licking her pussy even faster as I fought off my own orgasm. I focused completely on making Diane squirm with pleasure, trying to ignore Leigh's soft lips and tongue and the way her delicious tits pushed against me.

Leigh pulled away from me just before I couldn't hold it any longer. She had a wicked smile on her face. "You ready to breed her, David?"

"Yes," I growled as I drew back, Diane still squirming under me as she suffered through the last of her relentless orgasm.

My entire world was Diane's beautiful body, quivering and trembling and ready for me to push my cock into her and breed her. Leigh gave an encouraging purr as she tugged on my cock again, and I knew the time had come...

My lust rising, I grabbed Diane by her slender waist, my eyes feasting on her delicious curves and soft skin.

Her body, still trembling from the orgasm, was a delightful sight to behold. Her fox ears twitched, and the bushy tail curled around her leg, adding an exotic allure to her fit and lusciously curvy body.

I grunted in delight, my tongue trailing a wet path down to her breasts. I nuzzled against the soft mounds, taking a hardened nipple into my mouth, sucking and rolling it between my teeth. A gasp tore through her lips, her fingers clutching at the grass around us.

"Good Lord, Diane, you're a vision," Leigh purred from a distance, her accent thick and husky. She was reclining next to me, spreading her legs wide, her fingers dancing over her pussy. Her skin glistened under the sun; her blonde hair spread out on the soft turf.

Her blue eyes were fixated on us, her plump lips parted as she breathed heavily. "David, she's primed and ready. Ya gonna do her good, ain't ya?" She drawled, her digits picking up speed as her voice dropped lower.

I moved my mouth from Diane's breasts, leaving a trail of wet kisses down her stomach. "I'm going to breed her, Leigh," I declared, my voice heavy with desire. "I'm going to make her scream."

"Yes," Diane moaned. "Oh, please! I want it so bad!"

Diane's breath hitched as I positioned my body over hers, my hardened cock pressed against her entrance. She looked up at me, her sapphire eyes wide and full of anticipation.

The first thrust was slow, a test of waters. Diane's body welcomed me, her inner walls warm and tight around me. A shiver ran through her body, a soft moan escaping her lips as I filled her.

"Oh, David," she gasped, her nails digging into my back. The sight of her delicious body bouncing with my next thrust was intoxicating. The scent of lavender wafted from her skin, adding to the heady mix of pleasure and lust.

And the thought that I would breed her, that I would give her the child she and I so dearly wanted, was greatly arousing. It felt primal and pure — a fulfillment of the deepest and most profound need that we both harbored.

I leaned in, nibbling on her ear, and she gasped with pleasure as I delved deeper, her body accepting me completely. With every thrust, her breasts jiggled with the force, her nipples hard and begging for attention.

Unable to resist them, I leaned in and sucked on them, making Diane give a breathy gasp of pure, unadulterated lust, her hand raking through my tousled mop of hair. I licked her breasts, sucked on her nipples — all to the tune of Leigh's approving hums and dirty talk.

And as our need rose, Diane bucked up, meeting me thrust for thrust. "Deeper, David," she begged, her voice a sexy whimper. "Take me!"

I picked up speed, my movements becoming more frantic. Diane's body moved rhythmically beneath me, her moans growing louder with each thrust, and I felt her beginning to clamp on me — a sensation now familiar because of the deep and intimate knowledge she and I had of each other.

"Oh, David," she cried out, her pussy clamping down on me. "I'm close... so close..."

"That's it, darling," Leigh cooed nearby, her fingers working feverishly on her pussy as she watched me fuck her harem sister. "Cum for him... Then let him fill you up and breed you. Give you every last drop."

The thought was intoxicating, the idea of claiming Diane completely. It added to the pleasure, to the feeling of her body clenching around me. Our skins slapped together as I went harder and deeper, her juicing coating my cock, and everything in me feeling like I was ready to explode.

With a few more powerful thrusts, Diane's body tensed beneath me. Her mouth opened in a silent scream, her pussy clenching around me as she came. Her body shook, her eyes rolling back as the waves of pleasure washed over her. Her tongue even lolled out as she went completely numb in her deepest pleasure.

"Fuck, Diane," I grunted, still thrusting into her, prolonging her orgasm. I watched as she bit down on the back of her hand, trying to muffle her cries.

Next to me, Leigh's moans reached a crescendo, her body arching off the grass as she fingered herself while watching me breed Diane. With a loud cry, she climaxed, her body trembling from the release.

The sight of both women in the throes of pleasure was a sight to behold. It sent me over the edge, my climax hitting me like a freight train.

I thrust into Diane one last time, and I released. With a growl of pure lust, I spurted my first rope of cum deep inside her, seeking to impregnate her and make her the mother of my child.

"Yes, David," she panted, her body still shaking from her orgasm as her nails raked down my back. She seemed to pull me closer — into her — wanting every drop I could give her. "Fill me up... Breed me..."

With a few more thrusts, I gave her what she needed. I emptied my balls inside her, my body shuddering with the intensity of my orgasm as I had given her every drop of cum in my body. The feeling of her body clenching around me — how much she wanted nothing to spill — was exquisite, heightening the pleasure.

Finally exhausted, I collapsed on top of her, my cock still buried deep inside her. I could feel her heart pounding against my chest, her breath coming out in ragged gasps.

With a deep moan, Diane arched her back. "David," she hummed, her voice almost a whisper. "Oh, I can feel it inside. Hmm... This was so good."

With a smile, I wiped my forehead, taking my time to study that beautiful body underneath me. "It was," I agreed, shooting a look at Leigh's voluptuous body as well. "You two are a delight."

"Hmm," Leigh purred as we collapsed into a heap on the grassy bank. "You fucked Diane good, baby!"

Diane chuckled at her harem sister's dirty words in between panting for breath. My arm instinctively found its way around both of them, pulling them close against me. Their soft bodies were a welcome contrast to the firmness of the ground beneath us.

I pulled them both closer, burying my face in their hair. Their scents mixed together, creating a heady aroma that I found intoxicating. I closed my eyes, letting the sensation of them wash over me.

We lazed about a while longer, letting the sweat dry from our skin. After that, we all went for a quick dip to freshen up.

And of course, one thing led to another, and we soon gave it another try. After all, breeding my beautiful fox girl might take more than one go, and I didn't object to that in the least.

Chapter 29

The morning sunlight streamed in through the cabin windows as I stirred awake, a feeling of deep contentment washing over me. Last night had been incredibly passionate and intimate, bringing Diane, Leigh, and me even closer together.

And you could never really tell about these

things, but something in me gave me the feeling that I had shot true last night, and that I had given Diane what she had so yearned for.

Still, the only way to be sure is to try often...

After we had made love, Ghostie, Sir Boozles, and I had piled the mattresses and blankets in front of the fireplace, and we had all slept together in a little heap there. Following a night of passion like that, it simply wouldn't do for the three of us to sleep apart.

I smiled over at Diane's sleeping form nestled against me, her hand resting lightly on my chest. Behind me, I felt Leigh shift and stretch languidly before she propped herself up on one elbow.

"Mornin' handsome," she murmured drowsily, leaning in to plant a tender kiss on my shoulder. "I'd say last night was pretty special, wouldn't you?"

I reached back to squeeze her hand affectionately. "It certainly was," I agreed, remembering the pleasure we had shared. "I had a real good time, to be sure."

Leigh's answering smile radiated pure

happiness. She nuzzled against me a moment longer before slipping from beneath the quilts. "Best get some coffee brewin' then. I know Diane will be eager for some once she wakes up."

I cradled Diane gently, inhaling the sweet lavender scent of her hair. Soon she began to stir, blinking up at me with a blissful smile.

"Good morning my love," she purred, tail swishing contentedly beneath the blankets.

We traded a long, lingering kiss before finally motivating ourselves to rise and get dressed. The smell of frying bacon and percolating coffee drew us eagerly to the cozy kitchen where Leigh bustled about.

Leigh stood humming at the stove, golden hair falling in messy waves over her shoulders. She shot us a cheery grin as we rose lazily. "Perfect timing! I got a nice hearty breakfast coming together here."

Settling around the worn table near the hearth, we soon had steaming mugs of coffee and plates loaded with fluffy eggs, crispy bacon, and toasted cinnamon bread. Our appetites were voracious after the intimate exertions of the night before.

Over the hearty meal, we chatted and laughed lightheartedly about the passionate hours shared. A rosy glow suffused Diane's refined features as she recalled it all. "I've never felt more loved and fulfilled," she confessed earnestly.

I smiled, reaching over to squeeze her hand. "It was a very special night for all of us," I agreed. "I'm thankful every day for the family we've built together out here." Leigh's eyes shone with open affection across the table.

As we lingered over second helpings, talk turned toward hopes and plans for the future now that Diane and I had decided to try for kits. The prospect filled us with anticipation.

"With David's handy skills, y'all will have a big old mansion here in no time," Leigh said enthusiastically between bites of toast. She gave Diane a playful wink. "Though with your stamina lately, you may need more than one nursery before long!"

Diane blushed charmingly, absently fiddling with the end of her braid. "Oh hush," she giggled. "One will be enough to start." But her tail swished happily at the thought of having a large, loving family.

"Either way, I'll be happy to help out however I can," Leigh volunteered. "Bottle-feeding the little scamps when you two need a break, watching them while you work..." Her voice grew wistful. "They grow up so fast. I'd love to be a part of it!"

"Any child would be lucky to have you as an aunt," I told Leigh sincerely, making her smile.

I looked around as I finished the last bite of my breakfast. "Say, where are Ghostie and... *Sir Boozles*?" I winced as I spoke that last name, and both girls chuckled.

"I have no idea," Diane said. "Usually, he's in by this time. And Boozles follows him around."

"Oh, well," I muttered. "I'll go look for him in a sec."

"I'll clean up," Diane offered, rising from her chair. She gathered up the dishes, smiling dreamily to herself. I could tell her imagination was fully immersed in anticipation of the new lives we had set in motion. The cozy cabin already seemed warmer envisioning it filled with the patter of little feet.

While Diane tidied up, Leigh poured us all some more coffee, and I rose and stretched, getting ready for another day of long, satisfying work. I double-checked to see if the door was open so Ghostie and Boozles could come back in.

As we happily went through our morning routine together, a sudden excited chirping and whooshing sound made us look over. Ghostie drifted into the room, full of pent-up energy, its spectral form bobbing with impatience. Clearly, the domesticant was eager to convey some manner of request my way.

I cocked my head curiously at Ghostie's antics. "What's got you so worked up, little friend?" I asked. Its chirping grew more insistent.

Diane laughed, shaking her head. "I think someone wants your attention, love."

"Alright, alright, I hear you," I chuckled, rising from the rug to see what Ghostie was trying to communicate so urgently first thing in the morning. Its spectral eyes glowed cheerfully as it hovered nearby awaiting my approach.

"Let's see what's on your mind then," I said as I followed Ghostie toward the source of its excitement.

Ghostie continued chirping eagerly, zooming back and forth toward the cabin's front door. Its spectral eyes seemed to shine brighter in its state of excitement.

"What is it?" I asked, curious about what had the domesticant so worked up. "Did you see something outside?"

At my words, Ghostie emitted an enthusiastic series of affirmative-sounding chirps. Clearly, it was trying to convey that some event of interest had occurred beyond the confines of our cozy homestead. Intrigued, I moved toward the door and opened it to peer outside.

There, parked at a cautious distance just off our dusty drive, I spotted Caldwell's dusty Jeep. As I watched, the driver-side door swung open, and the suited man of the Frontier Division stepped out into the morning sunshine, eyeing the storm elemental warily as it drifted nearby on patrol. As always, his suit was impeccable.

"Morning, Caldwell!" I called in greeting, waving to catch his attention as I stepped from the porch. With a mental command, I directed Mr. Drizzles to stand down and continue patrolling the perimeter at a greater distance. Ghostie continued fluttering about over my shoulder, evidently pleased I had discovered the source of the commotion. "Come on over! It's safe!"

Caldwell turned at the sound of my voice, a broad smile creasing his weathered features when he spotted me. With a few long strides, he closed some of the distance, though he continued eyeing Mr. Drizzles as the tempestuous summon circled watchfully.

"David, good to see you, my friend!" Caldwell called. "I don't mean to intrude; just thought I'd pay a quick visit to thank you. And I see you have a new guardian protecting the homestead now?" He gestured toward the crackling storm elemental.

I chuckled, waving at Mr. Drizzles. "Yes, this is my newest guardian summon. Don't worry, he's just being cautious by nature. I've instructed him to allow you to visit."

Caldwell visibly relaxed once the summon had floated farther off. Together we walked out to meet halfway between his Jeep and the cabin.

"It's always good to see you, my friend," I told him sincerely, clasping his hand. "The summon will know you now, so no need to worry if you come by again."

A broad grin lit Caldwell's weathered face. "I'm glad to see you're taking security seriously! And I bring good news from New Springfield. Waelin has joined us in the city, and he is busy teaching several of the mages of the Frontier Division the warding ritual. Your quest has secured the help which will protect many new settlements. We are very thankful!"

"That's wonderful to hear!" I replied, genuinely glad our efforts were making the frontier safer for others seeking life beyond the city walls. "It wasn't an easy one, I'll admit, but we're happy to have helped make life a little easier for all those people still in the cities."

Caldwell nodded, looking satisfied. "Indeed, it grants much-needed peace of mind. We lost good folks attempting to settle unsecured lands in the past." His expression turned introspective. "Still, risks remain. But you've helped shift the tide in our favor, my friend."

I felt moved by his words, but Caldwell's mood lightened swiftly. "Enough official talk — I see your lovely homestead continues to thrive!" He surveyed the cozy cabin and cultivated fields approvingly. "You and Diane have accomplished something truly special out here."

I felt a flush of pride hearing the praise. "Much of the credit goes to Diane... and Leigh," I said sincerely. "They're the ones who really make this place a home."

"Ah, Leigh has joined you as well?" he said with a grin. "I am an avid enjoyer of the elven marriage myself. I have five wives, and life couldn't be better." He then peered past me at the cabin. "Ah, I see they're coming out!"

Right on cue, the cabin door opened, and both girls emerged onto the porch, bright smiles lighting their lovely faces at the sight of our returning guest. After quick hugs and greetings, I invited Caldwell to join us in the chairs arranged in the shade.

"We just finished a late breakfast, Caldwell," I said. "But I'm pretty sure we could whip you up a little something if you're hungry?"

"Your hospitality humbles me," Caldwell said. "But I don't want to be a burden. I just came around to thank you personally for all the hard work you've put in. I should be on my way to New Springfield soon... Although it *is* nice here." Caldwell's eyes turned momentarily wistful as he gazed out over the valley we called home.

I waved away his initial protest. "Nonsense, you must be hungry after your drive this morning! Please, come on in and have a bite to eat before you continue your journey." I gestured toward the cabin's open door in invitation.

Caldwell hesitated briefly, but then chuckled and conceded graciously. "Well, far be it from me to

spurn such warm hospitality from good friends."
Together we rose and headed indoors to enjoy a
midmorning meal Diane had thoughtfully
prepared.

Chapter 30

Settling around the worn but lovingly crafted table, Diane quickly whipped up a hearty sandwich and potato salad brunch for our guest. Caldwell thanked her profusely as she set the platter before him.

"My compliments to the chef," he remarked after

his first bite. "You have a real talent, Diane."

Diane's cheeks colored prettily at the praise as she took her own seat. She helped herself to some of the potato salad, and Leigh quickly joined her. We had eaten enough, of course, but the girls didn't mind a little extra.

As Caldwell ate with evident relish, I retrieved the statuette of Ilmanaria from atop the fireplace mantle. I was curious to hear his thoughts about the ancient idol.

"Caldwell, take a look at this statuette I discovered in some old elven ruins during our quest," I said, handing him the exquisite carving.

He turned it over thoughtfully in his hands, his sharp eyes glittering with interest. "Remarkable craftsmanship," he mused.

I nodded. "We found it in some elven ruins outside of Gladdenfield Outpost. According to Waelin, it provides a passive increase to our mana capacity since we placed it here. He called it a Hearth Treasure."

Caldwell's thick brows shot up in surprise. "Is that so? I've read vague mentions of such elf artifacts in the archives, but this is the first I've seen in the flesh." He handed the statuette back almost reverently. "This is a grand treasure to possess. Keep it safe, and you will profit from it."

"Do you know who it depicts?" I asked as I held the statuette again.

He studied the idol for a moment. "I would say this is Ilmanaria," he said.

I grinned, impressed by his knowledge. "You know her?"

He smiled. "The Frontier Division is part of the Coalition. As such, there are plenty of elves among us. So, we get a glimpse of elven lore occasionally, even though they are secretive. I know Ilmanaria to be a protector of mages, and several of those I fought in my early days as a Magebreaker have called on her for protection." He smiled. "She will look favorably on you, as a Frontier Summoner."

I smiled and nodded, replacing the statuette on the mantle. "I hope to find a few more of those," I said. "They are extremely useful."

He grinned. "Good," he said. "You show ambition!"

As he finished up his meal, talk turned to reminiscing on the harrowing quest we had undertaken at Waelin's behest. Caldwell listened raptly as we described traversing the Blighted Land and the strange aberrations lurking within.

"It seems the malignant forces in that valley have strengthened since anyone last delved there," Caldwell remarked grimly once we had finished relating the tale. "Perhaps one day it can be cleansed fully. It's likely the Frontier Division will post a quest for someone to deal with it." He looked at me with a smile, then at Diane and Leigh. "Perhaps something for you, provided I can pair you with a spellcaster equipped to cleanse the land?"

I grinned. "We'll see. We have some plans to work on this place first. But a quest might be interesting later on. Anyway, we were lucky to pass through the Blighted Land safely. We all advanced in the Dungeon, and being higher level helped on the return trip."

At this, Caldwell's expression sharpened with recollection. "Ah yes, Waelin mentioned your uniquely swift advancement when I spoke with him in the city. Tell me, have you learned anything more about the potential source?"

I quickly explained that I had not yet had the opportunity to look further into the concept of Bloodlines granting advantages. "I plan on meeting my grandparents and discussing it with them, but they are a distance away. Although travel will be easier now that I have a Class. And Waelin said he would be on the lookout for a Blood Mage to help unveil the mystery."

Caldwell nodded thoughtfully, steepling his fingers. "Well, consider me intrigued. Once you've investigated further, I would be fascinated to hear your findings." His eyes sparkled with scholarly interest in this mysterious phenomenon.

"Of course," I assured him. "Truthfully, I remain very curious about it myself. I'll be sure to share anything I uncover about potential Bloodline benefits."

As we continued conversing, Diane and Leigh also chimed in now and then to add details about obstacles overcome and enemies defeated within the perilous confines of Nimos Sedia.

Caldwell sat back after one colorful account of the battle with a drakeling horde, shaking his head in amazement. "It's clear your teamwork and quick thinking are unparalleled," he declared sincerely. "You three make an astonishingly effective trio, if I may say so."

Diane and Leigh beamed proudly at the high praise. "We do seem to complement each other's abilities quite nicely when the goin' gets tough," Leigh agreed, reaching over to give Diane an affectionate pat on her arm.

Eventually the morning began to carry on outside, and Caldwell sighed regretfully. "I'm afraid duty calls me back to the city," he announced, rising reluctantly from his chair. "But I cannot thank you enough for the hospitality and fascinating conversation. But mostly, I — and those living under the protection of the Coalition — are very grateful for your completing your quest with such skill!"

"It was our pleasure," I said warmly as we walked Caldwell out onto the porch. His dusty

Jeep waited nearby ready to bear him onward down the winding trail toward civilization. But I could tell part of him would have preferred to linger here in the valley's tranquility.

"We're always glad for a chance to reminisce about our adventures with you," Diane added sincerely as Caldwell descended onto the grass.

Caldwell turned back, clearly touched by their words. "Likewise. The tales you three have to tell are always a joy." He clapped me on the shoulder. "Stay vigilant out here, but also relish each new day. This life you're forging is special."

I smiled and nodded, looking around with pride at all Diane, Leigh, and I had built together. "We know how fortunate we are, believe me. Be well, my friend. Safe travels."

With a final warm handshake, Caldwell took his leave down the winding trail. We stood waving until his Jeep rounded a bend and passed from sight. But his visit had left me with much food for thought.

As we headed back inside, Diane gave me a curious look. "This Bloodline business does sound rather fascinating," she remarked. "Plus, I would love to meet your grandparents."

I laughed and nodded agreement, making a mental note to follow up on it soon. "I'll take you there one day," I said. "For now, though, a long afternoon of pleasant work awaits us. We have some work to do on the cabin!"

Together we returned to the cozy cabin, letting thoughts of past adventures and future investigations slip away for the moment.

Chapter 31

With the day beginning in earnest, I was keen to begin planning the expansion of our modest cabin. With Diane and me deciding to try for kits, the additional space would be crucial. I headed downstairs to wash up, mind already churning with ideas.

In the kitchen, Diane was preparing us some more coffee. She smiled knowingly. "Ready to start designing?" she asked, tail swishing amusedly. I chuckled and nodded, quickly taking a swig of coffee before fetching paper and pencils.

Settling at the worn table near the hearth, I started sketching initial concepts for adding a second floor with a master bedroom with a larger bed and two extra rooms — one for the baby once it moved out of our room and one for guests. Downstairs could be expanded with a larger kitchen and pantry.

I also wanted to build a workshop and woodshed. Right now, we were using the mudroom to store tools and keeping the firewood under a rickety awning.

As I scribbled, Diane peered over my shoulder, offering thoughts about the design. Her input was invaluable for visualizing the daily flow through the expanded spaces. I made some adjustments based on her insights about adjacency planning.

After roughed-out floorplans were complete, we headed outside to walk the grounds while picturing the new additions in context. The sunshine felt energizing as we strolled together, and Diane's suggestions helped refine the initial sketches.

Meanwhile, Leigh had dedicated herself to a day of fishing by the Silverthread, and she looked utterly relaxed as she sat in the sunlight, her cowboy hat providing some shade.

Back inside, I began the meticulous work of precisely measuring and scaling my drawings to determine accurate dimensions. This would allow me to calculate materials needed. The additional square footage would require a considerable amount of new logs and timber.

While I worked, Diane hummed idly in the kitchen, evidently daydreaming about our home bustling with playful kits. Her evident happiness inspired me, making the work fly swiftly by. Soon I had detailed schematics laid out across the table.

However, accurately estimating the required foundation logs, wall timbers, rafters, flooring, and other materials was challenging without architectural training. My math needed double-checking to ensure it was precise before proceeding.

As I poured over the sketches, recalculating everything, Diane kept me fueled with a steady supply of coffee and snacks. When Leigh took a break from fishing, she and I went through the numbers as well. Being the shopkeeper, Leigh had a good head for numbers, and despite her usual levity and bubbliness, she was sharp and had a good eye. By early afternoon, I finally felt confident in my building material estimates.

Next, I met with the domesticants — Ghostie and Boozles — to walk them through the expansion plans. Their assistance would be crucial. I described how the new workshops would connect and the best route for transporting logs from the forest. They seemed to comprehend their roles.

The remainder of the morning was spent creating a comprehensive written plan detailing the complete vision, from foundational excavations to finishing touches. Diane helped proofread it, lending her keen eye for detail.

At noon, we stood outside visualizing how the

additions would transform the modest cabin into a comfortable homestead. The rich yellow light over the valley seemed to lend our dreams substance. Soon this vision would be real.

Over a light lunch, the conversation turned to finances. The building materials alone — the ones the wild would not provide — should cost a sizable sum, not to mention additional furniture and decor later on. We would need to get creative with earning extra income.

Diane suggested baking pies to sell at the weekend market. I proposed brewing more mana draught potions, but Leigh helpfully commented there was a limit to how many of those she could offload. If I flooded the market with them, the value would drop.

"Food, however," she said, "is something I can always get rid of at a good price. Them dwarves in Ironfast buy it in bulk. Same goes for mead and ale. Tools sell well too, as do livestock and beasts of burden."

I nodded. "Sounds like we'll need to expand operations a little before we can make our blueprint a reality."

"We could also try another Dungeon?" Diane suggested. "Just to make sure we have a little more money to invest."

I chuckled. "Why, I wouldn't have expected that suggestion from you!" I exclaimed. "I thought you preferred safety."

She laughed. "Well, I do! But still, there is good money to be made Dungeon diving. It could be a good boost to our capital, which would allow us to expand the homestead."

I nodded slowly. "Well, how can we be sure the Dungeon is of an appropriate level?" I asked.

"Now that I'm a level 4 Scout, I can get an impression of what's lurking in a Dungeon and what levels we'll face. It's not perfect, but it usually serves well enough!"

"You two will have to pay a visit to Gladdenfield," Leigh suggested. "There's usually some postings for Dungeons, and some adventurin' folks will know where to find good places. You could ask around."

"Thanks, Leigh," I said. "And would you be

interested in joining up?"

"Yep," she hummed, beaming me a warm smile. "Provided it ain't too far away. Besides, I wanna venture out into the Wilds to find me a pet."

"Alright," I said. "This sounds like a good way to make some extra coin on the side. I'll think about it. For now, let's just focus on what we can do: expanding the plots for farming."

The afternoon sun filtered through the windows of the cozy cabin as Leigh finished packing up her things. She was planning to head back to Gladdenfield before the afternoon was over to open up her store but promised she would be back in just a couple of days, bringing plenty of seeds for us to sow on the land we would expand.

"I wish you didn't have to go so soon," Diane said as she gave Leigh a big hug goodbye. "It's always so nice having you here."

"Don't you worry, I'll be back before ya know

it," Leigh replied warmly, returning the hug. "You two try not to miss me too much!"

I chuckled as I stepped forward next to embrace Leigh as well. "We always miss your sunny presence when you're gone." I gave her a quick kiss on the cheek. "Travel safely and say hello to Gladdenfield for us."

"I will for sure," Leigh said cheerfully as she hoisted her pack over her shoulder and headed for the door.

Diane and I followed her outside, walking with her over to where her horse Colonel was hitched and waiting patiently. The air was warm and fresh, and we all reveled in it as we made our way to Colonel.

With fluid grace, Leigh swung up into the saddle and gathered the reins. Colonel pawed the ground, eager to be off. Leigh tipped her hat to us playfully. "Y'all take care now! Don't have too much fun without me."

"We'll try our best." Diane laughed. We both waved as Leigh tapped her heels and Colonel started off at an easy trot down the winding path away from the cabin.

In no time, Leigh's bright blonde hair and Colonel's chestnut hide were lost from view around a bend in the forest trail. But we knew it wouldn't be long before her cheerful presence graced the homestead again.

As we turned and headed back inside, I slid my arm around Diane's slender waist. "So, what shall we do in the few hours of sunlight we have left?" I asked her with a smile.

Diane hummed thoughtfully, leaning into me. "Well, the garden could use some tending, and the smokehouse needs restocking," she mused. "We just *fly* through the alderwood! Also, Leigh left us most of her catch, so that'll need to be made ready!" Ever the pragmatic one, her mind was already turning to the day's tasks.

I nodded agreeably. "That's very sweet of her. Well, sounds like a good plan," I said. There were always more chores needing to be done to maintain our self-sufficient homestead. Best we didn't idle away this mild weather.

After a quick pick-me-up, we readied ourselves

for a productive day's work. I donned my hat, selected my axe, and made sure my rifle was loaded before slinging it over my shoulder. Meanwhile, Diane took the tools she needed to prepare the fish and do some gardening after.

Together we headed outside into the sunshine, faces upturned to enjoy the melodic birdsong and a wholesome morning breeze. Our valley offered small delights like this wherever one took the time to appreciate them.

I set off into the forest to chop firewood while Diane began tending the vegetable gardens, carefully inspecting each plant and plucking away any pests or withered leaves she found. Soon we were both engrossed in our respective tasks.

Wielding my axe felt good, muscles remembering their old rhythms as I felled slender alders and split them into burnable lengths. Soon my growing pile would be transported back via domesticant to stock the woodbin. There was satisfaction in such honest work.

Wanting to work as fast as possible to use the daylight we still had, I only paused to drink water.

I worked as fast as I could, letting Ghostie and Sir Boozles carry the logs back to the cabin.

As the afternoon wore on, I added log after log to the stockpile until my muscles pleaded for reprieve. The chopping had gone swiftly, my skills honed day by day. Wiping sweat from my brow, I decided I had done enough for today. Luckily, the little domesticants had diligently cleared out every log, which meant I didn't need to carry anything.

Hefting the heavy axe over one shoulder, I turned and hiked back through the still woods toward home. Shafts of early evening sunlight slanted between the ancient trunks around me. Soon the trail opened up, and there stood our little cabin looking warm and welcoming.

There, Diane hummed happily as she weeded and watered the rows of thriving vegetables. Under her dutiful care, the plants stretched leafy vines towards the sunshine, their produce swelling plump and vibrant. Our self-reliance grew with each season's bounty.

I gave her a kiss, and we shortly talked through our respective afternoons. Then, we headed inside and began preparing dinner — the scent of simmering fish soup soon filled the cozy space. After washing up, I happily settled in my creaky chair near the hearth, leaving her to finish up the meal.

Before long, Diane called me over to dish up hearty bowls of the fragrant soup, along with thick slices of flatbread. My appetite sharpened by a long day of designing and swinging the axe, I ate with relish, complimenting Diane's flavorful cooking.

Bellies satisfied; we sat contentedly together as darkness crept over the sky outside. The cheery firelight flickered over Diane's refined features, making her blue eyes sparkle. She gave me a sleepy smile, evidently ready to retire for the night.

Taking her hand, I rose. Together, we ascended the ladder to our cozy loft. We moved around each other smoothly in the familiar nighttime rhythm — changing and tidying away clothes. Before long, we were nestled in bed.

Diane curled against me, head pillowed on my shoulder, one arm draped lightly across my chest. Her breathing deepened as she slipped into slumber. I held her close, cherishing these quiet moments before I too followed her into restful sleep.

Chapter 32

The morning sun was bright, shining through the trees as I stepped outside, ready to start expanding the farm plot. I had spent yesterday surveying the area and planning out where I wanted the new section to be located.

After a filling breakfast of oatmeal and some fruit

prepared by Diane, I finished the last sip of my coffee and stepped off the porch across the dewy grass. I inhaled the fresh morning air, gazing out at the area I had marked off the day before for the new farm plot expansion. It was time to get started on the hard work of clearing and preparing the land.

Arriving at the perimeter of the new plot adjacent to my existing fields, I set down the tools I would need for this first crucial step: an axe, a machete, a shovel, large knives, shears, and gloves. I had also brought along stakes and ropes to mark the plot boundaries once cleared.

I began working methodically to clear the area, starting at one corner. Using axe and machete, I chopped and sawed at the underbrush, thorny bushes, stumps, saplings, vines, and other growth covering the plot. It was grueling labor, hacking and tearing vegetation from the earth beneath the climbing morning sun.

I paced myself, stopping periodically to wipe sweat from my brow and drink some water. Diane came out to make sure I drank and ate enough, and

Ghostie and Sir Boozles worked hard to clean up behind me.

Chipping away steadily, I gradually transformed the densely overgrown plot into a blank canvas ready for cultivation. I made sure to dig down and extract even the roots of trees and bushes I felled to prevent regrowth.

Around midday, Diane brought me out some cold water and a plate of bread, cheese, and smoked meat to refuel me. I gratefully wolfed it down, knowing I would need the energy to finish clearing this land. Diane inspected my progress, clearly impressed by the large swathe of cleared earth.

After eating, I continued working tirelessly under the blazing afternoon sun. The machete felt like an extension of my arm, slicing through stalks and vines. My shoulders burned from hours of axe swinging, but I persevered. Slowly, the last brambles and saplings fell, leaving raw, exposed earth.

Late in the day, I finally cut the last stubborn root from the dirt with my pickaxe. I stood back, surveying my handiwork. The former wooded plot was now completely cleared and empty. Next, I would need to outline the farm plot boundary with stakes and rope.

Using my planned measurements, I began pounding in wooden stakes around the plot perimeter, unfurling ropes between them. My muscles screamed in protest, begging for rest, but I pushed myself to complete the task while sunlight remained.

At long last, as the sun dipped behind the trees, I tied off the final corner stake, completing the roped outline of the plot. I had succeeded in fully clearing and delimiting the expansion after an arduous day of nonstop labor.

Utterly exhausted, I trudged inside to wash up before indulging in a big, rewarding dinner. My sleep afterwards was deep and earned, and Diane was there to massage my sore muscles.

The next day, I began preparing the soil. This was crucial for successful crops. I used the shovel and hoe to churn up the top layer of earth, breaking up clumps. It was hard work, and I soon built up a sweat as I labored under the morning sun.

Luckily, Ghostie and Sit Boozles were there to help me, making the job a little lighter. However, I found that they required some mental instruction — they didn't know how to do this intuitively.

After turning over the entire plot to loosen the soil, I used a rake to smooth and flatten the ground. Good seed and plant contact with the soil was important. I took my time on this step, making sure the plot was uniformly level and smooth.

To further prepare the earth, I conjured up my earth spirits. These would enrich the soil with nutrients for strong plant growth. Shoveling load after load of the enriched earth, I mixed the organic matter thoroughly into the top layers of the plot.

After hours of vigorous work, I finally stopped for a rest and hydration break. Diane brought me out a canteen of cold water and sandwiches, for which I was very grateful. She gazed out admiringly over the plot.

"This is coming together nicely," she hummed. "You'll have that plot ready in no time!"

I nodded, wiping the sweat from my brow. "I want to have it ready by the time Leigh comes around again with the seeds. We can plant them, and then I want to go to Gladdenfield with her for a few days."

She nodded, guessing my plan. "To check up on Waelin's niece," she said.

"Yeah," I said. "I promised to. Plus, I'm interested in getting to know an elf better. They're usually so aloof and distant, and now I have a good reason to engage with one."

A twinkle appeared in her eyes. "I'm sure that's the *only* reason…"

I laughed and shook my head. "I'm not *that* bad, am I?"

She grinned. "I don't think it's bad at all. She's pretty. If she's nice, I don't see why you couldn't meet her more often." She raised a finger. "But elves tend to be a little… arrogant. I hope this one's different."

"We'll see," I said. "If I don't feel like we'd all get along, I'll just follow up on my promise to Waelin and make sure she's OK. Other than that, I wouldn't be very interested."

"Good," Diane said, then gave me a peck on the cheek before heading back inside.

After the sandwiches Diane had brought me, my strength was renewed. I consulted my plans for the last major task — installing protective fencing around the expanded plot's perimeter. Securing the area from wildlife would be crucial for the crops.

I began by driving sturdy wooden posts into the ground around the plot's edge using a sledgehammer and stake driver. The posts needed to be sunk deep and braced well to properly anchor the fencing.

With the posts in place, I started unfurling rolls of wire fencing, pulling it taut between each post. Using pliers and wire cutters, I trimmed the fencing to length and secured it to the posts with u-nails hammered in place.

Moving methodically around the perimeter, I

made sure the wire fencing was pulled flush to the posts so animals couldn't squeeze through gaps. The protective barrier needed to be tight and without weak points.

To further reinforce areas, I wove additional strands of wire above and below the fencing in vulnerable spots. This should prevent creatures from crawling under or leaping over.

Pausing to wipe sweat from my brow, I stepped back to inspect my handiwork so far. The posts and fencing now encircled the entire expanded plot, though the installation remained unfinished. There were more components I planned to add.

Next, I installed a gate to allow easy access to the plot interior. Using sturdy boards leftover from previous projects, I fashioned together a reinforced wooden gate wide enough for a wheelbarrow to pass through.

After hanging the gate properly and testing its function, I moved on to the final touch — a scarecrow to deter birds from pecking crops.

Finding an old flannel shirt and denim overalls in storage, I stuffed them with straw to create the scarecrow's simple body. I added a whittled wooden head with a carved pumpkin face for personality.

Once assembled, I erected a tall wooden stake in the plot's center and secured the scarecrow in place with nails and wire. Its pumpkin grin and outstretched wooden arms should help ward off pesky birds once crops were planted.

For extra protection, I also hung old pots and pans from the scarecrow's limbs on wires. These would rattle in the wind, scaring birds away with the noise. The clanging sounded quite ominous when a breeze kicked up.

Satisfied with my work, I stepped back again to survey the fully installed fencing and gate surrounding the expanded farm plot. The wooden barrier looked sturdy and without gaps or weaknesses.

Now I could focus on the final preparation of the bare soil itself in anticipation of planting. There was still raking, tilling, and more enriching of the ground to be done before it was ready for seeds.

First, I smoothed over the ground's surface using

a wide metal rake, breaking apart clumps and removing small stones or debris. Good seed-to-soil contact was essential, so I took time to rake everything uniformly flat and level.

My next step was tilling deeper into the topsoil layer to further loosen the dirt and allow seeds to take root more easily. Using a heavy hoe, I churned up the ground, pulverizing large clods.

I worked methodically across the plot, eventually tilling the entire area to an ideal depth for planting. The formerly packed earth was now well aerated and worked. Seeds would thrive in the loose soil.

To enrich the soil with nutrients, I summoned more helpful woodland and earth spirits. Infusing their powers into the ground, they added vital organic compounds that would foster strong plant growth and yield.

As my spirits did their work, I moved on to measuring out crop rows using stakes and string lines. Evenly spaced rows ensured an orderly plot with maximum yield per square foot. It took time to align each row flawlessly straight.

While mapping the rows, I left generous paths

between sections for easy access without trampling plants. Careful planning now would make maintaining crops simpler once sprouted and growing.

Brow dripping with sweat, I eventually declared the soil preparation complete as the afternoon faded toward dusk. The plot was marked, fertilized, raked smooth, and tilled deeply — ready at last for seeds and sprout plantings.

Heading inside, I washed up from the long day's labor, hands stained dark with good earth. I grinned seeing matching smudges on my nose in the mirror. Joining Diane, we enjoyed a hearty meal together by candlelight, discussing plans for obtaining robust seeds.

As we ate, Diane described her ideas about which hardy vegetables would thrive best in our valley. Her knowledge of regional growing conditions was impressive. I listened eagerly, valuing her practical insight.

"With the rich soil and moderate climate here, I think more tomatoes will do very well," Diane said after swallowing a bite of stew. "Especially if we can start them inside and transplant the seedlings out once the last frost passes."

I nodded in agreement. "That's an excellent idea. I'd like a little more variety, though, considering that we're already growing tomatoes. Any other crops you'd suggest?"

Diane tapped her chin thoughtfully with one delicate finger before continuing. "Let's see… peppers should also fruit well. And leafy greens like spinach and kale will bolt fast in the spring warmth. Ooh, and beans are a must — they'll climb those sunflower stalks we can plant along the edges for trellising."

She took a sip of water, ears perked with enthusiasm. "I think potatoes, carrots, and squash could all produce fine yields here too. Oh! And perhaps a few rows of sweet corn." Diane smiled dreamily across the table. "I can already imagine how lovely the rows of tall emerald stalks will look swaying in the summer breeze."

I chuckled indulgently at her evident excitement visualizing future bounty from our expanded plot. "It all sounds wonderful, but the plot isn't *that* big!"

She laughed generously. "Yeah, I guess I'm getting carried away a little!" She absently tucked a strand of raven hair back into her unruly bun. "Well, I just want to nurture as much abundance from the valley as we can. Oh, and maybe we could try a pumpkin patch next year too! I bet they would thrive. We could make pies and preserve the flesh."

I smiled and reached over to squeeze her delicate hand. "I share your optimism completely," I said. "Let's see what Leigh has on offer when she gets here."

"Just imagine," Diane murmured. "With your magic, we'll soon have rows of lush tomato vines bowing under the weight of ripening fruit... fragrant herb patches alive with bees... sunflowers standing tall as sentinels along the edges."

I met Diane's eyes, seeing my own dreams reflected there. "It's going to be really special," I said. "But let's take it one step at a time. I've found that Ghostie and Sir Boozles still need to warm up to farming, so we can't take on too much work.

Especially not if we plan to go on adventures every now and then!"

Diane sighed happily. "You're right! Let's not get carried away." She leaned over to plant a tender kiss on my lips. "Still, I'm so thankful to be sharing this adventure with you."

"Likewise," I said after returning her kiss.

Bellies full, we banked the fire for the night and soon retired upstairs, both eager to rise again with the sun and begin carefully sowing our first seeds in the expanse of dark fertile soil.

Much work still lay ahead, but the achievement of this milestone instilled confidence in me. Our self-sufficiency and prosperity grew each season as the valley bloomed under our care.

Chapter 33

The next few days passed swiftly as I settled into my usual rhythms of work around the homestead. Each morning, I awoke eager to continue stockpiling firewood and alder for the smokehouse in anticipation of expanding the cabin.

Donning my work clothes and hat after

breakfast, I would select my axe and rifle and hike out into the lively woods surrounding our secluded valley. The chatter of the woods and fresh scent of pine needles underfoot never failed to invigorate my steps as Diane and I settled even more into our frontier routine.

Arriving at the stand of young alders I had been harvesting, I would begin felling slender trunks with practiced swings of my axe. The repetitive movements felt good, muscles easing into the familiar motions as the axe bit satisfyingly into the wood.

I started with smaller trees, then moved on to hacking down slightly larger alders once I got into the rhythm. Their trunks soon lay scattered about the shady forest floor around me. Next, I moved on to the tedious process of delimbing each felled tree.

Using the axe or saw when necessary, I methodically stripped away all the living branches until only bare trunks remained. The limbs and leaves were left where they fell to decay and nourish the soil. Only the logs and larger limbs needed hauling. Every day I worked, I made sure to summon a woodland and earth spirit to imbue the saplings and ensure their steady growth.

For the trunks too large to carry over my shoulder, I cut them into sections roughly five feet long. These still required significant effort to lug through the woods, but the lengths were manageable for Ghostie and Sir Boozles, although I helped them often. My boots scraped over lichen-mottled boulders and exposed roots as I labored, chuckling at the domesticants' antics.

Arriving back at the homestead's edge, I neatly stacked the logs I had harvested. Soon, an impressive cord of firewood and alder was accumulating. The pile would continue growing over the next days as I steadily felled, delimbed, and transported more trees each day.

Wiping sweat from my dirt-smudged brow, I would pause to drink some chilled water before grabbing another load. My shoulders burned from the exertion, but it felt good providing such essential stores for our home. The cabin's merrily crackling hearth was incentive enough to motivate me.

When the pile looked sufficient for one morning's work, I would wash up using a bucket of crisp water drawn from the well before heading back to the cabin for a hearty lunch with Diane. She always had a fortifying lunch waiting after my mornings of chopping and lugging wood.

Over a simple but filling meal of bread, vegetables, and cured meat, Diane and I would discuss plans for the homestead. I would describe my progress chopping alder logs and stacking logs while she told me of her morning tending the garden and foraging useful herbs.

Our conversations were easy, frequently punctuated by affectionate laughter. The cozy fire and good food replenished my energy for the afternoon work ahead. I was fortunate to share such a rewarding life with my love.

After eating, I would tidy up then prepare for several more hours of chopping and hauling. The constant chores here provided little time for idleness, but the work kept me fit and brought tangible results. Our self-sufficiency grew daily.

Hefting my axe, I would hike briskly back to the

stand of alders, waving to Diane as she headed off on her own tasks, distracted by something only she could detect thanks to her Class abilities. Her passion for nurturing the valley's bounty impressed me endlessly.

Upon reaching my logging area, I would start felling more slender trees in a steady rhythm, my practiced swings sending them toppling to the shaded forest floor with resounding cracks. Though tiring, the exertion felt good.

As the afternoon wore on, my growing cord of delimbed logs and my aching muscles provided tangible proof of a hard day's work. But I persevered even as the light began to fade, determined to chop and transport as much wood as I could before nightfall with the aid of my domesticants.

Heaving the last laden bundle up onto my shoulder as dusk descended and flanked by Ghostie and Boozles, I would turn toward home, eager for the warm fire and Diane's soothing companionship. Our humble cabin was a welcome sight after hours alone in the quiet woods.

After stacking the final logs and washing up, the smell of something delicious simmering on the hearth signaled that dinner awaited. Diane had prepared the evening meal while I finished chopping wood for the day.

Settling around the worn wooden table near the merrily crackling fire, we would enjoy bowls of savory stew or fragrant herbal chicken. The hearty fare satisfied appetites honed by a long day of frontier labor.

Our conversations over dinner were often spirited, frequently filled with speculative plans for improving the homestead or hopes for future adventures we might undertake together. But we also simply treasured this time alone.

With the empty dishes cleared away by the chirpy duo of domesticants, we would share mugs of steaming tea or coffee as we lounged comfortably together on the braided rug before the fireplace. The intimacy of those quiet evenings was something we both greatly enjoyed, especially after the excitement of our adventure in Nimos Sedia.

Before turning in upstairs, I would secure the

doors and ensure the domesticants and the elemental were on patrol outside. Sleep came swiftly those nights; my body weary but fulfilled from the necessary tasks completed around the homestead. And of course, Diane and I shared each other often — making sure that our shared desire to expand our family would be fulfilled kept our nights full of passion and ardor.

When I awoke the next morning, I would begin the familiar routine again — hearty breakfast, readying provisions, walking the same shaded trail to resume chopping and hauling logs. Routine can easily turn to tedium, but Diane's presence kept each day fresh.

To change things up, I regularly checked on the traps and snares I had set, making sure to bring the bounty back to the smokehouse after resetting the traps. Diane spent much time fishing and exploring the surroundings, making sure she knew the movements of local critters.

Once or twice, she reported more dangerous creatures in the vicinity of our homestead. To anyone without a Class — as I had been before I came to the frontier — these creatures would have been lethal, but the storm elemental kept them at bay simply through its presence; the creatures knew not to tangle with it.

My purposeful labors continued steadily as the fragrant days passed. Our wood stores swelled, alder logs stacked in preparation for smoking meat and fish when needed to get us through next winter. The supply of wood would prove useful in expanding the cabin, and I regularly spent an evening mulling over my plans, making an inventory of what I needed to make our place bigger and better.

During breaks in my wood chopping, I checked the progress of the vegetable plots and my alchemy garden. The tomato and onion plants were thriving thanks to regular care and enrichment from the helpful woodland and earth spirits I summoned using my magical talents as a Frontier Summoner.

Kneeling amidst the dark, moist soil, I carefully inspected each plant in turn. The tomato vines were heavy with slowly ripening fruit, while the onion stalks stood tall and healthy. I commanded my spirits to continue nurturing the crops through their important growth phases.

Rising, I entered my alchemy garden and scrutinized the mystical herbs cultivated there — plump Thauma Roots, shimmering Magebread blossoms, and ethereal Wispsilk fronds. All were flourishing and nearing peak maturity for harvesting alchemical components. The plants were thriving thanks to my efforts and my spirits' tending. Each part served an essential purpose in my various alchemical transmutations.

Once my tasks were complete in the garden plots, I gathered my axe and provisions and hiked briskly back into the woods to continue chopping pine and alder logs. The sun slanted through the canopy in shafts of gold as I neared my stand of slender young trees awaiting the bite of my axe.

As the afternoon faded toward evening, I transported my last bundles of logs from the shady woods and stacked them with the others. Studying the impressive pile, I estimated there was a sufficient supply for the next several weeks at least.

After tidying my tools, I headed inside just as

delicious scents from the hearth heralded another of Diane's home-cooked meals. My appetite sharpened by long hours swinging the axe, I ate heartily and retired early that night.

One afternoon after several days of work had passed, as I hauled my last bundle along the trail toward home, movement near the cabin caught my eye. A smile broke across my face when I recognized the rider, even at a distance — Leigh had returned!

Quickening my strides, I hurried to greet her, my mind already turning happily toward her company around the evening's fire and all that it signified — seed stock for the expanded plots, fresh tales from town, and more laughter to grace our tranquil valley.

Chapter 34

I stood waiting at the edge of my property, listening to the sound of approaching hoofbeats. A smile broke across my face when I caught a full view of Leigh astride her horse, Colonel. Her blonde locks peeked out from under her wide-brimmed cowboy hat, and she waved exuberantly when she spotted me.

"Howdy there, stranger!" Leigh drawled playfully as she reined Colonel to a stop and swung down from the saddle. "Brought ya a little somethin' special today."

She patted the bulging burlap sack hitched behind her, regarding me with a playful wink.

I chuckled, resting the axe head on the ground as I approached to give her a quick one-armed hug, feeling great pleasure to have that voluptuous body pushed up against me once more. "Let me guess, you've come bearing seeds for our new farm plot?"

"You got it!" Leigh confirmed with an enthusiastic nod that made her locks bounce. She untied the sack and opened it wide, letting me peer inside at the several dozen small paper envelopes stacked within. "Picked all the essentials for ya from the store — at least, insofar y'all didn't grow 'em yet. It's all the fast-growin' stuff, too. I got beans, carrots, and lettuce!"

My eyes widened as I took in the veritable cornucopia of seed varieties Leigh had managed to procure. "This is incredible, thank you Leigh! With a stock like this, we'll have that new plot overflowing with produce in no time."

"Aw, I'm just doin' my duty to help out," Leigh said, puffing out her chest importantly before breaking into giggles as she trailed a finger along my chest. "But I don't normally do deliveries, David! I'm expecting some royal compensation from ya."

I laughed and nodded. "Oh, you will be royally compensated. Don't worry about that!"

At that moment, the cabin door creaked open, and Diane emerged onto the porch, her emerald eyes lighting up when she spotted our visitor. "Leigh, you're back!" she exclaimed happily, hurrying down the steps on swift feet to sweep her dearest friend into an affectionate embrace.

"Sure am, sugar!" Leigh said, returning Diane's hug warmly before holding her at arm's length. "The trip back to town was just fine and dandy. Hope y'all have been staying out of trouble while I was away?" She regarded us with playfully raised eyebrows.

Diane laughed, linking her arm through Leigh's as they strolled together toward the house. "Oh yes, we always manage to find some hijinks to get up to when you're not around to chaperone us," she joked.

Behind them, Colonel ambled over to a shady patch to lazily graze after I untied from his saddle the heavy burlap sack of seed packets Leigh had brought. "Come on, girls," I said. "Let's head on inside!"

Chatting merrily as they caught up, Diane and Leigh followed me.

Inside, we gathered around the solid table. While Leigh busied herself getting a pot of coffee brewing, Diane excitedly gestured to the bulging sack I'd set down.

"Goodness, you brought back so many seeds!" she marveled as I upended the bag, sending dozens of small paper envelopes cascading out across the tabletop. She picked one up reverently, eyes shining. "With these, we'll have more fresh vegetables than we know what to do with."

Leigh nodded, retrieving a trio of chipped

earthenware mugs from the cupboard to fill with hot, fragrant coffee. To see how much she felt at home here with us made me smile broadly.

"I made sure to bring plenty of variety too," she remarked, passing us each a steaming mug before taking a seat. "And as I told David just now, these are all Tannorian cultivars that'll grow more quickly and yield more. They ain't like the moonlight spuds I sold y'all earlier, but they'll grow near as quick. Oh, and I also brought some fresh fruit for us to enjoy!"

"Oh, nice!" Diane hummed happily.

Meanwhile, I nodded thoughtfully, picking up one envelope labeled beans and examining it with interest. The magical strains from across the realms, finding their origin in Tannoris, held exciting potential, though they required more care and management.

We spent some time sorting through the various seed packets, discussing the ideal conditions and care required by each vegetable type. Diane took meticulous notes, ever the perfectionist when it came to nurturing nature's bounty.

As the afternoon drew on, our conversation wound down. There was still ample daylight left thanks to Leigh's timely morning arrival.

"Why don't we head out and start the planting today?" I suggested, eager to get the seeds sown.

Leigh and Diane readily agreed, spirits high at the thought of seeing the first sprouts emerge before long. We swiftly gathered up the envelopes of seeds, hand trowels, rakes, and anything else we would need to work the plot.

Stepping outside into mellow sunshine, we made our way to the prepared vegetable patch, eager to get the planting underway.

I knelt and pressed a palm to the dark loose soil, finding it dry on top but still moist down below. "Feels perfect for planting seeds," I announced.

Scooping up a handful, Leigh crumbled the soft earth between her fingers, sniffing it appraisingly. "I'd say you're right as rain," she agreed. "This soil's ripe for seeds to set down roots and start growin'."

We started by thoroughly raking over the entire plot, breaking up any large clods we might have missed yesterday and smoothing the surface. The plots for each crop were already meticulously measured out thanks to yesterday's work, which meant we were ready to sow!

Carefully opening each seed envelope, we gently tapped a share of the contents into a spare tin cup, taking pains not to spill or mix up the types. The Tannorian beans, lettuce, and carrots required extra diligence while sowing.

Calling over Ghostie and Sir Boozles to assist us, I set them to the task of poking uniform starter holes along each labeled row. Meanwhile, Leigh and I followed behind, dropping seeds into each hole before gently covering them over with a sprinkle of loose soil.

The spirits continued their planting work tirelessly up and down the rows as the mellow afternoon wore on. By late morning, we had finished sowing the entire plot with lettuce, beans, and carrots.

Stepping back to survey our progress, I nodded in satisfaction at the sections of neatly planted rows ready and waiting to send up their first tender shoots. We had accomplished meaningful work today.

As the sun peaked overhead, we enjoyed a quick lunch by the banks of the Silverthread, looking over the sparkling water as we laughed and talked. We recalled much of our adventure to Nimos Sedia and the things we had seen and experienced there. We had many shared memories already, and the bond between us had been forged in both hardship and pleasure.

After lunch, we finished the job of seeding the land with the help of the domesticants. When we were finished, we gathered up our empty seed packets and idle tools to head back inside. There was a collective sense of eager anticipation surrounding what the coming days and weeks would soon unfurl across these cultivated beds of dark, life-giving soil.

After washing up on the porch, we returned

inside just as Leigh finished cooking up a fragrant vegetable stew. Our appetites were hearty after hours of planting labor. We ate our fill around the fire, reflecting contentedly on the satisfying work accomplished.

As we scraped the last morsels of stew from our wooden bowls, talk turned towards hopes and plans for when the seeds burst into leafy shoots and eventually fruits. The valley seemed full of potential, simply awaiting careful nurturing.

When our excited speculation wound down and yawns escaped unbidden, we decided to get some rest. Weariness had settled comfortably into our bones, though pleasantly so after a productive day in the nurturing outdoors.

As before, I piled blankets and pillows in front of the fireplace so the three of us could sleep together. While it wasn't the most comfortable, it would have to do until I made us a proper bedroom with a bigger bed.

After Leigh expressed how much she had missed me in the non-verbal way, eloquently aided by Diane, sleep found me swiftly, accompanied by lively dreams featuring verdant rows of vegetables thriving beneath the warm summer sun — the fruits of our shared dedication and dream of abundance.

Chapter 35

The morning sunlight streamed in through the cabin windows as I awoke to the inviting smells of sizzling bacon and percolating coffee. Stretching, I rose from the makeshift bed of blankets and pillows on the floor where the three of us had slept.

In the kitchen, Diane was frying up bacon and

eggs while Leigh sliced fruit for a morning salad. They chatted amiably as they worked, golden hair and raven tresses glinting in the sunshine pouring through the open windows.

"Morning, handsome!" Leigh chirped when she noticed me shuffle in. Diane flashed me a warm smile over her shoulder, spatula poised above the cast iron skillet.

"Breakfast is just about ready," she told me. My stomach rumbled appreciatively at the prospect of the hearty frontier fare being prepared. I poured myself a mug of hot, invigorating coffee and took a seat at the table.

Before long, the sizzling breakfast feast was ready. Diane and Leigh served up platters of crispy bacon, fluffy eggs, and mixed fruit salad along with thick slices of buttered toast. The aroma was mouthwatering.

As we ate with gusto, the conversation turned to the day ahead. "So, David, you and I were planning to ride into Gladdenfield today, right?" Leigh asked before taking a sip of coffee.

I nodded, swallowing a mouthful of smoky

bacon. "That's right. We're going to check in on Waelin's niece Celeste and see how she's settling in now that he's off teaching in New Springfield."

"It'll be nice to visit town again too," Diane remarked. Though she preferred the tranquility of our valley, I knew she still held some fondness for the lively frontier settlement. "But I think I should let the two of you run along together now. I want to stay here and keep an eye on these crops!"

"That's a good idea, " I said. "Besides, I shouldn't be more than a couple of days. I want to get back here and keep working on the cabin expansion plans." I smiled across the table at Diane. "Plus, I'd miss your company too much."

Diane laughed. "Aw, so sweet of you to say so!" She speared a juicy melon chunk with her fork.

"Don't you worry though," Leigh put in. "David will be back before you know it."

I grinned and nodded in agreement. "I'll keep Ghostie, Sir Boozles, and Mr. Drizzles here," I said, emphasizing the last two names pointedly. "And remind me I'll name my next familiar myself…"

The girls laughed at that, and we continued

chatting idly as we finished up breakfast and drank the last sips of our coffee. Though in truth, neither Leigh nor I relished the idea of leaving Diane, we knew the trip to check on Waelin's niece Celeste was necessary. Plus, I was very curious about the elf maiden.

She was pretty, sure, but elven culture still held many mysteries to me. Perhaps, by getting to know her, I could learn more about it. And who knew what else could grow between us if she was nice.

"Why don't we ride Colonel double?" Leigh said, throwing me a smile. "You can save some gas that way, and you can polish up on them horse ridin' skills, cowboy! I reckon you should get yourself a mount in time."

I nodded in agreement. "Sounds fun. But how will I get back?"

"Well, maybe I'll come with you."

"Again?" I said, eyebrow perked. "Won't you get in trouble with the store?"

She gave a mysterious smile at that. "Maybe. Maybe not. You'll see! Just take my word I'll be comin' on back with you."

I grinned and nodded, letting her have her secrets for now.

As Ghostie tidied up the kitchen, Diane whipped up sack lunches for us to eat on the road. Fresh bread, cured meats, cheese, and wild apples would keep us nourished during the ride to Gladdenfield.

Once the breakfast dishes were cleared and our provisions readied, Leigh and I discussed preparations for the journey. Donning a hat, I did a quick weapons check while Leigh ensured Colonel was saddled up and ready.

Stepping outside into the warm morning sunshine, I did a quick perimeter check then waved over Ghostie, Mr. Drizzles, and Sir Boozles. I gave them firm instructions to continue patrolling the homestead and assisting Diane while we were away. The domesticants chirped affirmatively, while the storm elemental conveyed its understanding with a brisk swirl.

With my summons watching over things and keeping any wilderness threats at bay, I felt at ease leaving Diane alone for a couple of days. She was fully capable of caring for herself and the homestead in the valley, but the summons might help and make life a little easier. Still, I would miss her company on the trail.

Diane walked with us over to Colonel, a serene smile on her lovely face. "You two be safe out there and hurry on back," she told us warmly. Standing on tiptoes, she gifted me with a tender and loving kiss before embracing Leigh.

"We'll be back before ya know it!" Leigh assured her, giving Diane an affectionate squeeze. Her sky-blue eyes were bright with optimism despite the necessary parting. "But let's do a practice round first, okay David? Just in case you're a little rusty."

Laughing, I nodded. I had ridden horses before, but I had to admit it had been a while. Still, Colonel was a calm beast, and she waited for me with the practiced patience of a horse that had carried riders often.

Adjusting my hat, I approached Colonel and ran my hand along her neck, feeling the smooth chestnut coat and powerful muscles beneath. I checked the straps of the saddle and stirrups, ensuring all was in order.

Placing my foot in the stirrup, I heaved myself up and swung my leg over Colonel's broad back. I settled into the saddle, finding my balance and getting a feel for Colonel's gentle swaying motions. The height and openness felt unfamiliar after so long on my own two feet. Gripping the reins, I lightly tapped Colonel's flanks with my boots.

Colonel began ambling forward obediently with an easy rocking gait. I practiced steering her around the yard in wide circles, re-accustoming myself to guiding a mount. Leigh called out occasional reminders about posture and rein handling as I rode.

Making another circuit around the cabin, I began to relax and find my rhythm atop the patient horse. The motions came back naturally, and I soon felt secure and steady in the saddle once more. Colonel responded fluidly to the subtlest shifts of my weight or light tugs on the reins.

As I looped back around with Colonel, both girls looked at me admiringly. "Well, ain't that a sight?" Leigh hummed. "There ain't nothing like a man who can handle a horse."

Diane nodded happily. "Hm," she purred. "He looks very handsome."

Bringing Colonel to a halt, I chuckled. "Don't you girls make me blush now," I teased them before I climbed down. Together, we started loading the supplies we had prepared for the journey.

We said our goodbyes again, I swung up first, and then Leigh mounted Colonel behind me. Finally, Diane waved us off as the two of us headed down the trail.

As we rode down the winding trail away from the cabin, I relaxed into the easy rhythm of Colonel's steady gait. Behind me, Leigh's arms encircled my waist as she held on. Her warm presence against my back made me smile.

"So, tell me, how were things around the shop while you were back in town?" I asked, turning my head so she could hear me over the clopping hooves.

"Oh, you know, same old," Leigh replied breezily. "Had to restock a few shelves, balance the books, chat with the regulars. The nice thing is that with a town the size of Gladdenfield, it's never really too busy, so I get plenty of time to make sure everything's running just fine. That way, I can get a little quiet time with my favorite customer!" She gave me a playful poke in the ribs, clearly indicating she meant me.

I chuckled. "Well, I've been looking forward to seeing you again too, so it's nice to hear affairs are in order." I glanced back to see her grin. "Did you hear any interesting news or rumors making the rounds in Gladdenfield?"

"Let's see..." Leigh mused. "Old Darny at the Wild Outrider is still trying to fix that darn squeaky porch floorboard. The man's got two left hands, though, so he just makes it worse. Oh, and there's talk of Clara plannin' a new Dungeon raid with a couple o' hopefuls out of Gladdenfield."

She absently adjusted her hat against the sunshine filtering down through the leafy branches arching overhead. "Mostly the usual small-town scuttlebutt. Quiet week, truth be told. How're things faring back at the homestead? Between you and Diane?" She giggled. "Y'all still workin' hard on getting' them kits?"

I laughed. "We are," I said. "And life's been good. The crops are really thriving thanks to our tending and the spirits' influence, and the expanded plot is looking good. I was able to stockpile a good amount of logs too."

I patted Colonel's neck as the trail widened into a sunny stretch. "I think we're just about ready to start planning the cabin expansion in earnest. Maybe we can finalize details when I'm back after this trip."

"Music to my ears," Leigh said happily. "I can already picture it... cozy little kitchen with a proper icebox, bedrooms that ain't in no drafty loft..." Her arms squeezed me affectionately. "Big bed... Gonna make that place perfect."

I smiled at the thought. "It's really coming together out there. I think we need to consider security a bit more in the future as well."

"How so?" Leigh asked. "Don't leave me in suspense. Have y'all been getting critters?"

I chuckled. "Diane scouted a few monsters. Low-level, and the storm elemental that patrols the property dissuaded them, but I think I'd like some kind of enclosure. Maybe more summons patrolling once I unlock more slots."

Leigh nodded and gave my waist a loving squeeze. "That sounds wise," she said. "This section o' the Wilds ain't too bad, but sometimes things bleed over from the higher-level areas. Ain't for nothing that Gladdenfield's got those walls and elven sentries."

"Exactly," I said. "Can't be too careful."

We continued on in comfortable silence for a stretch as Colonel carried us steadily closer to Gladdenfield. The morning sunshine felt pleasantly warm across my shoulders. The lively sounds of the forest echoed around us.

"How's Diane been doing since we left town?" Leigh asked after a bit, genuine fondness coloring her tone. "She get lonely or bored at all with just you for company?" She gave me a playful squeeze to signal she was just kidding.

I laughed. "Well, she seems to be doing really well," I answered thoughtfully. "Always keeps busy tending the garden, fishing, cooking meals... I think she just enjoys our quiet life together out there."

I smiled softly, picturing Diane's refined features in the flickering firelight. "Though I know she'll appreciate when the cabin renovations allow more space and comforts. Especially with our hopes to expand the family before long."

Leigh smiled warmly. "Well, ain't that just sweet as honey," she drawled. "You two are gonna make the best parents, baby. And I hereby once again volunteer myself as honorary auntie to all your lil' ones!"

I laughed. "The position is already yours. We'll be relying on you for plenty of babysitting and wilderness lessons, I'm sure." The thought filled me with real happiness. I didn't yet say that I would love for her to live closer to us or even with us. That would bring the family we were forming even closer together. It was a subject we would soon broach, I hoped.

As the morning wore on, the forest thinned and the Silverthread River glinted in the distance between the trees. The fine weather and easy banter with Leigh made the time pass swiftly, and the ride into town wasn't that long to begin with.

As we turned onto the main road by the old cottonwood, Leigh snugged up against my back once more. "I know I tease ya sometimes, honey, but I just want ya to know I'm real happy you and Diane have this life together," she said sincerely.

"You're as much a part of it as she and I are," I said, giving her hand an affectionate squeeze.

She smiled softly, pressing her delicious body against mine. "That means the world to me," she whispered in my ear. "Just want ya to know that." Her voice held a rare vulnerability that touched me deeply.

Under the bubbly and vivacious surface of the frontier gal was a vulnerable side that wanted to belong — to have a family. I shared that desire with her, and I would love nothing more than to have her with us for good. Hopefully, we would be able to make that happen.

I reached back to briefly squeeze her hand resting on my shoulder. "We're thankful every day to have you with us, Leigh," I said genuinely. "Our family wouldn't be complete without you."

Leigh's answering hug communicated wordless affection. Together we rode on toward Gladdenfield beneath the sunlit forest canopy.

Chapter 36

The dusty streets of Gladdenfield came into view as Colonel carried Leigh and me steadily closer to town. Soon, the familiar timber palisade walls rose ahead. There were not many folks coming into town today, and it promised to be a quiet day. We passed beneath the open gates to enter the lively frontier settlement.

The elven guards scrutinized us, but they were, of course, familiar enough with Leigh and me. With smiles and nods, they gestured for us to move on.

Dismounting Colonel, we led the horse down the bustling main thoroughfare. Townsfolk called friendly greetings to Leigh, clearly recognizing the bubbly shopkeeper.

Many knew me by now as well, especially those who had been at the Aquana Festival or had heard the stories. After all, I had won both the Gauntlet and the tournament organized by the dwarven lord Vartlebeck. As such, the townsfolk offered respectful greetings, and many of the children and kits looked at me with big eyes.

"Looks like you're building quite the fan base," Leigh joked cheerfully as we walked. "Heck, if you keep goin' like this, you might end up leading our little town!"

I laughed, entertaining the thought for a moment. "Well," I said, "let's just make sure we have the homestead in order before we get any broader ambitions."

Soon we arrived at Leigh's tidy shop. She hitched Colonel to the post out front before fishing a key from her pockets to unlock the door. Stepping inside, I smiled at the familiar space.

Shelves lined the walls, neatly organized with all manner of frontier goods and provisions. Sacks of grain, coils of rope, lanterns, tools, and clothing filled the roomy interior. The scent of cured leather mingled with pine wood.

While Leigh busied herself behind the counter, tidying displays and checking ledger books, I admired some of the fine handcrafted items for sale. Her inventory highlighted local artisans' skills and creativity. There were also plenty of produce, smoked meat and fish, and mana potions manufactured at my homestead.

As I turned a beautifully carved jewelry box over in my hands, the storeroom door suddenly banged open. I glanced up in surprise as an elderly human man shuffled briskly out front, arms loaded with merchandise to restock a shelf.

He smiled amiably through his bushy gray

mustache and nodded in greeting before turning to arrange cloth bolts along the wall with gnarled but deft hands.

Blinking in surprise, I turned to face Leigh. She stood there grinning with one hand on her curvy hip.

"Surprise," she purred.

I raised an eyebrow. "You... got help?" I asked curiously, suspecting this was the surprise she had hinted at.

Leigh grinned and nodded. "Surprise, surprise! Went ahead and hired Ol' Randal here to help mind the place while I'm away. He's a real hard worker, and the townsfolk have taken a shine to him."

As we spoke, Randal finished his task and ambled over to offer me a handshake in greeting after fixing his round-rimmed spectacles. "Pleased to meet ya, sir," he rasped cheerfully in a rough frontier drawl. "The name's Randal Cooper. Leigh speaks well of ya, sir."

I returned his firm handshake. "The pleasure's all mine, Randal," I replied politely. "How are you finding work here at the store?"

Randal's eyes crinkled merrily beneath bushy brows. "Can't complain one bit!" he declared. "Never had a job quite like this in my years, but Leigh here's been teachin' me the ropes real patient-like. Used to be a trapper, sir. I even got a Class to match: Hunter. Although I ain't never advanced beyond level 2. By the time I got the Class, my wife already done warned me I was too old to get out there and look for trouble. A man's gotta listen to his wife, y'know?"

I chuckled. "Well, that's great!" I said. "You live right here in Gladdenfield?"

"That's right, sir. My wife and me, we used to live in Memphis before the Upheaval and all. She and I, we both got Classes — a strange thing, 'cause many of the young'uns didn't and were forced to stay in the city. Anyways, we moved on out here and joined the Frontier Division for a while. I was already old when these things began, and I reckon I'm definitely too old for adventure now!"

As we conversed, customers began trickling into

the store seeking supplies for the day's work. Leigh and Randal smoothly handled the commerce, fetching requested items, and tallying purchases.

I found a place near the window to stay out of their way, observing with interest. Though Randal moved with age-stiffened joints, he interacted warmly with the ragtag townsfolk, laughing heartily at their jokes. Perhaps the frontier spirit suited him. And folks didn't seem to mind he was a tad slower than Leigh in getting them their things. After all, pleasant conversation smoothed things over.

I smiled as I watched this new dynamic. This was indeed a happy thing because it meant that Leigh would have more free time on her hands to spend with us, either at the homestead or adventuring. In fact, it was exactly what I had wanted, and I was very pleased to see she had come to the same conclusion on her own.

During a brief lull, Leigh showed Randal the store ledger, slowly walking him through recording the morning's transactions. The old man listened intently, weathered hands carefully inking each detail into the book.

"You're getting the hang of this real quick!" Leigh praised, clearly impressed by his dedication to learning a wholly new trade late in life. "Why, you'll be running the place solo before long if you keep applyin' yourself like this."

Randal smiled at the validation. I had to admit I was impressed by his willingness to learn a trade so different from his past as a trapper and hunter. He had risen earnestly to the opportunity granted him rather than balking at the unfamiliar. It was another great example of the frontier spirit, where everyone did their part to contribute and form a community.

As Randal returned to capably assisting customers with stiff but polite motions, I raised an eyebrow at Leigh approvingly. "Well, you certainly seem to have found some real help here," I remarked. "Gladdenfield is lucky to have you looking out for it."

Leigh nodded fondly as she watched Randal heft a heavy sack of grain for a customer. "Ol' Randal may move a mite slower these days, but he's got a real heart of gold," she said. "I know he'll pick this up quick if he sets his mind to it."

I studied Randal with newfound respect as he tirelessly rung up purchases for the steady stream of shoppers. His dogged cheer and focus were clearly winning over the colorful frontier residents coming through Leigh's door.

I grinned at Leigh. "So, is there any special reason you finally got someone around to help at the store? I always suspected you couldn't afford it?"

She blushed a little. "Maybe," she purred, drawing out the word. "Why don't you and I head to the Wild Outrider and talk a bit about it all, hm?"

"Sure," I said, feeling she was about to confess something of personal importance to me. "Lead the way!"

Chapter 37

Leigh and I left the shop, leaving Randal in charge as we headed down the dusty street toward the Wild Outrider. The rowdy tavern came into view, its timber facade sun-faded with age.

Pushing through the swinging saloon doors, we were greeted by the familiar mingled scents of ale and smoke. A few trail-worn regulars sat nursing drinks despite the early hour. Behind the bar, Darny looked up and waved.

"Hey you two, welcome back!" the portly barkeep called in his usual jovial bellow. He slid two frothing mugs our way as we took seats at the counter.

"On the house for two of my favorite customers," Darny declared with a wink.

I smiled and nodded. "Appreciate that, Darny," I said. "Leigh and I were looking to have a few drinks and maybe have some lunch later on. Can we grab a table?"

"Sure, sure!" he called out, giving us a wave. "Sit anywhere you like! The wife is gonna cook up some burgers, so y'all are in for a treat."

"That does sound great!" Leigh hummed.

Laughing, the two of us took our ales and found a nice and secluded table in the corner of the tavern, close to a window that let in some of the fresh daylight. We settled in the creaky old chairs, and I took a deep pull of the crisp ale. It was good to be back here again.

Beside me, Leigh toyed pensively with her drink, uncharacteristically quiet. I could sense she had something weighing on her mind that she wanted to discuss privately.

"So what made you finally decide to hire help for the store?" I prompted gently after a few moments of silence between us.

Leigh's sky-blue eyes took on a distant look. "Well, truth be told, it's 'cause of you," she admitted. "All this time we've been spending together, it really got me thinking."

She absently twisted a golden lock around one finger. "I want... more of it. More of *you*. Only being out at the homestead now and again has been lonely since..." Her cheeks colored charmingly. "Well, since my feelings gone and changed."

I smiled and nodded, understanding loneliness well enough from my days back in New Springfield, before all of this.

"Ya know," she continued, "I used to think I had it all figured out. I was gonna be single and happy, y'know? I'd run the store, have lotsa friends, do lotsa fun stuff... But ever since I met you, I'm kinda second-guessin' all of it... I don't think bein' alone is fun anymore." She fixed her blazing blue eyes on mind. "My... My mind is changing. It *has* changed. I don't want to be alone, David. I don't even want to be apart from you as long as I am by havin' to run the store."

My pulse quickened pleasantly at her confession. I reached over to squeeze her hand encouragingly. "Leigh, you know you're welcome out at the homestead anytime. Diane and I would love having you around more."

Her answering smile was tremulous but full of hope. "Do you really mean that?" Leigh asked almost shyly. "I know I can be a bit much sometimes. Loud, cluttering up the place..."

"Nonsense," I interjected firmly. "Our home is your home too. Diane adores you." I held Leigh's hesitant gaze. "We both want you there as part of our family. However often you can manage it."

Her cheeks flushed as she twirled her golden lock around her finger. "I'm... I'm really happy to hear that, David. And I suppose that's the reason I went and hired Randal. I just wanna be with you more often."

I smiled and nodded, reaching out to take her hand in mine. "I understand, and I'm very happy to hear it. With the renovations coming up, we'll have plenty of room." I gave her hand a little squeeze. "There's just one concern I have, Leigh. I know the store does well, but does it do well enough to allow you to hire someone?"

She wagged her free hand. "Well," she hummed. "I don't wanna… It's fine. Don't worry 'bout it."

"Leigh," I said, pressing on. "If you're going to be part of my family, then your troubles are mine. I don't want you to struggle financially just so you can be with us more often. We can help, you know? The homestead stands to make more money, and if you spend more time with us — if you come to live with us — it's as much yours as it is mine and Diane's. Let us help you."

Her blue eyes got a wet sheen, and she pursed her lips for a moment as she battled her emotions. "Ya mean that, David?" she said, her voice much smaller than what I was used to from the bubbly blonde.

"Of course," I said. "We can divest some of the homestead's income to paying Randal's salary. You won't have to worry about a thing."

Joy bloomed across Leigh's face at my reassurance. Impulsively, she hopped up from her chair and came over to mine, settling on my lap before I could utter a word. She threw both arms around me in a fierce hug that elicited amused glances from Darny and the few other patrons.

"You don't know how happy it makes me to hear you say that," Leigh confessed emotionally once we separated again. She dabbed at her eyes with a kerchief.

Seeing Leigh so vulnerable and overcome with emotion stirred powerful feelings within me in return. I cared for her deeply, and I wanted her to be happy above all things. If I could help her achieve that happiness, I would.

"This is all still new, but you need know that what Diane and I are building — our home, our future — it's yours to share too," I told Leigh sincerely. "However much you want. Just say the word."

Leigh nodded slowly, a dreamy smile curling her lips as she pondered my words. "Ain't gonna lie, nothing would make me happier than being out there with you two full time," she mused wistfully after a moment. "Buildin' up the place, going on little adventures, watchin' them kits grow up... And maybe..." She let the words trail off, but I understood the hidden meaning there.

I squeezed her hand reassuringly. "Leigh, you're family to us. Diane loves you like a sister, and you know *I* love you too." I chuckled. "We might have to move the expansion up a little to make sure the place doesn't get too cramped, but it's nothing we can't handle."

Leigh nodded slowly, looking thoughtful as she sipped her ale. "That sounds like a dream," she said softly. "Would be a big change leaving town. But waking up to your face, watching the sunrise over the valley..." She exhaled wistfully. "It would be so nice to live out there with y'all..."

We both chuckled. I certainly couldn't fault Leigh's preference for the pace of life Diane and I enjoyed away from the settlement's noise and bustle. Still, uprooting one's whole existence was no small decision.

I gave Leigh's hand a gentle, reassuring squeeze. "There's no rush or pressure," I told her kindly. "Just know the invitation's open. We'll support whatever choice makes you happy, Leigh."

"You're a real good man, David," Leigh replied, toasting me with her drink before taking a long pull. "And I'm a lucky gal..." She bit her lip. "I don't think I need to think long on it, y'know?"

I grinned. "Well, at least one night."

"Only if *you* stay the night while I do some... thinkin'."

"Of course..." I smiled broadly, feeling her words touch my core already. Most times Leigh and I had shared had been in the company of Diane. As much fun as that was, I was looking forward to a night alone with Leigh and explore her passions more deeply.

She smiled. "You know, I think I fully fell for you durin' that quest to the elven Dungeon. I mean, I was head-over-heels before that, but the way you controlled that situation and protected us..." She shook her head. "Hmmm... I just melted." Her eyes twinkled mirthfully. "Still can't believe we made it outta that spooky Dungeon in one piece."

I laughed and launched into reminiscing about our shared adventures navigating Nimos Sedia's lightless depths. Leigh's features practically glowed as she listened, clearly savoring this renewed closeness between us.

Time slipped by swiftly as we swapped stories and shared comfortable silences. Darny kept our mugs filled and left us to our conversation. Soon enough, we were laughing and sharing more stories. When Darny came around to take our orders, we decided to stay for lunch.

Darny soon returned with two piping hot burgers and a basket of thickly cut fries for Leigh and me.

"These are cut from taters I bought from you, Leigh," Darny said as he placed the food in front of us.

Leigh threw me a wink. "Chances are they are from David's farm, then! Best dig in!"

Grinning, I wasted no time doing just that. The savory aroma made my mouth water. I bit into the juicy burger, relishing the explosion of flavors.

"Mmm, Darny wasn't kiddin' about these burgers!" Leigh remarked appreciatively before taking a big bite of her own. "Darny's wife sure as somethin' knows what she's doing in that kitchen."

Mouth full, I hummed agreement. We ate ravenously, the satisfying fare hitting the spot after the ride into town and the conversation that had followed it. Crisp fries and cold mugs of ale perfectly complemented the hearty burgers. Darny kept a close eye on us from the bar, clearly pleased to see his wife's cooking being enjoyed.

As I finished up my burger, movement at the entrance caught my eye. An older but brawny woman clad in an armor of steel rings had just entered the tavern. Her graying red hair was bound back in neat braids, and a nasty scar cut across her weathered cheek.

"Hey, there's Clara!" Leigh exclaimed after following my gaze. She stood and waved the woman over eagerly. With a smile, Clara ambled on over to our table. I slid my empty plate aside to make room, curious to get to know the woman better — I was aware that she regularly led raids into Dungeons.

"Leigh, good to see you," Clara rumbled amiably as she pulled up a chair, offering me a nod. Though gruff in demeanor, I knew her to be a stout-hearted adventurer well regarded in Gladdenfield. She eyed our empty plates and whistled. "Those burgers get gobbled up mighty quick around here."

Leigh laughed. "You betcha! Can't get enough of 'em." She then gestured at me. "This is David Wilson."

She nodded. "I know. Weren't you the one who won Vartlebeck's tournament? And the Gauntlet Run?"

I smiled. "Yes, that was me."

"Some mighty fine fighting, I heard," she said. "I wasn't there. Otherwise, we might've crossed blades."

"Maybe some other time," I said with a light grin that made her give a nod of respect.

Leigh tilted her head curiously at Clara. "Say, what brings you out here so early today?"

Clara's scarred face split into a broad grin. "As it happens, I'm getting set to lead an expedition to clear out Hrothgar's Hope first thing tomorrow," she declared.

Leigh nodded slowly, clearly impressed, but I raised my eyebrows. "Hrothgar's Hope?"

She nodded. "Aye," she hummed, taking a swig of ale. "It's a dwarven Dungeon. Dwarves from the Forgeheart clan built it shortly after the Upheaval, but it got infested with kobolds three years ago. I reckon it's level 4 to 5, but I'm takin' a big party." She grinned broadly at me. "Three of 'em you know," she said. "Branik Storsson of Ironfast, Karjela of the foxkin, and a human called Ergun. All three of them participated in Lord Vartlebeck's tournament."

I nodded slowly, recalling the names well enough. They had been formidable combatants.

Karjela had been the other finalist I bested, while Branik and Ergun had been semi-finalists. My battle with Ergun had been harrowing, and I expected he would fight well in the Dungeon.

"No foolin'!" Leigh exclaimed, clearly intrigued. She leaned forward eagerly. "You really think your group can handle Hrothgar's Hope?"

Clara nodded confidently, graying braids swaying. "I've been planning this run for a while. Got three warriors besides myself, a mage, and a priest. All solid level 3's itching to advance." She rapped her knuckles on the table. "We got this."

"Well, ain't that excitin'!" Leigh said. "Y'all are gonna do just fine, I'd wager. That's a well-balanced group."

I wasn't sure if I agreed with that. Of course, with Clara's combat experience combined with the group's varied skills, they stood a good chance against the Dungeon's dangers. But if it was rated level 4 or 5, they might be biting off more than they could chew. Then again, Nimos Sedia had been a tough one for me, Diane, and Leigh, and we had managed all the same.

"What kinds of enemies and traps does Hrothgar's Hope contain?" I asked Clara curiously. Our own foray into Nimos Sedia had taught me such details were invaluable when undertaking a dungeon delve.

Clara took a swig of ale before responding. "From what I gathered, we'll be facing a slew of monsters — kobolds, drakelings, fire salamanders. There might even be a young dragon. There often is when kobolds are in play." She nodded somberly. "Nasty stuff, but we came prepared with plenty of healing draughts and mana potions."

My curiosity was piqued envisioning this motley band fighting through throngs of kobolds deep underground. It would be quite an ordeal, but Clara's confident demeanor showed she had planned thoroughly. Still, in time, I would love to undertake another expedition myself.

Leigh nodded thoughtfully as we listened. "Those healing potions will come in mighty handy if things get hairy," she remarked. "Oh, and be sure to watch for traps... those kobolds can be pretty darn cunning when it comes to settin' those."

"Good tip, thanks Leigh," Clara said appreciatively, filing away the advice. "We still have to find a Rogue or a Scout to help deal with those." She went on to outline their plan to take on the Dungeon.

Apparently, it was situated in the Shimmering Peaks, carved into the flank of the mountains. Originally a mine, it had drawn in many dwarves from the Forgeheart and Silverheart clans — two prominent clans of dwarves in this part of the frontier.

As Clara described her plan of attack, I noticed Leigh listening raptly, an almost wistful look in her blue eyes. It seemed part of her craved the excitement of adventure still. I couldn't say I disagreed with her; hearing Clara tell it all made my heart rise with excitement as well. I resolved that, once work on the homestead was done, we would try for another Dungeon.

"Well, it sure sounds like you got all your bases covered," Leigh remarked once Clara finished detailing their strategy. "Y'all are gonna knock it outta the park, I just know it!"

Clara grinned confidently. "That's the plan. This is my crew's big shot at some major advancement." She finished her ale and stood. "Anyhow, best be on my way — lots of prep still to do before we ride out at first light."

"Good luck," I told Clara sincerely as I shook her calloused hand. "Hopefully we'll see you back here celebrating soon." Clara was certainly earning the advancement that completing a major Dungeon would bring.

Leigh gave Clara an impromptu hug. "Y'all stay safe in there," she said fondly before stepping back. "Can't wait to hear all about it when you return."

Clara waved in farewell as she departed, the saloon doors swinging behind her.

"Exciting times, eh?" I said, turning to Leigh once we had settled back into our seats. "Dangerous work, but Clara seems to have a good head on her shoulders."

Leigh nodded, looking thoughtful. "She sure does. You said it though — awfully dangerous." She shook her head ruefully. "Wouldn't stop me from offerin' to tag along if we didn't already have plans. But another time maybe!"

Leigh gave me a playful wink, hinting at her ever-present thirst for adventure. I just laughed, knowing that wanderlust spirit was part of what I loved about her.

Chapter 38

As our laughter over Clara's bold dungeon plans died down, I waved Darny over. The portly bartender came sauntering over, eyes twinkling merrily beneath bushy brows.

"What can I do for you folks?" he asked, towel flung over one broad shoulder.

"We were hoping to get the scoop on Waelin's niece, Celeste," I explained. "How's she been settling in around town since her uncle headed off to the city?"

Darny's face lit up in recognition. "Ah right, the elf girl! I was wonderin' if you'd come around askin' after her."

I smiled and nodded. "Waelin asked me to check up on her while he is in New Springfield with Caldwell."

"He told me as much," Darny said as he leaned conspiratorially on the tabletop. "Well, seems young Celeste took right to life here in Gladdenfield soon as she got that treatment from her uncle. Full of vim and vigor now, that one."

I smiled, relieved to hear the magical cure of the Star Jewel had worked.

Beside me, Leigh nodded approvingly. "That's mighty fine to hear," she remarked. "We're glad she's up and about."

"You bet she is!" Darny said. "Why, just yesterday mornin' I saw her wandering the market picking up fruits and vegetables. Had a smile bright as the sun. She's a pretty one, too," he added, shooting me a wink.

"She sure is," Leigh agreed. "Normally, I find elves kinda... drab. But she has the radiance of one of the elven goddesses."

I had to agree with that, but I decided not to speak my mind about it. "I'm happy to hear she's doing well and fitting right in."

Darny wagged his head. "Well, I don't know about 'fitting in', if you'll pardon me. She's an elf, and she's got that elven distant thing going on, if you catch my meaning. She stops in here every once in a while — sometimes plays a bit of music for folks. It sure does liven the place up. But she don't hang around to talk or nothin'. I mean, she just sings, gets some coin for it, and heads on out. We don't see much of her beside that."

I had to admit this piqued my interest. Musicians tended to possess creative souls as I knew well from my time with Diane. "We'll have to catch one of her performances someday," I said.

"You'd enjoy it for sure," Darny assured us. "That elf has a real pretty voice. Sings songs I ain't never heard — probably from her homeland. But don't expect her to stick around."

Darny obviously took some kind of offense to her disinclination to hang around in the Wild Outrider and talk to the patrons, and I could understand from the bartender's perspective. If he had a pretty elf with a nice singing voice, it might sell an extra tankard of ale or cup of wine if she hung around to talk after her performance was over. But then again, not everyone was the tavern type.

"So, where's she living here in town?" I asked Darny, turning my attention back to the burly innkeeper.

"Let's see..." Darny muttered, rubbing his bewhiskered chin pensively. "Waelin told me you'd be askin' about it. He said he set her up in a rented room over in the northwest quarter, above the cooper's shop. I know that old miser ain't gonna rent his place out for cheap, so the poor girl's probably strugglin'." He shrugged. "I suppose there just ain't much room left within the walls... It drives up the rents, that's for sure!"

Darny gave directions to the building where Celeste had taken up residence since arriving in Gladdenfield. I listened closely, already visualizing navigating the timber buildings and thoroughfares based on time spent in the outpost. I knew my way around the charming frontier town well enough by now.

"Much obliged for the scoop, Darny," I told him sincerely with an appreciative nod. "We'll be checking up on her."

"Anytime, anytime!" Darny replied affably, clearly always happy for a chance to chat. "You folks enjoy the rest of your day. Town's pleased as punch to have you around, David. Folks like to talk about that stunt you pulled at the tournament. Hey, maybe you'd like to come around some evenin' and entertain the people with your tales about it, huh? That'd be a nice thing, for sure."

Laughing at the wily innkeeper's attempts to get me to act as an attraction for his patrons, I gave a playful shrug. "Maybe sometime, Darny," I said. "Pretty busy right now."

"Of course, of course," he said. "No rush!" And

with a final nod, he lumbered off to handle a rowdy dwarf's drink order down the bar. I sipped my ale for a moment, contemplating Celeste's plight.

"She seems typically elven from what Darny says," Leigh remarked after a moment, absently twirling a lock of golden hair around one finger. "Ain't too sure there's gonna be a lotta talkin'. Anyways, we oughta go and introduce ourselves before we leave town."

I nodded thoughtfully. "I did tell her uncle I would check in and make sure she's faring alright here by herself," I said. "Let's pay her a proper visit."

The notion didn't feel like an obligation. Truthfully, I was intrigued to learn more about Celeste and her history. Elves tended toward insularity, so any chance to broaden understanding felt worthwhile. She likely had tales to tell if we took the time to listen.

Leigh and I finished the remainder of our drinks. After that, we paid our tab with one of Darny's staff and headed out into the afternoon sun, ready to call on Celeste.

Leigh and I made our way through the dusty streets of Gladdenfield, following Darny's directions toward the cooper's shop where Celeste was renting a room. The air was warm even though the sun had already passed its zenith. Shadows stretched between buildings, signaling that we had taken our time enjoying lunch and conversation in the Wild Outrider.

We walked past various frontier establishments, exchanging greetings with shopkeepers and residents along the way. Raucous laughter drifted from a saloon, while a tantalizing aroma of freshly baked bread wafted from the bakery.

Everywhere, the energy and charm that made me love this settlement was on display. People knew us both and greeted us with nods and smiles wherever we went.

Before long, we arrived at the cooperage,

recognizable by the stacks of wooden barrels out front. A narrow stair along the side of the building led up to the second-story rooms for rent. Taking a breath, I ascended the creaking steps with Leigh and knocked firmly on the faded timber door.

After a few moments, we heard light footsteps approach before the door swung open. Even though I was prepared to see her again, my mind still swam for a moment as I laid eyes on the elven beauty once more. She had been beautiful in repose when Waelin had shown her to us, but awake and full of life, the vibrant elven maiden was a vision out of a fairy tale.

I swallowed as Celeste looked us over. She was even lovelier than I recalled with her flowing amber hair and finely pointed ears. Her brilliant green eyes widened in surprise to see us.

"Oh! You're the one who helped Uncle cure my illness!" Celeste exclaimed, a smile lighting her delicate features. "Uncle told me about you! Please, come in!" She ushered us eagerly inside the modest room.

"I'm David, and this is Leigh," I introduced us

with a polite nod, proud that I managed control over my voice.

Leigh nodded at Celeste before shooting me a grin that signaled she knew full well that I was impressed by the fine elven maiden's beauty. Luckily, Leigh was the type who did not mind. And neither did Diane, although she had voiced reservations about elves in general.

"Come, come," Celeste said again, her voice warm and her eyes blazing. "It's a humble place, but you are welcome!"

Nodding my thanks, I stepped through the doorway, Leigh right behind me. Celeste's accommodations were simple but cozy, with a bed, wooden table, and chairs by a small fireplace. The curtains were drawn back to let in sunshine.

"It's wonderful to meet you both," Celeste replied graciously. "My name is Celeste, as I gather you know. My uncle spoke very highly of you, David. He's quite grateful." Her voice rang melodically with traces of an elven accent. "As am I. If it weren't for you, I would still slumber. And there would be no saying when — or *if* — I would wake again."

I smiled. "Well, I was glad to help. It's good to see you up and about after your illness." I decided not to mention the Star Jewel directly, unsure if Waelin wished to keep the lengths to which he had gone to cure his niece a secret. "How are you finding life here in Gladdenfield so far?"

Celeste clasped her hands pensively before responding. "Oh, the people seem friendly enough, if a bit... boisterous at times." A delicate frown marred her brow briefly. "It's quite different from home. I play music at the tavern for coin, but I'm unaccustomed to such crowds."

Leigh and I exchanged a knowing look. Clearly, the Wild Outrider's raucous energy clashed with Celeste's more reserved elven sensibilities. I sought to steer the conversation toward more positive territory.

"We'd love to hear you perform sometime," I told Celeste. "Darny speaks very highly of your singing talent. But please don't feel pressured to spend time in the tavern. The frontier life takes adjustment."

Celeste gave a gracious smile, seeming to relax somewhat. "You're too kind. I mainly keep to myself here, but the open air and nature help." She gestured to a carved elven harp in the corner. "Music is my passion. When I play or sing, I can forget any troubles."

I followed her gaze to the elegant instrument. Though plain, its graceful curves spoke to the skill of elven artisans. Soft afternoon light glinted off the polished wood.

"That's a beautiful harp," Leigh remarked warmly. "Bet it makes the sweetest sounds. You'll have to play us a little song sometime!"

Celeste flushed slightly at the praise. "I'd be happy to play for you, if you wish." She moved to take a seat before the harp, adjusting her skirts and long amber braid. "I can do so now, if you wish?"

"I, uh…" I blinked, a little taken aback by the offer. Perhaps this was some elven hospitality thing I did not grasp. Leigh seemed equally taken aback for a moment, but then she gave her radiant smile.

"Sounds lovely!" she purred.

"Sit, please!" Celeste urged us before heading to the harp.

Leigh and I settled into the simple wooden chairs by the window, eager to hear Celeste perform. She sat with poise before the carved elven harp, her willowy frame silhouetted gracefully against the warm afternoon light from outside.

Celeste's long, dexterous fingers began gliding skillfully over the harp strings, plucking out a delicate introductory melody. Her playing was impeccable, each note ringing out with precision. As the introduction swelled, she took a breath and began to sing in her sweet, lilting voice:

"Astardhiel, Lone Haven of shrouded shore,
Where mist-veiled ships with spectral sails glide,
And twilight gulls cry out forevermore
Above the inky tide.

Astardhiel, domain of restless waves,
That surge and crash against weathered stone,
Where elven mariners find early graves,
In the sea's depths unknown.

Astardhiel, bastion bleak yet fair,
Where mournful wind through crumbling spires sings,

And dreams of glory lost still haunt the air,
Of ancient elven kings.

Astardhiel, where melancholy dwells,
And shadowed groves guard fogbound secrets old,
Where emerald moss each fallen pillar swells,
And paths of pearl and gold."

As the final melancholic notes faded into silence, Leigh and I exchanged an awestruck look before breaking into enthusiastic applause. Celeste's singing had transported us wholly into the mournful seaside realm she described with such vivid detail.

"That was absolutely beautiful," I told her sincerely once her blush at our praise had faded. "You have an incredible gift. Thank you for sharing that song with us."

Leigh nodded her enthusiastic agreement, visibly moved by the haunting ballad. "You painted such a clear picture with your voice," she added warmly. "Makes me wish I could visit that place, even if it sounds gloomier than a rainy day!"

Celeste smiled, her fingers drifting idly over the harp strings once more. "You are both too kind.

Music is my greatest passion. I'm pleased you enjoyed the song — it's very old elven lore."

"Well, you have a rare gift," Leigh hummed warmly. "I can see why Darny enjoys having you play at the tavern, even if you find the crowd a bit much at times."

Celeste blushed a little, absently running her fingers over the harp strings again. "Thank you." For a moment, her expression grew sad. "So much has changed recently… Playing helps keep darker thoughts at bay. I… I fell ill shortly after the Upheaval. Many of my kind still mourn the loss of Tannoris and the beautiful cities my kin wrought on its surface. But they have moved on, it seemed, keeping their grief in sealed boxes within their hearts, as we elves are wont to do. However, I cannot shake my melancholy."

My heart went out to her. Having experienced similar pains, I could imagine being uprooted so suddenly from home and transplanted into this boisterous frontier settlement without her family. I sought some way to raise her spirits again.

"We understand this is all still new for you," I

said gently. "Why don't you come sit with us for a moment. I'd love to hear more about this place you sang about. Astardhiel?"

She swallowed, suddenly seeming a little more self-conscious. "Well... I am afraid I have nothing to offer you. I... There is little coin for me right now. I have only water."

"Aw, water will do just fine, sugar," Leigh purred. "David and I just drank and ate our fill at Darny's. We don't need nothing but company."

"Yeah," I agreed. "And maybe we can take you out for a bite to eat after we talked?" I suggested. "There's not much elven cuisine in Gladdenfield, but maybe we could show you some of the frontier cooking that goes on here?"

She warmed up at that and gave a gentle nod. "That sounds lovely," she agreed in a small voice before moving over to sit with us.

Chapter 39

Celeste settled gracefully into the empty chair across from us, smoothing her skirts. She clasped her hands pensively in her lap before looking up to meet our gazes.

"You're very kind to take an interest," she said. "I apologize if I seem melancholy. The frontier life is still so new..." Her voice trailed off wistfully.

"Think nothing of it," I assured her. "We can only imagine how overwhelming all this must be — waking up in Gladdenfield only to have your uncle leave you so soon."

She nodded. "Indeed. He told me that the work he had to do was noble, but I cannot change the way I feel. It's been quite lonely. There are elves here, but they seem distant and removed. It is often so with our kin — long lives make us... insular, even among our own kind. It is a habit I seek to break, for I have no other kin left but Waelin. If I would never dare to meet new people, then I shall never have other company than Waelin's."

She wrinkled her cute nose as she nervously fidgeted with an amber lock of hair. "He is nice... but... Well..."

I chuckled at that. "I believe I know what you mean."

She gave a flustered chuckle, covering her mouth.

"Please, tell us more of your homeland if it would lift your spirits." I smiled encouragingly, hoping to coax Celeste out of her reticence.

Beside me, Leigh nodded agreement. "We'd love to hear any stories or tales you got from Tannoris," she added warmly. "Neither of us know much about the elven part of that world at all. The elves I met ain't very talkative."

"Yes," she said. "They wouldn't be. It is a painful memory to most of us. Tannoris was our empire, and we had raised cities and temples and wonderful works there. Things that took centuries to plan and build, all wrought with the love and the care that my kin have for their works." She shook her head gently. "Many feel the loss, and we speak of it mainly in song and art."

I nodded. "I understand. Still, speaking of something honors its memory as well."

Celeste contemplated my words silently for a moment before responding. "Very well. I agree with that. What would you like to know?" Her tone remained guarded, but there was a spark of interest in her brilliant green eyes now.

I rubbed my chin thoughtfully. "Why don't you tell us about the city you mentioned in your song earlier — Astardhiel? It sounded very striking."

At this, a faraway look entered Celeste's eyes. She gazed past us out the window, seeing vistas only visible in memory now. "Ah yes... Astardhiel was a great elven port city. Lost in the Upheaval, it was a center of trade. We elves have always loved the sea, although she does not love us back. Many were the names written on the Wall of Remembrance, where we honored the mariners who did not return from their voyages. The very stones of that great city had drunk from the melancholy of their loss, and it was a city at once of great joy and pleasure — the kind only mariners know — and of grief and things long passed. Such a beautiful place of contradiction."

As she spoke, Celeste's voice took on a lyrical cadence, as though relaying a tale that had been told many times yet lost none of its wonder. Leigh and I listened raptly, picturing this lost domain.

"It stood upon the shrouded western shores of Tannoris, overlooking a sea of perpetual fog and mist. At dawn and dusk, ghostly ships with ethereal sails would emerge briefly through the mists before vanishing back into obscurity. Often I stood there when Uncle's travels took him there. There was no sight in all of elvendom equal to standing on the Widow's Watch, where wives once looked out over the sea for the men who held their hearts and sailed across the world, faster than love could pursue."

Celeste's hands danced elegantly as though painting the scene. "There, twilight gulls wheeled endlessly through silvery skies above the inky tide that ceaselessly pounds the weathered sea walls. There, more tears have been shed for men lost and more laughter has been heard for happy returns than in any other place on Tannoris."

Her audience of two sat enraptured by Celeste's lyrical account, transported from the cozy frontier room to this melancholy elven haven sprung from her words. I could almost hear the mournful sea wind keening through abandoned spires and imagine the veil of fog enshrouding everything.

When she fell silent at last, Leigh and I exchanged an awestruck look before applauding enthusiastically. Celeste started slightly, as though pulled from a trance, and flushed at our praise.

"My goodness, you made it seem so real," Leigh said earnestly. "I felt like I could almost see that whole ghostly place in my mind's eye while you told it!"

Celeste smiled tremulously. "You are too kind, but I'm pleased my descriptions could bring some small vision of my homeland to you both." Her hands moved idly in her lap, and the delicate movements of her graceful fingers showed her skill as a musician quite plainly.

I leaned forward, still hoping to gently draw her out further. "Astardhiel sounds incredible, but surely other elven cities must have existed in Tannoris too before the Upheaval?" I suggested this gently, not wishing to dredge up painful memories.

The elven beauty smiled softly. "You do not find this talk boring?" she asked, an insecure hint to her voice.

"Not at all," I said. "I have been looking forward to learning more about elves, in fact."

She chuckled. "Well, in that case... Let me get

you two some more water, and then I shall tell you more!"

After refilling our cups, Celeste's expression grew wistful once more, but she continued speaking softly. "Indeed, there were many more elven cities! Although it lacked the solemn and sad beauty of the sea, few elven cities could match the glory of Thilduirne, the dreaming spire." Her voice filled with a mournful longing. "It is there that Uncle held his grand position with the Arcane Academy. To us, it was closest to a home we ever knew."

As we listened, she wove tales of shimmering towers winding endlessly skyward, of buildings that seemed grown rather than constructed, streets paved in pale luminescent stone with patterns that flowed like water.

Vast arched windows and open colonnades afforded views of the surrounding realm that could steal away breath and set the soul soaring. Gently glowing orbs illuminated sprawling plazas where musicians played, and artisans created wonders.

Though Celeste could only describe fragments now, her words conjured fleeting glimpses of grace and artistry in Thilduirne that seemed otherworldly. Leigh and I glimpsed but the faintest echo of the magnificence now lost forever even to most elves.

When at last her lyrical account came to a close, silence lingered. It was not an uncomfortable one, but rather a silence of contemplation of beauty. The elven maiden had a way with words, even more so than most other elves I had known.

Thankful, I laid a hand gently upon her slender arm. "Thank you for sharing those beautiful visions with us, Celeste," I said sincerely.

She placed her delicate hand atop mine and managed a bittersweet smile. "Of course. I hope they may offer you some small window into the world that existed across the veil before the Upheaval sundered all." Her lovely voice held only wistfulness now, not bitterness.

Leigh leaned over to give Celeste a sympathetic

pat on the leg, blinking away a hint of tears. "Well, I'd say you succeeded, sugar. Makes my heart ache to think of all that grandeur and artistry being lost."

Celeste gave a gracious nod, seeming to relax somewhat after unburdening memories long kept sealed away. Some of the melancholy still clinging to her had lifted. She regarded us now with open warmth.

For a long time, we continued speaking of the world of Tannoris as it was before the Upheaval, and I soon learned that the elves had ruled most of that world. The kin — catkin, foxkin, and the rare deerkin — lived on the fringes of civilizations, while the dwarves dominated the mountains and deserts. Monsters — like goblins and kobolds — lived wherever civilization did not thrive, but the elven realms were safe, protected by a powerful host of warriors.

After that, she spoke more of lost cities, including Talamas-Adaa, the wood elven capital I remembered from the tale spun by the Storyteller at the Festival of Aquana. Apparently, Celeste and

Waelin were of wood elven descent — another reason why they struggled with making acquaintances with many local elves, who were not wood elves. To Celeste, the destruction of Talamas-Adaa had been one of the greatest losses of Tannoris. And then there was fabled Talas Ilmanarion, the golden-spired city devoted to Ilmanaria, a shining jewel of arcane power and knowledge.

When she had recounted the tale, she turned to us with a wistful smile. "Surely, you of Earth must have suffered similar losses?"

"Well, sure," I said. "There are places I won't miss, either, but maybe we can talk about that later."

"Yup," Leigh agreed. "I ain't gonna tell her about the tragic loss of Cleveland, Ohio, until I've had a drink."

I chuckled at that, and Celeste laughed along even though it was unlikely she knew what we were talking about.

"Celeste, thank you again for so generously sharing these stories with us," I told her earnestly.

"Perhaps we could take you out for a meal at the tavern now, if you don't find the crowds too overwhelming? A change of scenery might be nice."

Chapter 40

Celeste's eyes lit up at my suggestion to grab a bite to eat at the Wild Outrider. "Oh, that does sound lovely!" she hummed. "I haven't had a proper meal in days, trying to stretch my limited coin." She clasped her hands excitedly. "And truthfully, the idea of sampling this frontier fare you spoke of earlier intrigues me."

Leigh grinned and clapped her hands. "Well, that settles it! You're in for a real treat. Darny's wife makes the best burgers and fries around these parts." She rubbed her smooth stomach appreciatively. "We already had some, but that ain't gonna stop me from having 'em for dinner again! Let's get ourselves back to the Wild Outrider for some grub!"

Laughing at her enthusiasm, Celeste and I readily agreed. The three of us stood, spirits buoyed by the prospect of good company and hearty food. Celeste tidied her harp and grabbed a light shawl before we headed out into the mellow late afternoon sunshine.

The lively sounds of Gladdenfield filled the air as we made our way toward the timber-fronted tavern. Celeste walked between Leigh and me, clasping each of our arms lightly and seeming to relax in our company. I was glad to see her brightening, and she was true to her word of attempting to let go of her kind's usual distant behavior to make new friends.

I admired her for that. I knew it wasn't easy to try to force a change in the way you act, but she had seen the problem after waking up: she was lonely. And with Waelin gone, she would be lonelier still. While she seemed soft and gentle, she obviously had the backbone to act on the things she wanted to improve in her life, and she was opening up to us despite her natural instincts.

Pushing through the saloon doors, we were greeted by the mingled scents of ale and woodsmoke. The place was a lot busier than it had been a few hours ago before we headed out to call on Celeste. There were a few rowdy dwarves, laughing and sloshing ale, but most were humans and a couple of catkin and foxkin local to Gladdenfield Outpost.

Darny looked up from behind the bar and grinned through his bushy beard. "Back so soon?" he bellowed cheerfully. "And back for more of them burgers, I bet! Hey, and you brought the songbird! Welcome, welcome!"

Celeste flushed prettily at being recognized as we claimed a table. Soon enough, Darny came by to take our order personally, clearly eager to show off his wife's culinary skills to our elven guest.

"We'll take three of your finest burgers and a hearty helping of fries all around," Leigh told Darny with a wink. He gave us a thumbs up and bustled off, yelling our order to his wife, the cook.

While we waited, I asked Celeste about her uncle and if she had received any word from him since his departure. Her expression grew pensive. "Only a brief letter to say he arrived safely in the city," she replied. "I know his work is important, but I do miss his company."

I nodded sympathetically. "I'm sure he misses you too. Hopefully his time there will pass swiftly."

Beside me, Leigh gave Celeste's arm an affectionate pat, eliciting a small smile from the elf girl.

I decided to open up a bit more to help put Celeste further at ease. "You know, I first came to Gladdenfield not long ago myself, so I understand feeling out of place," I told her.

She perked up, looking curious. "Oh? What

brought you here?"

"Well, I actually lived in the city of New Springfield," I explained. "It's a settlement guarded by the Coalition of humans and elves, not too far from here. But I never got a Class after the Upheaval, and I was kind of stuck there."

Celeste nodded. "Many of your people remain confined to the cities without Classes, yes?" At the mention of Classes, something seemed to pass over her pretty face — an expression I could not quite place.

I did not know her Class, and I had not asked her about it yet. I had to admit to some curiosity, and in my mind, I had her made out for a mage or a sorceress of some kind. But her expression told me there was something else going on — something unknown to me. It could be cultural, but it could be personal as well — perhaps a combination. I knew little about elves, and so I decided to tread carefully around the subject.

"Exactly," I agreed. "Those without a Class who do leave the cities generally come to a bad end. But I was scouted by a representative of the Frontier

Division named Caldwell. He saw talent in me, and I was allowed to undergo an awakening ritual. After that — even though my Class didn't activate right away — he brought me out here to set me up with a homestead and a companion."

Celeste's emerald gaze swiveled over to Leigh. "Leigh is your companion?" she asked.

I chuckled. "Well, she is too," I said, "but Caldwell set me up with Diane. She is a foxkin, and she's currently at the homestead, about a twenty-minute ride out of town."

"Oh," she hummed, knowingly. "You have more than one wife? I did not know humans had marriages similar to ours." I believed I noticed a spark of interest in those big, green eyes, but Leigh's giggling drew me away.

"I ain't his wife... yet." She threw me a teasing wink.

Celeste blinked, confused. "And yet you touch each other like you have relations," she mused.

I grinned, remembering this little detail from most elves in the city. "Yes, some humans have *relations* when they're not married... yet." I winked at Leigh, teasing her right back, and she grinned and bit her lip as her dainty foot nudged me under the table.

"I see," Celeste hummed. "Like the catkin?"

I nodded. I knew foxkin required some kind of formal opening of courtship — something I had done accidentally with Diane at first and later repeated on purpose. Apparently, the catkin were a little looser.

"Anyway," I continued with a wistful smile, remembering my eye-opening first journey to Gladdenfield. "Gladdenfield was the first real frontier town I saw. It was quite an adjustment, but the people welcomed me kindly enough. And then I met Diane and Leigh and... well, the rest is history."

Celeste smiled warmly. "Fate brought you here, as it brought me. And now we all have a new home." Her expression had softened after learning of our similar circumstances.

"You're right about that," I agreed, feeling a pleasant sense of kinship with her.

Our conversation was soon interrupted by Darny

arriving with three piping hot plates stacked with juicy burgers and crispy fries. He set them down with a flourish. "Dig in, folks! Ain't nothin' better than my good wife's cookin'."

Celeste's eyes widened at the size of the burger. It was a big, juicy heap of goodness — a far cry from the reserved helpings of elven cuisine.

Hesitantly, she picked it up with both hands and took a dainty bite. We watched eagerly for her reaction.

As she chewed, her green eyes slowly lit up. "By the gods, this is incredible!" she exclaimed after swallowing.

Leigh and I laughed jovially at her enthusiasm. "We thought you'd like it!" Leigh said, already biting happily into her own burger, cheese stretching as she pulled it back. "I knew you were a regular frontier girl deep down!"

Any remaining reservations forgotten, Celeste took a much bigger second bite, sauce and juices running down her delicate chin. I chuckled and handed her a napkin, which she accepted with an embarrassed but delighted smile. Soon we were all devouring the mouthwatering fare with gusto.

Over our meal, the conversation flowed easily between us, frequently punctuated by Celeste's exclamations of amazement at each new taste sensation — the smoky meat, salty fries, and tangy condiments were wholly foreign to her palate. But she clearly relished every bite.

Leigh regaled us with humorous anecdotes about customers at her store, eliciting smiles and laughter all around. The warm atmosphere kindled an almost familial camaraderie between us. For the first time since arriving, Celeste seemed wholly at ease.

When at last we sat back with empty plates and satisfied stomachs, Darny came by beaming. "So, what did y'all think of these here famous burgers?" He turned expectantly toward Celeste.

Celeste laughed musically. "They were utterly divine! My compliments to the chef."

Darny grinned from ear to ear and promised to pass along the glowing praise to his wife. Still smiling, he gathered up our dirty dishes and headed off.

As we lingered, idly sipping mugs of honeyed mead, I studied Celeste. The warm glow of lantern light played across her refined features. With food in her belly and pleasant company surrounding her, she seemed transformed from the melancholy creature I had first met.

Catching my eye, Celeste smiled brightly. "Thank you both again for such a lovely evening," she said earnestly. "It feels wonderful having friends here now. You and Leigh have shown me such kindness since my arrival."

"You just let us know if you need anything at all," Leigh told her. "David and I are happy to help you get settled in around here however we can. Ain't that right, baby?"

I nodded agreement. "Of course. We want you to feel at home in Gladdenfield." Impulsively, I covered Celeste's delicate hand with my own. Her answering smile lit up the room.

For a time, we simply sat comfortably together watching the tavern crowd. Though still boisterous, their energetic spirit no longer seemed to trouble Celeste. She pointed out some of the regulars she had come to recognize, assigning them amusing nicknames that had Leigh and me laughing heartily.

"So," I said after the tavern grew busier and busier. "Were you going to play a little for the people tonight? I'm pretty sure Darny would appreciate it."

She smiled and nodded. "Well, I certainly am in a happy mood."

"Good," Leigh hummed. "We loved the song about the elven haven, but perhaps somethin' a little more chipper would do for tonight."

Grinning, Celeste hopped to her feet. "I have just the thing!"

Chapter 41

Celeste eagerly took the small stage at the front of the tavern, the lively crowd turning their attention to her as she stepped into the lantern light. An expectant hush fell over the room in anticipation of her song.

With grace, Celeste lifted the elven harp settled

on a stool before her. Her fingers began plucking a cheerful, upbeat melody that immediately buoyed the mood of all gathered. As she played the introduction, she shot Leigh and me a playful wink.

When the jaunty intro swelled to a crescendo, Celeste's crystalline voice rang out in joyful song:

"Come one, come all, let's gather and sing,
Clasp hands, let cheer fill halls that long rang somber,
No more shall we dwell on sorrow past,
Tonight we celebrate life, love and laughter!

Sing praise for the bounty of forest and field,
Each seed sown, each harvest yielded,
Lift voices in thanks for hands joined as one,
The warmth shared between friends, lovers, and kin.

Come one, come all, let's gather and sing,
A light in the dark, let music ring,
No more shall we dwell on sorrow past,
Tonight we celebrate life, love, and laughter!"

The upbeat lyrics immediately stirred the crowd's spirits. All around heads bobbed and tankards thumped enthusiastically on tables. Beside me, Leigh whooped and hollered her encouragement.

Caught up in the festive atmosphere, I found myself clapping along as Celeste repeated the infectious chorus. Her voice soared sweet and clear over the adoring din of the crowd. Darny, too, was humming and swaying behind the bar, grinning through his great beard.

When at last the final notes faded, the tavern erupted into thunderous applause and cheers. Celeste laughed and curtsied gracefully in thanks; cheeks endearingly flushed from her energetic performance. As the calls for an encore rang out, she gave us a meaningful look before retaking her seat. I knew she would sing again before the night was through.

Still grinning, Celeste returned to our table breathless but elated. Her brilliant green eyes shone brightly as she accepted our profuse congratulations. "Oh my, performing never fails to invigorate my spirits," she confessed happily, one hand pressed melodramatically to her chest. "Music truly feeds the soul."

"You said it!" Leigh agreed enthusiastically.

"Why, the whole place was alive and toe-tappin' thanks to your song, sugar. I ain't never seen ole Darny look so cheerful." We all laughed at the image of the usually gruff bartender swaying and humming along behind the counter, clearly caught up in the performance.

Our lively conversation stretched long into the evening. Celeste appeared wholly at ease now amidst the tavern's energetic atmosphere. She regaled us with amusing stories of her uncle Waelin's many eccentricities that had me chuckling into my drink. It seemed that even dour elven archmages possessed quirky sides behind closed doors.

As promised, Celeste performed several more songs as the night wore on, varying from boisterous drinking tunes that had the crowd roaring and pounding tankards to gentler ballads that captivated with their melancholic beauty. Each time she finished, I found myself hoping she would play just one more.

During her breaks, Celeste mingled briefly but amiably with various tavern patrons who approached our table to offer praise and compliments on her talents. Though still reserved, she accepted their admiration graciously before returning her full attention to Leigh and me.

For my part, I made sure to keep Celeste's drink filled and saw her fed a steady stream of snacks that Darny brought over, not wanting the now merry elf maiden to overdo it on an empty stomach. She seemed surprised but touched by my solicitousness.

As the night stretched on, I was thankful for Leigh's tireless cheer and wit that never failed to elicit laughter from Celeste and me. She regaled us with exaggerated tales of sticky-fingered patrons trying to pilfer goods from her store until we were all gasping for breath between bouts of giggles. The ale and fellowship kindled warmth in my heart.

During one of Celeste's breaks, Leigh amused us by attempting to teach me a traditional elvish drinking song, though it quickly dissolved into silly improvisation since neither of us recalled more than a few lines. Celeste nearly choked laughing at Leigh's absurd lyrics, and I quickly joined in her contagious mirth.

The hour grew late, but none made mention of turning in just yet. This lively celebration of new friendship still had us enthralled. When Celeste shyly took my hand during one of our talks, I gave it an encouraging squeeze, hoping to convey without need for words the joy her companionship brought me. Her answering smile was radiant.

Eventually, even Leigh's indefatigable energy showed hints of flagging, though she valiantly stifled yawns behind one hand lest we tease her. Taking pity on my poor sleepy friend, I declared that the next song would be our last for the night. Leigh shot me a grateful look at the prospect of soon retiring to a cozy bed.

Celeste happily took the stage once more amidst enthusiastic applause as calls rang out for one final tune before closing time. Lantern light shone softly on her windswept braid and elegant face as she smiled down benevolently at the now subdued crowd awaiting her song.

Plucking a gentle melody, Celeste filled the cozy

tavern with her dulcet voice one last time:

"The hour is late, the candle burned low,
Linger we now at our day's end.
Sweet company, glad tidings shared,
Our time together at a close.

Farewell, good folk, till we meet again,
Rest now weary bones and mind.
Dream of joy found, friends around,
Safe at home, worries left behind."

A hush fell as Celeste's velvety voice conveyed images of warm hearths and restful sleep awaiting after a fulfilling day of kinship and cheer. Her mellifluous singing carried me along until I could nearly feel the tantalizing softness of pillows and blankets.

As the final notes faded gently, reverent applause broke out. Celeste curtsied before drifting back our way through the signs of farewell. Leigh and I congratulated Celeste once more as we slowly finished our final round that Darny announced was last call for the night.

Her singing had imbued the long night with such joy and life that words could not encapsulate our gratitude. As she smiled happily across from us, I glimpsed a new blaze of life shining in her eyes; she seemed to have revived from her melancholy.

The tavern had mostly emptied by last call, leaving just a few patrons nursing final tankards and laughing and talking still, desiring not yet to give up on the night. Soft lantern light cast a cozy glow over our table as we chatted idly, reluctant for this magical evening to end.

As we sat and basked in the afterglow of a pleasant night, I felt the bonds of friendship blossom. Celeste had surprised me by being so much more than another aloof elf. While there was still the characteristic distance and haughtiness to her, it was plain to see she was making an effort. And I found myself simply watching the interplay of firelight across her refined features as she looked across the tavern with a satisfied smile.

When at last even Leigh could no longer fully smother her yawns, she stood reluctantly and announced "Welp, I better visit the little girl's room 'fore we mosey on outta here." She punctuated her words with a pointed wink in my direction as she walked off, and I understood at once that she was going to give me a moment to close off the evening with Celeste. I smiled at the realization; she was sweet to give me that space.

Left momentarily alone with Celeste, I decided to be bold. Taking her delicate hand, I told her earnestly, "I had a lot of fun tonight."

Celeste's answering blush was charming. "The delight was mine," she replied softly. "I have not connected so deeply with new friends in a long time."

I chuckled softly. "You know, I was expecting to do a simple check-up — to fulfill my promise to your uncle Waelin. Instead, I had a very enjoyable evening. I would like to see you again."

She smiled softly, slightly abashed, and the way her cheeks lit up went straight to my heart. "I would like that as well, David," she said.

"I'll still be in town tomorrow — at least for a little bit before Leigh and I head back to my homestead. Maybe we could meet up in the early morning and go for a walk. Would you enjoy that?"

She nodded enthusiastically. "I would love that!"

"Great," I said with a smile as Leigh reappeared, making her way back to us. "When shall I come by?"

"I rise early," she said, her green eyes fixed on me. "With the sun. You can come before breakfast if you like — as early as you like, really."

I nodded enthusiastically. "I will be there at first light."

Just then, Leigh rejoined us, shooting me a knowing smile. "I think Darny wants us outta here," she said. "How 'bout we head on back?"

I nodded, and so did Celeste. Together, the three of us made our way out into the cool evening air.

Chapter 42

The three of us stepped out into the cool night air after leaving the warm and cozy tavern. Celeste smiled happily, her cheeks still flushed from the lively atmosphere and one too many honeyed ales.

"Thank you both again for such a delightful evening," she said earnestly, her green eyes luminous in the moonlight. "I cannot remember the last time I felt such a sense of belonging."

"We're just happy you had fun!" Leigh replied warmly, giving Celeste an impulsive hug that made the elf maiden laugh. "It was a real treat gettin' to hear you sing and play that harp."

I nodded in agreement. "Hopefully this is just the first of many nice evenings together," I added sincerely. Something about Celeste's creative spirit and delicate beauty stirred me, that much was clear, and I was keen to see how she would get along with Diane.

Celeste's answering smile was radiant. "I would like that very much," she said softly. For a moment, we lingered there together beneath the starry sky, reluctant for the night to end.

But eventually, I stifled a yawn, the lateness of the hour catching up with me. "Suppose we should get you home safely," I told Celeste. "Why don't the two of us walk you back to your place?"

Celeste consented with a broad smile, eager to let the night last just a little while longer. Her place was clear across town, but the fresh night air felt invigorating after so long cooped up in the smoky tavern. Celeste slipped her arms through ours as we walked, surrounding herself with friendship.

Along the way, we pointed out landmarks that had meaning for us — the spot where we had gathered for our exciting procession into the forest for the Aquana Festival, the gate through which I had first entered Gladdenfield Outpost with Caldwell, and of course Leigh's general store.

Celeste listened with bright interest, asking an occasional question in her dulcet voice. Though the hour was late, the quaint thoroughfares held magic, and our meandering path was unhurried.

Before long, we reached the modest building where Celeste was staying. The streets were silent now, and all were sleeping in Gladdenfield Outpost but us. Celeste hesitated at the base of the creaky steps leading up to her room.

"Thank you again for everything," she said sincerely, clasping my hands for a moment before her bashfulness took over again. "I cannot properly express what your kindness has meant to me." Her eyes shone with emotion. "Gladdenfield was very lonely to me, and your presence here has changed these things."

"Think nothing of it, sugar," Leigh assured her fondly. "You just let us know if you need anything at all."

I nodded, maintaining eye contact with her. "It was our pleasure," I assured her. "We had a great time!"

Celeste smiled tremulously and pulled us both into an impulsive hug. I rubbed her back reassuringly, sensing the depth of her gratitude. The nearness of her body and the sweet and enchanting scent of her made me long for more. This evening had clearly meant the world to her, as it had to me.

"Get some rest," I told Celeste gently as we finally stepped back. She nodded, wispy strands of amber hair blowing in the faint breeze. With a parting wave, she turned and gracefully ascended the steps out of sight.

Leigh and I lingered for a moment, thoughtful expressions on our faces as we recalled the unexpectedly heartwarming time shared with the elf maiden. The frigid loneliness that had clung to Celeste seemed to have melted away.

"She seems to be coming out of her shell," Leigh remarked appreciatively as we finally resumed our walk through the slumbering outpost.

I hummed agreement. "I'm glad we checked in on her. She just needed a little companionship." And yet, I sensed Celeste still guarded part of herself away behind elven reserve. But that was only natural with new friends.

We soon arrived outside at Leigh's cozy shop, the floorboards creaking familiarly as we walked up to the front of her shop. Sinking tiredly onto a bench, I smiled over at Leigh.

"I'm planning to see Celeste again tomorrow before we head back," I told her. "Thought I'd invite her on a morning walk if she's feeling up to it after the late night."

Leigh's answering smile was knowing. "Well now, ain't that just charming," she teased lightly, giving my leg an affectionate pat. "I think she'd enjoy that."

Despite the gentle ribbing, her tone held only

warmth. Like Diane, Leigh seemed to understand my curiosity about the elf musician. Perhaps she sensed my attraction, but there was no resentment or jealousy there. I knew that Leigh liked her, too, but there was still the matter of introducing her to Diane. That would come later…

I pulled Leigh into a grateful hug, feeling lucky to have the support of both my beloveds. "I care for you just as much, Leigh," I assured her sincerely. "Never doubt that."

Leigh just chuckled, nuzzling against me. "Baby, I know," she said simply. And from her tone, I knew she meant it. There was no acrimony or envy marring our connection. For that, I felt immensely grateful.

"Now," she purred. "Why don't we head on back to my bed?" She ground herself against me, and before I could even answer, she buried me in a passionate kiss that had been simmering to explode all night, evaporating any tiredness I had…

Chapter 43

Leigh and I stumbled into the store, already kissing and touching. My hands were under Leigh's shirt, seeking soft skin, and she ground her hips on me, making me hard. Conjoined like that and panting with lust, we barged through the store, making our way to the stairs up to Leigh's apartment.

Once in the apartment, Leigh's soft laugh echoed in the quiet room as she pulled back from our kiss. "Why don't you go light the fire, sugar," she purred.

"Good idea," I agreed. I nodded, making some effort to pull myself away.

"I'll be right back," she promised, her voice husky, her eyes dark with desire. The sight of her walking away, her hips swaying in a tantalizing rhythm, sent a jolt of anticipation through me.

I made my way to the fireplace, the soft crackle of the unlit wood only adding to the heated tension in the room. With one swift move, I lit the fire, the flickering light casting a warm and inviting glow on the leather couch. It was a cozy setting, perfect for what was to come.

The light from the fire refracted off the crystal decanter on the table, the amber liquid inside promising a sweet burn. The room was filled with the rich scent of fresh forest air and the sweet scent of Leigh, a heady mix that made my pulse quicken.

I turned around as I heard the soft sound of her footfalls. Leigh had changed into a flimsy thong and a wispy, transparent top, her curves accentuated, her freckled skin glowing in the soft light.

"Like what you see?" she asked, a teasing smile playing on her lips. Her blonde hair cascaded down her shoulders, framing her face and giving her an ethereal glow. The sight of her took my breath away.

I stepped closer, my hand reaching out to pull her against me. Her skin was soft, warm, inviting as my fingertips traced the curve of her waist, the swell of her hips, the roundness of her breasts.

Her top was a gossamer barrier, doing little to hide her hardened nipples. I brushed my thumb over them, her gasp echoing in the quiet room. She leaned into my touch, her eyes closing, her lips parting in a silent moan.

In response, my cock throbbed, the fabric of my pants doing little to hide my arousal. "You're wickedly beautiful," I murmured into her ear, my breath making her shiver.

She chuckled, her fingers deftly unbuttoning my shirt. "And you're wonderfully sinful," she replied, her hands roaming my bare chest, her fingers tracing the lines of my muscles.

Her touch was electrifying, sending jolts of pleasure down my spine. I savored the feel of her hands on me, the way her fingers explored my body as if she was learning a new language. Every touch, every stroke made me want her more.

She unbuckled my belt next, her fingers fumbling in her eagerness. I helped her, kicking off my boots and stepping out of my pants, leaving me in my boxers. Her eyes widened at the sight, a wicked smile crossing her face.

"Aren't you a sight for sore eyes?" she murmured, her fingers skimming the waistband of my underwear. I grinned, my hands on her hips pulling her closer until our bodies were flush against each other.

She pressed herself against me, her breasts against my bare chest, her hips grinding into mine. I groaned, my hands splaying on her back, pulling her closer, the thin fabric of her thong doing little to hide her heat.

Our lips met in a heated kiss, tongues exploring

and tasting. The world outside ceased to exist, everything narrowing down to the woman in my arms and the raw desire coursing through me.

I lifted her up, her legs wrapping around my waist. She was a perfect fit, her body molded against mine in a way that was intoxicatingly perfect. We continued to kiss, our bodies moving in perfect sync.

I walked us over to the couch, laying her down on the soft leather. She looked up at me, her blue eyes dark with desire. The sight of her, sprawled on the couch, her body flushed and ready, was enough to make me shudder.

I sat between her legs, my hands resting on her thighs. She looked at me, her chest heaving, her lips swollen from our kisses. She was a vision, her skin glowing in the soft light, her body awaiting my touch.

"David," she whispered, her hands reaching out to me. I leaned down to claim her lips again, my hands exploring her body, my fingers tracing her curves.

She arched into my touch, her hands on my back,

her nails digging into my skin. I moaned into her mouth, the pain mixing with pleasure, making me need her so much.

My hand slid down her body, tracing the line of her thong. She gasped, her hips bucking up to meet my touch. I chuckled, my fingers teasing her through the thin fabric.

Leigh whimpered in response, her fingers tangling in my hair, pulling me closer. My mouth left a trail of kisses down her neck as I slowly gave in, my hands continuing their exploration, slipping under her transparent top.

I reached her breasts, my fingers tracing the freckles scattered on her skin as I peeled the flimsy top out of the way. I looked up at her, her eyes were closed, her lips parted in a silent moan. I took a hardened nipple into my mouth, the taste of her skin sweet on my tongue.

She writhed beneath me, her body responding to my every touch. I switched to the other breast, giving it the same attention. Her moans filled the room, the sound making me harder.

I slid my hand down her body, tracing the line of

her thong again. She was wet, ready for me, and I felt my need rise, my power thrum with the desire to claim her.

"David," she gasped again, her hands pulling at my hair.

I looked up at her. Her eyes bright with desire. She bit her lip, a lustful look crossing her face.

"Let me sit on your face, baby," she whispered, her voice shaky with anticipation. "Let me suck your dick while you eat my pussy…"

I groaned in response, the dirty words making my cock twitch. My mind exploded with the dirty images — to have the voluptuous blonde sit on my face was a fantasy straight out of heaven, and I grunted with desire as she gently pushed me back and turned around.

I panted with lust as Leigh hovered over me, wearing nothing but her skimpy thong and her disheveled see-through top. Her big, round ass was a sight from heaven as she swung one leg over me, almost reverse-cowgirl style.

"Bring that ass down," I groaned, giving it a slap that made her yelp with delight.

A teasing smile played on her lips as she positioned herself, adjusting so her plump ass was directly above my face. The scent of her arousal hit me, heady and intoxicating, as she began to lower herself down.

"Your wish is my command," she hummed in her sultry accent, her voice dripping with anticipation.

My hands found their way to her hips, fingers digging into her soft flesh as I guided her down towards my eager mouth. The taste of her on my tongue was sweet, addictive, making me want more.

As my lips latched onto her, she gasped, a soft cry escaping her lips. My tongue swirled around her, exploring her folds, savoring every drop of her essence.

Her hands fumbled, seeking me out. When her fingers finally wrapped around my hardened length, I groaned into her, the sensation shooting straight to my core. Her touch was soft yet firm, stroking me with a rhythm that matched my own.

I pushed her thong to the side, giving me unhindered access to her. As I delved deeper, her moans grew louder, spurring me on.

"Oh, David," she breathed, her voice strained with lust. "Don't stop...please."

The room was filled with the sounds of our pleasure, the soft creaking of the couch, the rustle of fabric, and the hitched breaths and low moans echoing off the apartment walls.

I squeezed her ass, pulling her closer, my tongue delving deeper. Her body shivered in response, her grip on my cock tightening.

My thumb slipped into her tight little hole, and she cried out, her body bucking against me.

"Oh god, yes," she panted. "I want to feel you inside me. I'm gonna... Ahnn... I'm gonna make you ready for me, baby..."

The arousal in her voice was an aphrodisiac, spurring me on. I pumped my thumb in and out, matching my rhythm to her strokes on my cock.

Her body tightened, her breath hitching as she neared her climax. "I'm...I'm close," she moaned, her voice barely a whisper.

I doubled my efforts, my tongue flicking against her faster, harder. My thumb moved with a frantic pace, each thrust bringing her closer to the edge as I teased her tight little backdoor into submission.

Her hand returned to my cock, her touch slow and teasing. "I love to taste you, baby," she purred, her blue eyes sparkling with mischief. "I love your cock. I love your cum. Ahnn... I want you to fill me up good tonight, baby."

My heart pounded in my chest, my body humming with anticipation as I was captured between her delicious thighs. My cock bucked as she leaned down, her lips hovering over my hardened length.

Her tongue flicked out, teasing the sensitive tip. I hissed in a breath, my hands clenching on her hips as I pulled her closer, never giving her a moment's mercy from my tongue.

But the sensation of her taking me into her mouth was enough to make my head spin, my mind clouded with pleasure. Her mouth was warm, wet, a perfect contrast to the cool air of the room. The need to cum in her warm mouth was almost overwhelming, but I kept it at bay, desiring to last longer.

Her tongue swirled around me, making me groan in pleasure. The feeling of her, bare and flushed with desire, was overwhelming.

But I gave her as little mercy as she gave me. I kept lapping, licking at her tight little nub as my thumb teased her forbidden little hole. And by her trembling and shaking, I could feel that she would soon have to give up.

"Ahnn... Fuck... David..."

I went even faster, pinning her juicy round ass on my face with my hand and licking and sucking on her little clit as I teased and fingered her tight little pucker. I wouldn't allow her to pull back, and she had no choice but to ride the pleasure I was giving her.

"I'm... Oh, fuck!"

Her body convulsed, a scream of pleasure ripping from her as she tumbled over the edge.

"Oh, David!" she cried, her body shaking with the force of her orgasm.

I continued to lap at her, drawing out her climax. Her body shuddered above me, her grip on my cock faltering as the waves of her orgasm washed over her. Pressing her pussy and ass on my face, I kept at it, eating her up and making her cum harder than she ever had before. She moaned and trembled, sending ripples down her delicious ass, until she finally experienced the last of her lashing orgasm with a gasp.

Then, she collapsed on top of me, her body limp and sated. Her chest heaved as she tried to catch her breath, her skin slick with sweat.

I held her in place, my arms wrapped around her as I continued to toy with her. Her body twitched with every touch, aftershocks of her orgasm still coursing through her.

"David..." She took a deep breath. "Fuuuuck..."

"I'm not done with you yet," I growled, my voice muffled between those delicious thighs.

"Ohh, baby," she moaned. "Please... Fuck me. Fuck me until I can't see straight no more."

I didn't need to hear anything more than Leigh's desire for me to fuck her brains out. With a growl of lust, I pushed her off me, still dressed in her skimpy thong, the strap peeled away to reveal her delicious pussy, and her transparent top.

She yelped and laughed as she momentarily lost her balance, and I reveled in the sight of her beautiful round ass in that thong.

"You're gonna get it now, Leigh," I warned, my voice echoing in the cozy apartment.

Leigh giggled, the sound as sweet as honey as she shook her ass at me. "Bring it on, cowboy," she challenged, her blue eyes gleaming with arousal.

I edged towards her on my knees. She was on her hands and knees, her lush ass presented to me, her blonde hair cascading over her shoulders and her freckles glowing in the soft candlelight as she gave me a challenging look over her shoulder.

I positioned myself behind her, my throbbing

cock brushing against her ass cheeks. She gasped, wiggling her hips, tempting me with her curvy body. I couldn't resist. Not that I wanted to.

With one hand on her hip and the other guiding my cock, I pushed the head into her tight, wet pussy. I went fast on purpose, giving her little time to adapt, but I knew she liked that. She gasped; the sound swallowed by the blankets she'd buried her face into.

Her pussy was hot and tight, and I groaned as I sank deeper, her inner walls gripping me like a velvet glove as I fucked her with her thong still on. The sight of her ass bouncing in rhythm with my thrusts was intoxicating.

My hands moved to her hips, gripping them for leverage. Each thrust elicited a breathy moan from her lips, each sound pushing me closer to the edge.

I could see her fingernails digging into the floor, her body tensing and releasing in rhythm with my movements. I didn't hold back, my muscles straining as I pounded into her.

"Fuck, David," she moaned, her voice muffled by the blankets. "Yes, baby!"

I lost myself in it. My thrusts becoming more forceful, the sound of our bodies slapping together filling the room. She met each thrust with a push of her own, her ass slapping against my hips in a delicious rhythm. And every time our sweating bodies connected, a ripple passed through that delicious ass.

As I fucked Leigh, her hand snaked around, her fingers parting her ass cheeks. I groaned as she guided my thumb to her puckered hole, the sight of my thumb disappearing into her tightness making me groan. She really liked butt stuff, and I was more than happy to give her what she wanted.

Her moans grew louder, more high-pitched as I began to finger her asshole, her body trembling with pleasure. The sight of her writhing beneath me, her ass wiggling in delight, was overwhelming.

I could feel her pussy clenching around my cock, her body trembling as she neared her orgasm. The sight of her in the throes of pleasure was intoxicating, my own climax building.

"Fuck, David!" she screamed, her voice echoing

off the walls. "I want your cum in my pussy. Fill me up, baby!"

I growled, my thrusts becoming more erratic as I neared my climax. My body was on fire, the pleasure building in my lower abdomen, threatening to explode.

Her body was a sight to behold, her breasts swaying beneath her, her ass jiggling with each thrust. Her skin was flushed, her freckles standing out against her reddened skin, her blonde hair sticking to her sweaty forehead.

I could feel her pussy contracting around me, and I knew she was close. I slowed my pace to a more teasing rhythm, and I chuckled as she gave a frustrated mewl and slammed her big ass against my hips.

"Ahnn, David," she moaned, her voice filled with pleasure. "I wanna cum!"

With a grunt, I slammed into her again. I went hard, merciless, with my thumb still buried in her ass, and the dual stimulation made her scream in pleasure.

"That's it! Yes!" she cried out.

We achieved perfect rhythm now, slamming into each other, sweaty bodies slapping together, and I knew she was so close.

"C-cumming! David... Ahnn! I'm cumming!"

I rammed into her, and another orgasm ripped through her, her pussy clenching around me in waves, clenching me for all I was worth, practically begging for my cum. The sight of her coming undone beneath me was beautiful, her body trembling in ecstasy.

"Fuck, Leigh," I groaned, my body straining as I fought the urge to cum. "You're so fucking tight."

Her body was still trembling as I continued to fuck her, grabbing her thong for leverage and accidentally tearing it in my vigor. It only made her coo more with pleasure, her body still trembling under the force of her orgasm.

"Uhnn..." she moaned. "David... it's so goooood."

I grabbed her hips, my cock sliding in and out of her wet, hot pussy. The sight of her sated body, her ripped thong, her blonde hair a wild mess, her skin flushed and sweaty, was driving me over the edge.

"David," she moaned. "I need your cum. Cum in me, baby!"

I growled, my body tensing as I felt my climax nearing. I increased my pace, my cock slamming into her, my balls slapping against her.

Her pussy clenched around me, her body urging me on, pushing me towards my climax. I could feel the pressure building, the pleasure overwhelming.

"Fuck," I groaned, my voice strained. "I'm cumming."

With one final, powerful thrust, I came, my cock pulsing as I shot my load deep inside her.

"Yes!" she cried out. "Fill me up, David! Give it to me."

Her body was still trembling, her orgasm subsiding as I continued to fuck her, spurting rope after rope of my hot seed into her fertile, voluptuous body. I kept going until I was all empty, and Leigh gave a satisfied mewl when I groaned, having spent my seed inside Leigh's delicious pussy.

As I pulled out, she gave a little squeal, and a final spurt of cum glazed her perfect, jiggling ass cheek. Grinning broadly at the sight, I collapsed onto the blankets beside her.

"Fuck, David," Leigh purred as she collapsed next to me, her transparent top disheveled, and her thong torn and pulled to the side.

"I just did," I quipped, my voice husky, and that won a naughty giggle from her.

With a smirk, I traced a finger along her collarbone, down the valley of her breasts, and further still, until I found the lace edge of her thong.

"David," she sighed, her voice barely a whisper. "That was…" she trailed off, lost for words. I pressed a soft kiss to her forehead, a silent promise of more to come.

We lay there, tangled in each other's arms, basking in the afterglow. Her fingers traced lazy patterns on my chest, a soothing rhythm that had my eyes growing heavy.

"Sleepy, cowboy?" she teased, her southern twang bringing a smile to my face. "Mmm," was all I could manage, my body heavy with satisfaction.

Sleep came as we lounged on the blankets, and we only just managed to find enough energy to make our way to Leigh's bedroom, where a well-earned slumber awaited.

Chapter 44

The next morning, I awoke before dawn, eager to see Celeste again. After washing up, I quickly donned my shirt and jeans, ready for a pleasant morning stroll through town with the elf maiden. Leigh was still sleeping soundly, so I left a brief note letting her know I had stepped out.

The morning air was crisp and refreshing as I headed briskly across the sleepy settlement toward Celeste's lodging. All was still tranquil at this hour, with only a few early rising souls up and about on errands. Overhead, the sky was just beginning to brighten.

Arriving at Celeste's building, I headed up the creaky steps and gave a firm knock, hoping I hadn't woken her. After a few moments, I heard stirrings within before the door swung open, revealing Celeste's lovely face peering out. She blinked for a moment before a radiant smile lit her fair features.

"David, how lovely to see you," she greeted me warmly, her musical voice still husky with sleep.

Celeste was clad in a thin robe, and I caught glimpses of her lithe form silhouetted alluringly against the lamplight within. She seemed very much awake, which meant she was indeed an early riser like I was.

"I hope it's not too early," I said with a smile. "Most of the town is still sleeping, by the looks of things. But I always liked getting up early, and I can see you do too."

She grinned broadly. "Rise early, and you have done much work before others are yet to begin. It is something Uncle Waelin taught me."

"Wise of him," I said. "I hope you don't mind a little stroll while the morning is fresh?"

Celeste shook her head, wispy amber locks swaying beguilingly over her shoulders. "Not at all, a walk sounds perfect," she assured me. "Just allow me a few moments to dress."

I waited outside, enjoying the peaceful dawn air until Celeste reemerged looking radiant as always in a pale green dress that complemented her eyes. Together we set off down the sleepy lanes, our footfalls echoing companionably.

"Did you sleep well?" I asked as we walked. "Ale didn't play parts?"

Celeste giggled before she hummed an affirmative, clasping her hands behind her back. "I did not drink *too* much. And you?" she asked. "Were your accommodations comfortable?"

I chuckled. "Leigh always makes sure I'm right at home there."

"She seems very sweet," Celeste hummed, searching my expression for perhaps a clue as to my relationship with Leigh. She had expected an elven marriage, but I would not make her much wiser yet. There would be time to speak of such things later.

"She is," I agreed. "She was still asleep when I went out, though."

"Must be tired, then," Celeste said, a little twinkle in her eye.

I laughed. "Come on," I said. "Let's go to the palisade. I saw there's a platform unused, and it would be the perfect place to see the sunrise."

"I hope the guards won't get angry," she quipped.

Our playful banter came easily already. I was struck again by how Celeste's initial shyness had so swiftly melted away into casual warmth. Either she was placating me very well, or her desire for company truly was profound. I hoped for the latter.

We reached the palisade enclosing Gladdenfield within a minute, and there was indeed a fighting platform unoccupied. I helped Celeste climb the ladder up, and we sat on the edge, overlooking Springfield Forest.

There, the sunrise painted delicate pastels across the horizon beyond the trees. Celeste's refined profile glowed beautifully in the golden light as she gazed outward. Impulsively, I moved closer. She started slightly at my proximity before glancing up with a tremulous smile that encouraged me to stay.

However, I could tell that there was something a little more tender to her than to Leigh or even Diane. If I were to pursue her, I would need to know more about elven courtship.

As the little town came to life around us, we resumed strolling, no destination in mind. Celeste seemed content simply to walk together and take in the sights and sounds. Now and then she would pause and point out a quaint building or colorful character, providing commentary that charmed me.

"See that delightful bakery with the yellow shutters?" she remarked at one point, gesturing to a cozy shop emitting the heavenly aroma of fresh bread. "I enjoy stopping there when I can scrape together a few coppers. The kindly old baker always slips me an extra roll with a wink."

At another corner, Celeste indicated a ramshackle building tilting precariously between two sturdier structures. "I've named that peculiar little shop The Drunken House," she confided conspiratorially. "See how it leans to one side like it's stumbling home after one too many ales?"

I had to laugh at her whimsical naming and observations. Though still new to frontier life, she was clearly embracing Gladdenfield's quirks and charms, viewing them through the unique lens of her creative mind. Each nibble of insight into how she saw this world delighted me more.

Before long, the allure of freshly baking bread drew us toward the bakery. My stomach rumbled loudly, reminding me I had rushed out without breakfast. "How about an early pastry and some coffee?" I asked Celeste.

Her answering grin was immediate. "I would enjoy that very much," she replied, giving my arm an affectionate squeeze as I led us inside the cozy shop redolent with yeasty aroma. I insisted on paying for a generous assortment of still-warm baked goods and two piping hot coffees to share.

Settling at a table by the front window, Celeste and I enjoyed flaky croissants and cinnamon rolls still oozing with icing. The elf girl clearly relished the sweet tastes, made even sweeter by our continued amiable conversation about her musical talents. Her passion for song was readily apparent.

As we lingered over second cups of coffee, I was loath for this pleasant interlude to end. But the morning was escaping swiftly, and I knew Leigh would soon be looking for me to head back to the homestead. With regret, I explained we must be going shortly.

Celeste's smile faded briefly before returning tremulously. "I understand," she said. "I appreciate you taking time to see me once more before departing. Today shall remain a cherished memory." Her eloquence charmed me.

"I'd love to come visit again soon," I said. "We have some work to do at the homestead, but we always come back to Gladdenfield every few days. How about I drop by your house the next time I'm here?"

Celeste's expression instantly darkened at the notion. "That sounds lovely, but... I'm unsure if I'll be there."

I perked an eyebrow. "*Unsure*? How come?"

"It... It is a long story. I do not wish to keep you."

"Nonsense," I said. "Come on. Let's sit down for a moment, and we'll talk about it."

She gave a meek protest, but my heart went out to her, and she quickly sensed my sincerity and gave in.

Gently, I guided Celeste over to sit on a sunny bench and turned to face her directly. "Now," I said, "what's going on? Why are you unsure that you'll still be at your house in a few days?"

"Well," she hummed, obviously a little abashed.

"The truth is, the money Uncle left is nearly gone, and I cannot afford next week's rent." Her voice quavered with barely restrained panic. "I don't know what I shall do, but I cannot stay there."

"Why didn't you tell me things were this difficult?" I asked softly.

She averted her gaze, cheeks coloring. "I... I did not wish to appear beggared," Celeste admitted in a small voice. "It is not something I am proud of — to be an impoverished vagabond."

I took her slender hands in mine. "You could never be that in my eyes," I assured her. "Please, let me help. I care about you and don't want to see you struggling alone."

Celeste lifted her eyes hopefully. "Truly? I cannot bear the thought of imposing..."

I smiled. "Don't worry about that."

Celeste looked at me with desperation in her emerald eyes. "But how could you possibly help with my situation?" she asked, her voice taut with emotion. "I cannot pay what I owe on my rented room, and the landlord is not a patient man. I fear he shall turn me out the moment rent is overdue a single day."

I pondered a moment. Of course, I wanted nothing more than to offer her a place to stay with us at the homestead. But I felt it was too early for that. She and I had only recently met. Besides, she still had to meet Diane, and since Diane lived with me, I felt they needed to meet at the very least.

Celeste's big green eyes were on me as I thought it over, and I could clearly see there was a measure of despair there. However, an idea soon came to mind.

"Well," I said, "perhaps I could have a talk with Darny over at the Wild Outrider," I suggested. "He seems to like your singing talents. Maybe he could be persuaded to offer you a room in the tavern in exchange for regular performances."

Hope flared in Celeste's expression. "Truly? You believe he would consider such an arrangement?" She clasped her hands, scarcely daring to believe deliverance could be so close at hand.

I smiled reassuringly. "I'm almost certain of it. Darny knows firsthand what an asset your beautiful voice and playing are to the tavern's atmosphere." I rose from the bench, resolve renewed. "Come, let's go speak with him right away."

Celeste accompanied me eagerly back into town, new optimism lightening each graceful step despite her circumstances remaining unchanged for now. Her faith in me to aid her through this difficulty was both daunting and inspiring. I would not fail her trust.

Chapter 45

The tavern was quiet, it being morning, but the steady humdrum of folks enjoying their breakfast seemed jarringly loud after our idyllic walk along the tranquil river as Celeste and I entered the dim interior. Behind the long wooden counter, Darny looked up from scrubbing out a row of cloudy beer mugs and grinned broadly through his beard at the sight of us.

Beckoning him over with a wave of my hand, I politely asked, "Sorry to trouble you, Darny, but might Celeste and I have a quick private word with you? It's rather important."

Darny's bushy brows shot up in surprise, but he readily nodded and agreed. "Of course, of course!"

Turning to yell some instructions back to one of his barmaids, he then waved for us to follow him over to a small table tucked away in the back corner of the tavern, out of earshot from the few other early patrons scattered around.

As we settled around the table, I met Darny's curious gaze. Keeping my voice low so as not to be overheard, I proceeded to explain Celeste's increasingly dire financial plight to him while she sat tense and quiet beside me, slender hands folded tensely in her lap.

I told Darny how the money Waelin had left for her was nearly depleted, and she had no way to pay next week's rent on her room. My heart ached to see her usual radiance dimmed by fear and uncertainty.

As I spoke in hushed tones, Darny's jovial expression gradually shifted to one of genuine concern. Turning his sympathetic gaze toward Celeste, he asked gently, "Well, you've been playin' here for a while now. You could've talked to me about this, and I'm sure we could've made an arrangement."

Celeste's fair cheeks flushed an even deeper rose than their usual perpetual blush as she worried the embroidered edge of her sleeve self-consciously beneath the table. These words of Darny's were good for her to hear. After all, Darny would've likely offered help earlier if she had gone to the trouble of actually talking to him for longer than a few minutes.

Keeping her eyes averted shyly, Celeste replied in a small, tremulous voice, "Darny, I don't... I didn't mean to impose. I still don't." She shot me a worried look. "Perhaps we should..."

But Darny waved off her protests. "Let's see now..." He rubbed his bewhiskered chin, pondering a moment. Soon his face lit up.

"I know! We've a small room upstairs that's unused," he declared brightly. "You're welcome to it, my dear, in exchange for playing in the tavern every evenin'. The wife will set you up with some food as well — three meals a day! I'd be thrilled to have your talents here regular-like! How's it sound?"

Celeste's eyes shone, and she turned to me in wonderment. "Food and board?" she whispered elatedly.

I grinned, giving her hand an encouraging squeeze beneath the table. Her relief was palpable.

"Oh Darny, are you certain?" Celeste asked tremulously, scarcely daring to believe his generosity. "I promise I will earn my keep by singing every evening."

Darny waved off her effusive thanks. "It's done!" he stated adamantly. " Can't have Gladdenfield's star attraction out on the streets. I won't hear another word about it." His eyes twinkled merrily. "And besides, we folk of the frontier gotta look out for one another." He wagged his finger. "We may not be a band of fancy, sorcerin' elves, but we stick together in Gladdenfield. We're a community, and you're part of it, like it or not!"

She was unable to speak due to being caught between gratitude and a sense of shame for having been so aloof during her first days in Gladdenfield Outpost. I had expected that Darny — a real pillar of the community — would be able to help her, and I was happy my guess had been right.

"Well," he said, "I gotta head back for a spell. I'll be back in a minute to help you get settled into that room!" With that, Darny tactfully made himself scarce to afford us a moment as emotions overwhelmed the elf girl.

Overcome with gratitude, Celeste turned and threw both arms around my neck. "However can I thank you?" she exclaimed, eyes gleaming with unshed tears of elation.

I simply held her close, my own happiness multiplied by hers. When she finally sat back dabbing at her eyes with a kerchief, I took Celeste's slender hands in mine.

"Well, you've got Darny to thank," I said. "As for me, I'd just like to see you again soon."

That radiant smile I was beginning to adore instantly graced her fair features once more, banishing the last shadows of fear and uncertainty. In that moment, she had never looked more beautiful.

Composing herself, Celeste turned to me with solemn eyes. "I shall endeavor to prove worthy of the faith you and Darny have placed in me," she vowed fervently.

I gave her hands an encouraging squeeze beneath the table. "You owe me nothing. Your friendship is thanks enough."

At that moment, Darny returned beaming, apparently quite pleased with himself for concocting this ideal solution. He jovially offered to show Celeste to her cozy new accommodations upstairs so she could move in right away.

Grinning, I rose as well. "It's time for me to be on my way," I said. "Leigh and I need to head back to the homestead."

Celeste paused and turned back, gifting me with a look I can only describe as adoring. "I shall see you soon, David," she promised warmly. "I cannot wait! I had a lovely time with you."

Smiling, I received a hug from her, as well as a timid kiss on my cheek. After that, she followed Darny, and Darny's wife was already waiting with a handful of linens, ready to bustle about and concern herself with Celeste's wellbeing. Before they headed up, Celeste offered me a wave.

Watching her disappear happily up the stairs beside Darny and his wife, I exhaled slowly, happy the dire crisis had passed so swiftly. Stepping back out into the bustling frontier settlement, I whistled merrily despite our parting now at hand. Celeste would be safe and sheltered here in Gladdenfield until we met again.

My steps turned toward the general store, sure that I would find Leigh awake. She awaited my return so we could begin the ride back to our little spot by the Silverthread River, where Diane waited.

But I knew Celeste and I would reunite soon enough. For now, pleasant memories would sustain me until that joyful reunion could occur. With a lighter heart, I strode on, whistling a tune as

I reflected on the things to come.

The frontier still had much in store, it seemed…

Finished and eager for early access to my next book? Check out my Patreon: patreon.com/jackbryce

THANK YOU FOR READING!

If you enjoyed this book, please check out my other work on Amazon.

Be sure to **leave me a review on Amazon** to let me know if you liked this book! Like most independent authors, I use the feedback from your review to improve my work and to decide what to focus on next, so your review can make a difference.

If you want early access to my work, consider joining my Patreon (https://patreon.com/jackbryce)!

If you want to stay up-to-date on my releases, you can join my newsletter by entering the following link into any web browser: https://fierce-thinker-305.ck.page/45f709af30. You can also join my Discord, where the madness never ends... Join by entering the following invite manually in your

browser   or   Discord   app:
https://discord.gg/uqXaTMQQhr.

Jack Bryce's Books

Below you'll find a list of my work, all available through Amazon.

Frontier Summoner (ongoing series)

Frontier Summoner 1

Frontier Summoner 2

Frontier Summoner 3

Country Mage (completed series)

Country Mage 1

Country Mage 2

Country Mage 3

Country Mage 4

Country Mage 5

Country Mage 6

Country Mage 7

Country Mage 8

Country Mage 9

Country Mage 10

Warped Earth (completed series)

Apocalypse Cultivator 1

Apocalypse Cultivator 2

Apocalypse Cultivator 3

Apocalypse Cultivator 4

Apocalypse Cultivator 5

Aerda Online (completed series)

Phylomancer

Demon Tamer

Clanfather

Highway Hero (ongoing series)

Highway Hero 1

Highway Hero 2

A SPECIAL THANKS TO...

My patron in the Godlike tier: Lynderyn!
My patrons in the High Mage tier: Christian Smith, Eddie Fields, Michael Sroufe, and Pamela J Smith!

All of my other patrons at patreon.com/jackbryce!

Stoham Baginbott, Louis Wu, and Scott D. for beta reading. You guys are absolute kings.

If you're interested in beta reading for me, hit me up on discord (JauntyHavoc#8836) or send an e-mail to lordjackbryce@gmail.com. The list is currently full, but spots might open up in the future.

Made in the USA
Monee, IL
14 April 2024

56938697R10301